THE OPPOSITE OF TIDY

LARA GRAY

RAZORBILL

Carrie Mac

CARRIE MAC is an award-winning author who
lives with her family in Vancouver, British
Columbia. Some of her accolades include the
Arthur Ellis YA Award, the Stellar Book Award,
several CLA Honour books, and the Sheila A.
Egoff Children's Literature Prize, which she was
awarded for *The Gryphon Project*. She is also a
paramedic with the BC Ambulance Service.

CARRIE MAC

HOW DO YOU COME CLEAN WHEN
YOUR LIFE IS A MESS?

THE OPPOSITE OF TIDY

razOr
bill

RAZORBILL

Published by the Penguin Group

Penguin Group (Canada), 90 Eglinton Avenue East, Suite 700,
Toronto, Ontario, Canada M4P 2Y3 (a division of Pearson Canada Inc.)

Penguin Group (USA) Inc., 375 Hudson Street, New York, New York 10014, U.S.A.
Penguin Books Ltd, 80 Strand, London WC2R 0RL, England
Penguin Ireland, 25 St Stephen's Green, Dublin 2, Ireland (a division of Penguin Books Ltd)
Penguin Group (Australia), 250 Camberwell Road, Camberwell, Victoria 3124, Australia
(a division of Pearson Australia Group Pty Ltd)
Penguin Books India Pvt Ltd, 11 Community Centre, Panchsheel Park,
New Delhi – 110 017, India
Penguin Group (NZ), 67 Apollo Drive, Rosedale, Auckland 0632, New Zealand
(a division of Pearson New Zealand Ltd)
Penguin Books (South Africa) (Pty) Ltd, 24 Sturdee Avenue, Rosebank,
Johannesburg 2196, South Africa

Penguin Books Ltd, Registered Offices: 80 Strand, London WC2R 0RL, England

First published 2012

1 2 3 4 5 6 7 8 9 10

Manufactured in Canada.

LIBRARY AND ARCHIVES CANADA CATALOGUING IN PUBLICATION

Mac, Carrie, 1975–
The opposite of tidy / Carrie Mac.

ISBN 978-0-14-318091-3

I. Title.

PS8625.A23O66 2012   jC813'.6   C2011-906821-4

Visit the Penguin Group (Canada) website at **www.penguin.ca**

Special and corporate bulk purchase rates available; please see
www.penguin.ca/corporatesales or call 1-800-810-3104, ext. 2477.

ALWAYS LEARNING   PEARSON

FOR MY MOM,
WHO SHARED HER LOVE OF READING
WITH ME.

PROLOGUE

:
:
.

Juniper had gotten used to the smell of the house. Even something as foul as that had become normal after a while, and it was made worse by the incense and cheap scented candles that her mother kept lit to make it smell "nice," even though foul and fake did not mix well at all. But her mother plain stank, and there was no hiding it. This was a more recent and very alarming development. Her big fat self smelled rank. Junie couldn't recall the last time her mother had washed her hair. It was lank and wet-looking, but not from any water. Just grease. There was a slick on her skin, too, a light oily sheen from not having showered or bathed or even passed a damp cloth over her face for who knew how long.

Chinese food takeout boxes balanced on the arms of her mother's easy chair. Chow mein noodles inched down her ample bosom like worms. Red blotches of sweet and sour sauce dotted her sweatshirt, too, and bits of egg foo yung littered her lap. Junie glanced in one of the boxes. The fried rice looked like maggots. She could imagine them writhing around in there, pale and putrid.

"Do you want some?" Her mother offered up the box, never taking her eyes off the television. On *The Kendra Show* that day, a man who used to be a woman was showing off the twins he/she gave birth to. Kendra forced a grin as he handed her one of the bleary-eyed infants, who promptly started to bawl.

Junie swallowed back bile. She wanted to throw up. It was the smell, yes, but it was everything else, too. Absolutely everything.

"Is that dinner?" she asked.

"Lunch."

It was almost four o'clock. Junie could be sure that the only time her mother had left that chair was to use the bathroom. And to answer the door for the guy who delivered the Chinese food.

"Are you planning on making dinner tonight?" The question was pointless. Junie knew that her mother had no plans for dinner that didn't involve a takeout menu and delivery, if she had plans for dinner at all.

"How about pizza?" her mother replied.

Junie glanced at the stack of discarded pizza boxes piled to one side of the easy chair, at the flies buzzing lazily above. When the television was off, you could hear the scurrying of rats as they sought out the dried up pizza crusts and abandoned noodles. No matter how many traps Junie set out, it was never enough. She shuddered at the thought.

"No. No pizza." Junie made fists of her hands. Her mother didn't notice. The man who used to be a woman was going on about how badly people had treated him during his pregnancy.

"So, in essence …" Kendra leaned forward, excited, "you were the world's first pregnant man!"

"Mom?"

"Hmm?" Her mother looked up. There were deep dark bags under her eyes, and zits dotting her chin. On a grown woman! And that sweat suit had not seen the inside of a washing machine in over a week, at least.

Junie lifted her fists. She brought them to her face and pressed them hard against her mouth. Part of her wanted to sock her mother between the eyes. Punch her to attention. Knock her out of this mess and into the realm of common sense. And the other part of her just wanted to run away. She let the latter take over and backed toward the door.

"Where're you going, honey?" her mother asked, eyes ever fixed on the screen. *The Kendra Show* cut to commercials, so she flipped to the Shopping Channel. A tiny loud model was promising that the scarf flecked with real gold would slim down any woman when worn just so around the neck. One of those would show up within the week, Junie was sure. At least one.

Junie didn't answer her mother. One thing Junie's grandma had always taught her was that if you couldn't say anything nice then you shouldn't say anything at all. Right now, it was taking all of Junie's inner strength not to tell her mother how disgusting she was. And that wouldn't make any difference anyway. She knew this because she'd tried it, and all that had ended up happening was that she'd hurt her mother's feelings and made her cry. She'd tried begging, threatening and shaming, along with everything else she could think of, to snap her mother out of this eternal and fetid funk.

Junie let herself out the front door and took a deep breath of the fresh spring air. She closed her eyes and thought the worst thought. What if her mother was going to be like this forever? What if she never got better? What if this was the new normal?

ONE

What was—and always had been—normal was that Junie sucked at math, even though her own father was a very skilled accountant. What was worse was that her teacher, Mr. Benson, always made a great big show of handing back tests. His thought was that if everyone knew how you did, you would either be proud of yourself, or motivated by shame to do better the next time. Junie wouldn't have minded this so much if it had been English. Or Art. Or Social Studies. Or Biology, even . . . she was holding steady at a solid C+. But this was Math class. And she sucked at math.

Mr. Benson strode down the aisles, calling out the mark as he dealt each test paper off his pile, letting it drift onto the desk as if it were light and pleasant, which for some it was.

"One hundred percent." That would be for Ollie, behind Junie. She would've hated him for it but he tutored her every Thursday and was the only reason why she wasn't down the hall repeating grade nine Math. "Good job, Ollie."

Ollie coughed, which was what he did whenever he was embarrassed by how smart he was. He coughed often.

"Forty-one, Juniper."

Junie closed her eyes. She'd been hoping for a pass, at least. Just a lousy sixty percent or so.

"Forty . . ."—Mr. Benson tapped the paper—"one." The test was covered in red, and had an unhappy face up in the corner beside her name and another beside the mark. It was one miserable exam. Even the pencilled-in numbers in their erroneous foxholes under the problems looked sad. They all drooped now, exhausted from enduring so much erasing and rewriting and scratching out. The math problems remained just that. Problems.

Mr. Benson moved on while a neon-lit marquee of failure buzzed over Junie's head. "A healthy—if somewhat anemic—eighty-six." This was for Tabitha, in front of her.

Tabitha didn't even glance at her own paper. Instead, she twisted around in her seat and whispered, "It's okay." She plucked Junie's test up, turned around and wrote on it, as Mr. Benson carried on up the aisle to the front.

"Ninety. Well done."

"Seventy-four."

"Eighty-three."

Tabitha slid the test back. She'd added *Fantastic!!!* in teacherly printing, plus a halo and wings to the unhappy faces, along with an edit of the mouths, turning them into fat, kissy lips. All this, and a one in front of Junie's score: 141%.

Junie loved Tabitha. She was the consummate best friend.

"It's just a number." Tabitha grinned at her and winked. "Forget about it."

When the bell sounded, Ollie patted Junie on the back.

"We'll get you through this," he said, as if they were talking about cancer. "Everything will be okay." He coughed. "See you Thursday?"

"Sure, Ollie. Thanks."

The room emptied until it was just Tabitha and Junie and the test.

Tabitha grabbed it and shoved it into her binder. "Never mind that. Come on." She led the way to Junie's locker, where she undid the lock and took out Junie's backpack. "You'll be okay. Right?"

"Uh-huh."

"I'll skip my thing if you need me to."

"No way. I'll be fine." Tabitha's "thing" was a very important piano adjudication for the Royal Conservatory of Music. It was certainly no small *thing*.

"Just say you need me and I'll book it for next time."

"No way. I'm not going to be the excuse for your stage fright."

"You'll be sorry when I come back minus a leg or an arm because the judges gnawed it off with their bare teeth."

"You'll do great. Like always."

"But I'll puke, too, like always."

"And then you'll get a ginger ale from the pop

machine, take a few sips, get up on that stage and knock their socks off. Like always."

Tabitha fixed her with a sympathetic smile. "But you know I wouldn't go if you needed me, right?"

"I'll be fine. It's just another mathematical disaster in a long, drawn-out history of mathematical disasters. I'll be okay."

"Ollie will think of something. You'll see."

Usually Junie used the walk home to clear her head of all things school so that she could focus on all things home. After all, there wasn't much point in dwelling on her abysmal math results. She'd always been terrible at math. Her mother had kept her report cards from elementary school, and every single one of them had a comment about her struggles with math. Politely worded, but essentially saying the same thing: Juniper was a mathematical retard. A numerical dunce. *Is working to grasp her numbers. Struggles with addition. More work needed to apply fractions.*

Junie had tried to throw out her report cards once, but her mother had had a conniption fit. She'd also tried to throw out the Mathematic Marvel Flashcard and Workbook System (Success Guaranteed!!!), which her mother bought when Junie was seven. But when it arrived, it just went into a pile of other stuff she'd bought off the Shopping Channel, most of which she never bothered to open. Back then it wasn't as bad, but you could see where things were going.

About halfway home, Junie heard an engine gear down behind her. She turned to look. There was no mistaking who it was. There was only one student at school who drove an old orange Volkswagen van. Wade Jaffre. He'd transferred to Junie's school only the week before from Tupper, and Junie had noticed him right away. He was tall, with long, brown, sinewy arms, and closely cropped black hair that he angled up a bit in the front. He wore a black leather cuff on one wrist, and jeans that slouched just enough to look exceptionally good on him. And he had a video camera with him almost all the time, although she'd only seen him use it once or twice so far.

He pulled up alongside Junie, going slowly enough to catch her eye. Junie didn't know where to look, or what to do. This was Wade Jaffre! About three minutes after he'd arrived at school she'd developed a full-blown crush on him. And this was a big deal. Junie didn't crush easily. She could count all the crushes she'd ever had on one hand. And still have a finger left over. Until now. The first time she'd laid eyes on him her head and heart and gut had all sent her a very clear message: this guy was optimal crushable material. Her palms went damp, butterflies flitted in her tummy and she was at a loss for words.

Wade rolled down his window. Patsy Cline crooned from his stereo. On many guys, this would seem odd. But it just made Wade Jaffre all that much more sexy.

"Need a ride?"

All thoughts of math and her mother evaporated from Junie's mind. In fact, her brain had apparently shut down entirely, because she was at a loss for words again. Wade Jaffre was offering her a ride, and all Junie could think about was that he had remarkably handsome eyebrows.

"I . . . uh . . ."

And the next thing that occurred to her was that she wasn't allowed to accept rides from strangers. But Wade wasn't a stranger, was he? He wasn't some creepy old man with a boner tenting his polyester pants. She wasn't going to end up dead in a ditch somewhere. Wade was a student at her school. A classmate. So she could say yes. In fact, she should say yes. But she couldn't make herself say anything at all.

"Junie?"

He knew her name. Junie hoped her surprise at this wasn't written all over her face. She couldn't wait to tell Tabitha. "A ride?" she finally managed to say.

"As in, do you need one?" He grinned at her.

"Sure." Junie shifted her backpack from one shoulder to the other, not sure what to do next. "Please. Thanks."

Wade pulled the van ahead and off the road. He cut the engine and leaned way across the gearshift to open the passenger door. "Get in."

"This isn't the first five minutes of the end of my life, is it?" Junie set her backpack on the floor and started to get in. "You're not some serial killer disguised as a high school honour roll student, are you?"

"No." He raised three fingers and laughed. "Scout's honour."

"Good." Junie arranged herself on the seat, did up her seatbelt and stared at him. And then she realized what she was doing and looked away. She got the sense that he was staring at her, and when she glanced to check, sure enough his gaze was fixed on her. A nervous laugh escaped

THE OPPOSITE OF TIDY ● ● ● ● 11

against her better judgment. She wished she could slap herself across the face. Instead, she swallowed hard and said, "So."

"So." Wade merged carefully back into traffic. "Where do you live?"

"Lambert and Fourth Avenue."

"Lambert and Fourth it is, then."

What amazed Junie about this exchange so far . . . this whole *event* so far . . . was that she was actually kind of pulling it off. Yet. And it wasn't like she had any experience in dealing with her crushables. She'd never had the guts to even approach any of her crushables outside of forced school interactions. And this was the first time one of her crushables had ever paid her any kind of attention whatsoever. What amazed her further was that she hadn't made a complete ass of herself, and this was without Tabitha's help. This was the kind of thing they fantasized about. The kind of thing they spent entire sleepovers rehearsing. Well, maybe not this scenario exactly, but Major Life Events just like this. All involving boys, naturally. And things one might hope of doing *with* boys at some point in one's life. Preferably before the age of twenty, as that was the age she and Tabitha had decided was the Spinster Age of Doom. If you reached the Spinster Age of Doom without losing your virginity, it was not likely ever going to happen. Ever.

"So are you?" Wade asked.

Clearly Junie had missed something, because he couldn't have possibly been inquiring about her virginity.

"Sure," Junie said with as much dumb confidence as she could muster.

"Excellent."

A couple of seconds passed, during which Junie prayed that Wade hadn't asked her something horrible, like if she'd be a drug mule for him.

"I'm sorry." She needed to know what she'd just agreed to. "What did you just ask me?"

Wade laughed. "I asked if you'd help with the Think Globally, Act Locally bottle drive next week."

"Then for sure, for sure!" Again, Junie wanted to slap herself across the face. She sounded like a stupid valley girl. This was not what she and Tabitha strove for in their fabulous imaginary relationships with cool and excellent boys. Like Wade Jaffre. She tried again. "I mean, yeah, okay. I'm free that day."

"I haven't told you what day yet."

"Hmm." Junie glanced up to watch the idiot points accumulating above her head, like on the giant scoreboard in the gym. "Right."

"Next Saturday. Does that work for you?"

"Absolutely."

Wade signalled and steered off the main road.

"So . . . you think maybe Tabitha could come too?"

And all of a sudden, Junie was confused. He'd picked *her* up, was chatting *her* up, making *her* stomach churn with nerves, and now he wanted to talk about Tabitha?

Maybe he wanted Tabitha, and he was trying the classic Best Friend Bait and Switch move. It would make sense that he'd want the prettier one. The one with long, lovely auburn curls and long, lovely legs to match. The one who actually had tits, and the ass to back them up. Last

September, Tabitha had tried to convince Junie that she'd really blossomed over the summer, but Junie knew that Tabitha was just being nice. The fact was that her friend had blossomed even more over the summer, which was why they were at the mall buying Tabitha new bras when she made the empty compliment to Juniper. Yes, Junie had gotten taller, and yes, she'd recently gotten her braces taken off, and yes, she could finally actually justify a AA cup, but the truth remained that she was somewhat of an ugly duckling. She could only hope that someday she'd get to be the swan. For now, she was nothing but a go-between. Figures.

"I don't know. I'll check." She was sure that her tone gave away her disappointment.

"It's just, the more the merrier with this kind of thing. Ollie and Lulu are in. They're the ones who said I should ask you. You're friends with them, right? So they're in."

"Turn here," Junie said. Thank God the ride was almost over, because she was feeling awash with petulance that she was not entitled to. She and Tabitha had a rule. If a guy liked one of them better than the other, that was just the way it was. The less-liked would bow gracefully out of the way, no questions asked. It had been all hypothetical until now, and therefore hypothetically easy until now. But put into practice, Junie wasn't so sure.

Wade glanced at the street signs. They were at the intersection of Lambert and Fourth.

"Which house is yours?"

A lie could take any shape. Like the one Junie was forming at that moment as she glanced at the house on the

corner. The lie she was about to tell was shaped like embarrassment, bloated and pale.

Wade slowed. "Which one is it?"

In the driveway with the minivan and the red sports
car, fat Mrs. Rawley was screaming at Mr. Rawley, in broad
daylight for all to see. There was Mrs. Rawley in her housecoat, open over her dingy sweat suit, ratty slippers on her
feet, and Mr. Rawley—looking sharp as usual in a three-
piece suit—red in the face like he was about to explode.
He had a suitcase dangling from each arm, and the trunk
of the sports car was stuck open, jammed full of boxes. He
looked as though he was about to hurl the suitcases at Mrs.
Rawley. And who would blame him?

"It's a ways yet." Junie brought her hand to her face.
She slumped a little in the seat. "Next block."

"See those two?" Wade pointed at Mr. and Mrs.
Rawley. "Putting on quite the show."

"I see them." Junie slouched even lower. "Keep
driving."

"But you said Lambert. And Fourth."

"*Near* Lambert. Next block. Second house in. Cape
Cod, Wedgwood blue, biscuit trim. Cherry trees up and
down the block."

Patsy Cline was singing about being crazy in love,
which seemed extra sad, watching Mr. and Mrs. Rawley
fight like that. They must've been in love at one point.
Surely? The cherry blossoms were in full bloom on the next
block, making a pink fluffy canopy over the street. There
was enough wind that day that there was a lazy snowfall of
tiny petals. How could it be that this street looked so much

more beautiful, so much tidier and happier than the last block, where Mr. and Mrs. Rawley fought in front of the whole world?

As the song wound down, Wade stopped outside the blue-and-white house, as if the moment had been choreographed. His windshield was dotted with pink.

"It's like candy snow," he said.

Junie grinned. "Imagine if it tasted sweet?"

More blossoms fell. Junie sighed. These would be the perfect first moments of a perfect first love. She could imagine telling their grandchildren about this day. Only, it wouldn't be her telling her grandchildren, because there wouldn't be any. Because Wade was more interested in Tabitha than her. Having reminded herself of this, Junie squared her jaw and willed the beauty of the moment into oblivion.

The living room curtains parted and a woman waved at them.

"Your mom?"

"Yeah," Junie said quickly as she waved back. She turned to Wade. It was time for this to be over. Tabitha would have to get busy making her own perfect moments with the perfect boy. "So, thanks for the ride."

"No problem. Thanks for helping out with the bottle drive."

"I haven't done it yet." Junie was wishing she hadn't been so eager to say yes. "How do you know I'll even show up?"

He winked at Junie, and even though he was more into Tabitha than her, it still made her heart lurch. "I don't think you're the type to bail."

He was right, so she said so. "You're right."

"So, I guess I'll see you in class tomorrow."

They had World Studies together, which was where, until now, Junie had been pining over him. She'd have to do something about that. She'd have to devise a plan to stop being crushed out on him. Because right now her heart was betraying her, still awash with twitterpation, despite her application of logic.

"Um. I should get going."

Wade laughed, which was when Junie realized she'd been staring at him.

"Are you okay?"

"Yeah, sure. Why?"

"I don't know." Wade shrugged. "You just seem kind of—"

Junie didn't want to know what she "seemed" like, so she cut him off. "I flunked a math test today."

"Oh, sorry. That sucks. You've got Benson, right?"

"Yeah."

"When I first got here, I thought he was pretty cool. But he's not. He's one of those teachers who is cool for about two classes and then is never, ever cool again."

"I agree. But unfortunately, he's in control of my math grade." More cherry blossoms fell. The windshield was almost covered. "I've got to go. Thanks for the ride."

"No problem. See you tomorrow?"

"Okey-dokey." Junie climbed out, slung her backpack over her shoulder and waved as he drove off.

She marched up the sidewalk and flung open the front door. There was Mrs. D., eyeing her with a justifiably quizzical look. She was wearing pearls. And heels. She had makeup on that made her look like she wasn't wearing any makeup at all. She had the poise of someone in charge, like someone about to stand in front of a judge and jury and convince them of the defendant's innocence, which was probably exactly what she had done all day, even though she looked as though she hadn't lifted a finger or met a gust of wind, ever. Her briefcase sat in its usual spot, tucked out of sight. Her keys rested in the bowl set for that purpose on the waxed side table. Other than the bowl, the surface was clear. The antique mirror above was perfectly square, with not a single smudge on it. The carpet boasted fresh vacuum lines, like some kind of immaculately kept soccer field.

"Junie?" Mrs. D. flashed her a smile. "What are you doing here, hon?"

"I just said 'okey-dokey' to Wade Jaffre." June pointed behind her as if the words were following her like a bad odour. "He drove me home and I said *okey-dokey*. And Tabitha wasn't there to stop me!"

"Oh, dear." Mrs. D. winced. "Tabitha is at her piano adjudication."

"I know." Junie leaned against the closet door and groaned.

"Of course you're always welcome here, sweetheart . . . but I still have to ask. Why exactly are you here if Tabitha is downtown?"

"I just didn't want to go home."

"Ah, I see." Mrs. D. touched Junie's shoulder. "I saw your father's car in the driveway when I came home. Is everything all right?"

Junie shook her head. "No." Here came the tears. Almost. Once started, there would be no stopping them. Mrs. D. stepped toward her, arms open, just about to hug her, but Junie shook her head.

"If you hug me, I'll cry. And I really don't want to."

"Do you want to talk about it?"

"No." Junie shook her head again. "Thanks."

"Well, you know I'm here. And of course you're welcome to be here, even when Tabitha isn't." Mrs. D. retreated to the kitchen, from which the glorious aroma of roasting chicken wafted into the hall. Junie followed her, leaning in the doorway, watching her. Mrs. D. took up a knife and sliced a carrot in perfect slanted coins. "Are you staying for supper?"

"Definitely."

"Do your parents know that?"

"Mr. and Mrs. Rawley are otherwise occupied on the front lawn screaming at each other." Junie turned back into the hall to hang up her backpack and jacket on a hook in the closet. "I'm sure they won't mind."

TWO

. . . .

Tabitha came home just as Mrs. D. set the last spotless water glass on the table. While Junie told Tabitha about her horrifying verbal wreckage and the fact that she'd outright lied to Wade Jaffre, Mrs. D. "plated" the food. Mrs. D. loved plating the food she made. Each plate arrived at the table looking as if it had just been served to you in a five-star restaurant where the meal cost at least a week's wages. It made the food seem so much more valuable, unlike the takeout and freezer-to-microwave fare at Junie's house. At her house, the food was as good as trash.

"Did he notice?" Tabitha asked, her voice full of the appropriate sympathy. "The *okey-dokey*, I mean. He wouldn't know any better about where you live. Or who your parents are, for that matter."

"I don't know if he noticed."

"He probably didn't."

Junie groaned. "Only because his attention was on my idiotic parents!"

"Junie!" Mrs. D. and Tabitha said in unison. Tabitha shook her head. "That's an awful thing to say."

"But it's true. My parents are idiots."

Mrs. D. set out two plates and went back to get the third. "Your parents are going through a tough time right now."

"They've been going through a 'tough time' for over a year! When does that excuse expire?"

"I don't know, exactly," Mrs. D. said, truly giving it some thought. "But nonetheless, enduring a personal crisis is a far cry from idiocy."

"Not far enough," Junie muttered, eyes on her plate. She could feel Mrs. D. staring at her, so she dutifully looked up and apologized. Inside, she wasn't sorry at all. Her parents were idiots. And she was one too. It had to be hereditary.

As if reading her mind, Tabitha touched her hand. "So? Did he notice?"

"By the sounds of it, he did not." Mrs. D. set Junie's plate in front of her. A leg of chicken artfully set against a shaped brick of wild rice pilaf with almonds and apricots. Six stalks of asparagus arranged just so at the top of the plate.

"Thanks, Mrs. D." The food smelled so good, and looked even better, but Junie's appetite wasn't at the table with her. It was back on the corner of Lambert and Fourth, watching her parents make royal fools of themselves in front of the whole neighbourhood and, more importantly,

Wade Jaffre. Even if he did like Tabitha better, it still sucked to appear so lame in front of a crushable. "Even if he did notice, he's too cool to act like it."

Mrs. D. poured them each just an inch of wine and then seated herself. With a subtle flourish, she draped her napkin across her lap. "There's absolutely nothing wrong with saying *okey-dokey*."

"Yes, there is," Tabitha and Junie replied in unison.

"Okay, so perhaps it's a little gauche. But you're teenagers! Practically every other word out of your mouths is *like*."

"Not true." Tabitha jabbed an asparagus spear. "You've made sure that's not the case."

"And for good reason." Mrs. D. might've seen Junie and Tabitha as mature enough to enjoy a sip or three of fine wine with dinner, but she didn't think they were old enough to make decisions about how they spoke. She fined them twenty-five cents every time either one of them used "like" when it wasn't an "appropriate application of the word." It added up fast, but to her credit, when Junie and Tab were cured of the habit, she took them shopping with the money and they got matching sunglasses that made them look like Hollywood starlets. Junie and Tabitha loved the sunglasses. Mrs. D. did not, but she had said that they could buy whatever they wanted, and she was a woman of her word. Unlike some other mothers.

"What about your parents?" Tabitha said, reading Junie's mind the way she always did. "Did Wade say anything?"

"No." Junie didn't want to tell her the truth. Especially

if he did like Tabitha better than her. Tabitha wouldn't stand for a guy who came off kind of judgy, and despite everything, Junie wanted him to have a shot, so she kept her mouth shut. Honestly, Junie didn't blame him. Her parents had looked like something off of *The Kendra Show*. "I know you my baby's daddy, even though I slept with eighteen other guys!" Or, "My cousin is my cross-dressing secret lover and we have three kids!" But her parents weren't really like that. They were actually quite boring. Except for the one big thing that set her mother apart from everyone else. That pesky little business of her being a compulsive hoarder whose junk had long ago taken over her life.

Junie sat back and watched Mrs. D. and Tabitha talk about the piano adjudication, which Tabitha had aced. Junie knew that she should tell Tabitha that Wade liked her more. She knew that was the right thing to do. But when she thought about saying the words, her stomach rolled up into a wet ball and shoved itself up into her throat. She wanted Wade to like *her*, not Tabitha. She wanted things to be different. Like always, she wanted them to be different.

Like how badly she wanted Mrs. D. to be *her* mother. Since she was five years old she'd wanted Tabitha's mother to be her mother. Not for real, because no matter what, Junie did love her mother. As she'd got older and things got worse, she'd realized that she didn't exactly want Mrs. D. to replace her mother; she just wanted her mother to be more like Mrs. D. Junie wanted her to be thin and pretty and have a purse with just the right things in it. She wanted her mother to have an impressive job and a shiny car. She wanted her to know how to kneel expertly in her skirt and heels and take Junie in her arms and tell her how beautiful she was and how smart and how brave. Junie wanted a mom who kept house like Mrs. D. did, with or without the help of a cleaning lady who came once a week. Tabitha's house was perfect. Spotless, but still livable. The house was like a practised hug. New and cozy at the same time. Everything was so tidy. And every single object had a purpose and a home. No mess. No muddle. No junk.

And no father, either. Tabitha's father had died of a heart attack when she and Junie were eight. A stockbroker, out jogging during his lunch break, the picture of health and success. Dead ten minutes later.

What if Mrs. D. and Junie's dad got together? It could have its benefits. Tabitha and Junie would be sisters. Junie and her father would move into Mrs. D.'s house and every night would be like this one. Dinner at the table in the heart of a house that looked like something out of *Home & Style* magazine. They'd be a perfect little family who constantly beamed at each other as they complimented and praised each other until they were blue in the face.

Good grief. What was Junie thinking? Her dad had only left a few months ago! She poked at her rice pilaf, her appetite gone. She was crazy. She didn't want her father to marry Mrs. D. And besides, he was already occupied with That Woman. What Junie wanted was for her father to unceremoniously dump That Woman and come back home, where he belonged. What Junie really wanted was for her mother to be normal again.

And anyway, where would her mother be in all of

this? Festering away in the hovel down the street? Junie couldn't let that happen. No matter what, she loved her mother. More than anything. She just wanted things to be different. She wanted her mother to change. That was all.

⋮

After dinner, Mrs. D. shooed Junie and Tabitha off to the basement so they could do their homework. After half an hour of puzzling out Mr. Benson's evil math equations, Junie brought herself to let Tabitha in on the fact of the matter.

"I didn't tell you everything."

Tabitha put a finger in her textbook, marking where they were. "What'd you leave out?"

"The most important part." She told her what had happened, and exactly what and how Wade had said what he did. "Obviously he likes you better. I didn't say so before because I was enjoying five minutes of thinking he might like me."

"And he probably does." Tabitha shook her head. "You can't tell anything from what he said."

"It's how he said it," Junie said.

"*Or* how he said it." Tabitha moved her finger and took her attention back to the textbook. "You can't tell."

"I can so."

"I bet he likes you."

"And I bet he likes *you*."

Tabitha smiled. "I won't lie. If he did, I'd be thrilled."

"No more than I would be, if he liked me."

Junie and Tabitha appraised each other, and then Tabitha said, "We always knew this might happen."

"Yeah, well." Junie arched her eyebrows, hoping to look haughty. "Maybe you should develop an interest in a different type."

"Why don't you?" Tabitha mimicked Junie's face.

The two of them grinned at each other. "Whatever," Junie said. "If it's you, I'll be happy for you."

"And if it's you, I'll be happy for you."

There was a tiny, sharp lull then. Just enough time for both girls to wonder if that was true.

"But it'll be you," Junie said quickly.

"You don't know that," Tabitha said. "And do you know how I know? Because if the tables were turned, and I'd been in the van and you'd been at a piano adjudication, he'd have said the same thing!"

Junie had to admit that Tabitha had a point. "I guess that's possible."

"He probably just really wants extra people for his bottle drive thing. Nothing more, nothing less. He probably isn't interested in either of us. Maybe he's gay."

"I doubt it." Junie glanced down at her math worksheet. The numbers shimmered like hot pavement. She hated math. She hated crazy-making boy encounters. Well, maybe she didn't exactly hate them . . . perhaps she even liked them. But that didn't make them any less confusing.

"You know what?" Tabitha handed Junie her own sheet with the answers filled in. "Either way, we'll be okay. Right? If he likes you, I'll be cool. And if he likes me, you'll be cool. And if he likes Ollie, we'll both be cool."

They laughed at the thought.

The phone rang, but neither of them dove for it. They both knew it would be Junie's mom. Sure enough, they heard Mrs. D.'s reassuring murmurs trickle down from upstairs. Then silence. Then footsteps. Mrs. D. appeared on the stairs, a small plate in each hand.

"Juniper Rawley. Your mom had no idea where you were!"

"I'm always here. She knows that. Where else would I be?"

"But you hadn't told her. And you told me you had."

"I told you she wouldn't mind. And she didn't, right?"

"I'm not so sure about that." Mrs. D. tried to look full of lawyerly discipline, but Junie had a point. Her mother could have called earlier, but she hadn't. And they all knew why. First she'd been busy making a scene with Junie's father in the driveway, and then she hadn't bothered because she knew exactly where Junie was. "It would have been much better had you been clear."

"I'm sorry, Mrs. D.," Junie said. "I was flustered and messed up."

"Apology accepted." Mrs. D. set the plates in front of them. A little quenelle of vanilla ice cream rested in the centre, with a fan of roasted pear slices tucked beside it. "She said you could have dessert first, but then you are to go straight home. To your real home." Again, she tried to sound firm, but she didn't really. She set her hand on Junie's shoulder and gave her a tender squeeze. And her tone was more gentle than stern. "I am sorry you're going through this, Junie. You know you're welcome here any time."

⋮

Going through this. Which "this" did she mean? The divorce?

"Or the usual 'this'?" Junie asked Tabitha as she walked her home.

"Both."

Junie stopped at the end of her driveway, Tabitha beside her. Inside, the only light was the blue flicker from the TV in the living room. In the houses on the rest of the block, a warm orange glow emanated from various rooms. A couple of porch lights were on, beckoning. Each one of those homes looked more inviting than her own.

"I wish the moms would let me sleep over on weeknights," Junie said. "Even just once in a while." It was a rule, though, and there was no breaking it. Junie was sure it was a rule not because they'd never get any sleep, but because it would hurt her mother's feelings if she chose to sleep at Tabitha's every night. And she didn't want to sleep there every night. But after a day like this, she would. For sure, she would. After a day like this, she didn't really want to go home at all.

"You'll be okay." Again, Tabitha read her mind. "You'll go in, say goodnight and hide out in your room until morning. You don't have to listen to her go on about your dad. And you don't have to hang out in all that—"

"I know. All that crap."

"Yeah." Junie could hear the awkwardness in Tabitha's voice. "Well, not crap, really. But—"

"Call a spade a spade, right?"

"I guess so. Night, Junie." Tabitha hugged her. "Sweet dreams of Wade Jaffre."

"You too, Tab." She backed up the driveway, slowly. "And congratulations on your stellar piano performance!"

⋮

The front door had a creak, so it announced her arrival, no matter how stealthy she wanted to be.

"Junie?" her mom called, from what was called the living room in most houses. But in Junie's house, it was not livable at all. She and Tabitha called it the unliving room. "I'm home."

There was a pause. Her mother turned down the volume on the TV, but she could still hear some shrill lady pleading with her to buy a set of cubic zirconium earrings for only $29.99, including shipping.

"Come on in here for a minute."

This was easier said than done. Junie hated going into the living room. It was the worst place in the whole house. And only because it was where her mother dwelt amongst her accumulated junk, like a foul queen amongst her wretched legions. Her mother was a hoarder—there was no better way to describe it. No stronger word. No more accurate word to describe the mountainous squalor. The front entrance was cluttered with boxes and padded envelopes from couriers and the mailman and delivery trucks, stuff she'd bought off the Shopping Channel and the Internet, stuff she hadn't even bothered to open. The closet was jammed open with jackets and boots and hats. The hall leading to the living room was stacked with plastic bins and crates and boxes full of more crap she didn't need: MiracleMan Hair Rejuvenator from when Junie's father started to go bald, the Fabio Fab Abs Machine from when her mother finally realized she'd gotten very fat, the Number Whiz Kid Genius Kit (Success Guaranteed!!!), another "system" that she'd ordered when it had become clear that Junie was seriously numerically challenged. And amongst all that, plain old garbage. Bags of old shopping bags, teetering stacks of washed out tin cans she "might need one day for a craft project" she had in mind. Leaning towers of old newspapers. Black garbage bags bursting with clothes that didn't fit any of them any more but that might have "one or two good wears in them yet." Shoeboxes jammed with pencil stubs and twist-ties and paper clips, margarine tubs bursting with old elastics.

The entire house had been overtaken by her mother's *stuff*. Her crap, her doodads, her compulsive purchases, the detritus of her extreme and out-of-control hoarding. Junie couldn't blame her father for leaving them, considering the mess he'd had to live with.

It took three times as long as it should have to make her way from the front door to the small patch in the living room that wasn't occupied by stuff, stuff and more *stuff*. Broken lamps, rolled up carpeting from the old house they'd lived in ("In case we decide to use it in the basement . . ."), pillars of phone books, catalogues, takeout menus, yearbooks, old bills and receipts, entire sets of dishes still in the boxes ("But don't you LOVE the pattern? You can have them when you go to college!"). The only free space was the short distance between her mother's armchair and the TV. A very small expanse of nothing. So as not to obscure her view. Sometimes Junie did her homework there, sitting on the floor with her books spread out around her while her mother watched the Shopping Channel. She only did this when she was feeling guilty about not hanging out with her mother enough. But that was rare. Increasingly rare. Mostly, Junie stayed in her room.

"My errant child," her mother said drolly. "Returned to the hideous home front."

"Don't say that." Junie hated it when her mom made jokes about the state of their home. It was so terrible; there was nothing funny about it. It was no laughing matter. Not at all.

"Why didn't you come home after school?"

Junie didn't answer. She looked at the TV. *The Amazing Closet Butler! Organizes up to sixty-three items! Indispensable.* Her mother wrote something in the notebook she kept by her chair.

"We don't need that, Mom."

"We could organize the front closet."

"I *did* organize the front closet. Last year. And the year before that. It always goes back to being your stuff-it place for the mail and packages you never even bother to open."

"There are coats and boots and such in there too."

"Mom!"

"Junie!" Her mother held up her hands in a truce. "I get it, okay?" She paused. "Did you do your homework at Tabitha's or do you still need to get it done?"

Apparently, she was not going to mention that Junie's father had been there. Apparently she was not going to mention the very public fight they'd had in the driveway. Apparently she was going to pretend that everything was business as usual. As usual as it could be in this mess.

"Did it at Tabitha's."

"You should get to bed, then."

"So you can buy three Closet Butlers?" Junie couldn't help the sarcasm. She was sorry for it the moment she'd said the words. But it was true. Junie's mother would pick up the phone the minute Junie was out of sight. Her mother couldn't help it. It was an addiction. As bad as a crack addict jonesing for a fix. That's what her father told her. That was his explanation for it. That—along with the hoarding and the filth and every other problem her mother seemed to have—was why he wanted Junie to come live with him and That Woman.

Her mother looked at her, eyes damp. She knew how bad it was. She knew she needed to stop. She'd finally admitted that she was a hoarder—had actually used that very word herself—only about a year before. Right before everything had gone downhill between her and Junie's dad. In fact, it was after she'd seen a segment on *Kendra* about it. That was the night she'd started looking for a professional organizer. What a mistake *that* had been.

Junie's mom knew that if Social Services saw the state of things, they'd remove Junie and make her go live with her father and That Woman. She knew that the only reason Junie stayed with her was because she worried about her. Junie worried that her mother would stick her head in the oven and turn the gas on just to get away from the mess once and for all without actually having to deal with it.

She worried that one of the candles would tip over and the house would burn so hot and so fiercely that no one would be able to rescue her amongst all the junk. Sometimes Junie worried that one day her mother would pack a bag, walk out the front door and never come back, because to fix it was too hard, and to stay was even harder. But mostly, she worried that her mother was just going to get worse. That she'd hoard even more. And that one day Junie would come home from school and find her dead under a pile of rubbish that had fallen on her and crushed her to death. This happened for real. A man in New Jersey reported his wife missing only to find her three days later in their basement, where she'd perished under a pile of Christmas ornaments still in their original, unopened packages.

Junie left her mother with her guilt and went up to her bedroom. Her oasis of uncluttered calm. Her bed, a desk, a bureau, two shelves of books. That was it. Nothing else. Tabitha said her room looked like a monk's quarters. And that suited Junie just fine. She changed into her pyjamas and went down the hall to the bathroom to brush her teeth. Things were slightly better on this floor, with only one side of the wall stacked with archive boxes from when her father had tried to "apply some order to the chaos." Junie's mother wouldn't let them get rid of anything, but occasionally she let them sort it. The floor-to-ceiling stack of archive boxes had twenty years' of papers in it. Not just the papers produced from a normal household, but every single paper that her mother had *ever* come in contact with: notes, parking receipts, old gum wrappers, bills, used envelopes . . . you name it.

When Junie headed back to her bedroom she heard the telltale sound of her mother dialling the phone. She knew the different beeps of the different numbers. This was one of the 1-800 numbers she often dialled to buy off the TV. A few days from then, several Closet Butlers would show up via courier. Junie glanced at her watch. Eleven minutes. Her mother had tried to resist. Junie knew this because if she hadn't been trying, she would have dialled while Junie still stood there laying on the guilt. She'd made it eleven minutes before she'd caved and given in to her addiction.

Never mind if Wade liked her, or Tabitha, or neither of them. Junie was just glad that Wade Jaffre thought she lived at what was really Tabitha's house. Never mind the scene in the driveway—imagine if he ever actually wanted to come in! The only person—other than her mom, dad or herself—who had ever been in this house on a regular basis was Tabitha. She was the only one who knew her big secret. And Tabitha's mother. She'd come into the house once, and only once. She couldn't find Tabitha, and it was past the time that she and Junie were supposed to be home. After looking around the neighbourhood for the girls, she'd knocked on the front door, and when there was a muffled answer from deep in the house, she'd opened the door and stepped inside. She'd only stood in the front hall for the time it took Junie's mother to make her way to her, to tell her that the girls had called and were on their way home from the corner store, where she'd sent them on an errand. But from there Mrs. D. could see enough. Smell enough. After that, the girls almost only ever hung out at Tabitha's house.

Mrs. D. had asked Junie if she felt safe. Junie said yes. Then Mrs. D. asked if she was bothered by the "state of things" at her house. Junie said no. She said that it was worse right then because they were finally clearing things out. Junie said that everything was just fine. Junie lied, over and over again, worried that Mrs. D. might turn her parents in.

Maybe it was better if Wade liked Tabitha. Junie couldn't imagine having a boyfriend. Not when her house—and her life—was such a huge, unsalvageable mess.

THREE

:
:
:
•

Her mother had slept in her chair again. This was a secret that no one else knew. Not Junie's father, not even Tabitha. That chair. How Junie hated that chair. Recently, her mother had gotten stuck in it when a pile of junk had been teetering for weeks slid onto her lap, topped with an ottoman and broken coffee table that Junie had said were a hazard but had refused to deal with on her own. Junie wondered if her mom could've helped herself out and hadn't bothered. Either way, she'd sat there, underneath it all, until Junie had come home from school and helped dig her out. And was that a big enough deal to have inspired her to reach out for help? Apparently not. Junie had begged her mother to make things better, even as she dragged off the table and set aside bundles of old clothes, dirty empty food containers with ants and maggots in them, a box of musty old textbooks.

"You'll die under all of this crap, Mom. Is that what you want? You want me to come home and find you dead? It could've been today! What if I wasn't here? What if no one came for days and days? What if you starved to death here? Died from lack of water? It doesn't take that long, Mom."

"I'm not going to die anytime soon," her mother said in very small voice.

Junie replied in an equally small voice, "But when will it end, Mom?"

"I don't know," her mother said. "I wrote to Kendra about it."

"Who?"

"Kendra. On TV. *Kendra*, Kendra."

Junie had said nothing. Her face flushed red. As if a world-famous talk show host would be able to help. Junie could only imagine the mailroom at the *Kendra* studios, full of desperate letters written by desperate people about their desperate situations. Her mother was now deluded as well.

Junie had thought that the burying scare might kick her mother into gear, but it hadn't. Other than rearranging and steadying the detritus around her so that none of it was so tall that it would overwhelm her again, her mother had not only gone on hanging out in that horrible chair, but she'd taken to sleeping in it, too. Junie genuinely believed that one day she'd come home to find that her mother had purchased a commode and mini-fridge online and wouldn't have any reason to leave the living room ever again.

Junie's mother was still sleeping when Junie left for school. The chair was one of those armchairs that leaned

back, with a footrest that went up. She was in it fully
reclined, and was sleeping hard with her mouth open and
one of her legs dangling off the footrest. One arm was
splayed out to her side, and she was still clutching the
remote with the other. An old afghan covered her lap; her
computer teetered precariously on her thighs. She hated
that her mother slept in that gross old recliner.

She stood at the edge of the living room and shook
her head. It was a disgusting sight: the room, with all
its squalor, and her mother in the middle like she was
queen of the garbage heap. It was all so embarrassing and
awful. Even more so now that her mother couldn't even
be bothered to take herself up to bed at night. Junie had
glanced in her mother's room before she'd come down.
Even if her mother had wanted to go to bed, there was
no easy way she could. The bed was covered with the
contents of a series of plastic bins that her mother had
started to organize. She'd started that project eleven days
ago, and hadn't slept in her bed since. Not that it had been
very sleepable before that. Up until her father had left,
her mother had managed to keep a narrow moat around
the bed, and the bed itself clear, even though the room
was a mountain range of laundry, both clean and dirty.
There'd been an avalanche on one side, the heap tilting
and tilting until it had given. Now musty old clothes were
piled around the bed and spilled onto it, mixing with the
contents of the bins. The mattress itself was dingy and
stained, because her mother had not bothered to put a
sheet on it since her dad had left. When Junie had asked
her why, her mother had explained that there was no

point, because she was alone, and slept in her clothes, so what did it matter?

It mattered. Greatly. Maybe Junie would tell Tabitha today. That her mother had been sleeping in her chair. Or maybe she wouldn't. She felt as though she'd passed a threshold: the border between simple omission and a real secret.

Junie opened the door as quietly as possible. She didn't want her mother to wake up and catch her leaving, because she wasn't sure what she'd say to her. She could imagine all kinds of rude things about how fat she'd gotten and how lazy she was and what a slob she'd become. Junie hated that her mother made her have thoughts like that. But it was her mother's fault. She was the one who was living this ruined life. Junie just wanted to get out of there, so that she wouldn't say anything mean.

Outside, it was a glorious day. This made the inside of her house seem all that much worse. At the street, she glanced back. From the outside, you couldn't tell what horror lay behind the closed doors and drawn curtains. That was because the outside had been her father's domain. He still came once a week to mow the lawn. Junie didn't know why, given that he'd otherwise abandoned them to live with That Woman. Guilt, probably. Nonetheless, the house looked good from the street. He'd painted it the year before, and had put in new windows, and the shrubbery along the front was neatly trimmed. He'd planted bulbs when they'd first moved in, when Junie was just a toddler, so the same tulips came up every year. They were in full bloom now, and always made Junie smile. The tulips were

her favourite part of the house. It was so sad that they only bloomed for a few weeks of the year.

Her favourite part of the street was the cherry trees. The street was lined with the majestic old ladies, their branches forming a fluffy pink canopy as she walked below. The ones on Junie's street were a little behind that year, but the ones on Tabitha's block were in full bloom. She walked down the middle of the quiet street, craning her neck so she could look at the explosion of pink, with bits of the bright blue sky behind.

"Hey!" Tabitha called from her stoop. "Watch out, Junie."

A van turned the corner at the end of the block. A very familiar van.

"That's Wade Jaffre's van!" Junie ran up the sidewalk and clutched Tabitha's sleeve. "Don't tell, Tab. Please."

"But where am I supposed to live?"

"I don't know. But you can't live here."

Mrs. D. joined Junie and Tabitha on the step as Wade pulled to a stop in front of the house.

"I'm guessing you two don't need a ride to school today?"

"I guess not." Tabitha glanced sideways at Junie. Wade turned the engine off and opened the door.

"How is he old enough to drive?" Neither Junie nor Tabitha even had a learner's licence yet, even though Tabitha had just turned sixteen.

"He's in grade eleven," Junie and Tabitha said at the same time. Junie punched her, and then all of a sudden felt incredibly immature.

"And you know him how?"

"Junie is in grade eleven World Studies and Biology with him," Tabitha offered. "They were short AP teachers this year, so they put her up one year after she did those online courses in the summer, remember?"

"Oh, no!" Junie smacked her head and groaned. This called for a convincing, lightning-fast story. "Mrs. D., he thinks you're my mom—"

"Sometimes I think I am too."

"And he thinks I live here—"

"Sometimes I think you do too—"

"Please, just listen!" It came out more sharply than Junie intended, but Mrs. D. was paying attention now. Junie had never spoken to her like that. "I told him that I live here, because of the whole awful scene with my parents yesterday and how I couldn't bear to be related to either of them. So now I'm related to you. Okay? I'm sorry, it was stupid, I wasn't thinking, forgive me, but please, please, please just play along, okay? Please, please, please?"

Mrs. D. glanced at her real daughter. "And you're okay with this?"

"Parts of it." Tabitha caught Junie's pleading look and gave in. "All right, all right."

That, right there, was one of the biggest reasons why Junie loved Tabitha. She knew how to be the world's most excellent best friend. Even willing to give up her own mother for the sake of the greater good! Or share her, at least.

"All right." Mrs. D. straightened her blouse. "But for the record, I don't like lying. And I don't condone it, either. And neither should Tabitha."

"I don't!"

"Later," Junie said through her teeth as Wade approached with a great big smile.

"Morning, ladies."

"Good morning," Mrs. D. said, while Junie and Tabitha gawped silently at him. "I'm the mother," she added, with a pointed glance in Junie's direction.

"Wade Jaffre." He extended his hand. "Pleased to meet you."

"You can call me Georgia." This cost Junie another knowing glance in her direction. Of course he couldn't call her Mrs. D.—he knew that Junie's last name was Rawley. But Mrs. D. was smart. And quick. "And who are you in the larger context of the world, Wade?"

"I, uh . . ." Clearly caught off guard by one of Mrs. D.'s Bigger Picture questions, he took a second or two to come up with an answer. Tabitha and Junie were used to these questions, but they could be quite the challenge for the uninitiated. "Let me think. Student, thinker, friend . . . Son of Raj and Miriam Jaffre, who are in Darfur with Doctors Without Borders, grandson of Gurpreet Jaffre, civil rights activist in India, fighting against the caste system, and grandson of Mikhail and Gena Fuller, both psychology professors at MIT."

Leave it to Wade Jaffre to blow that one out of the water. June felt her knees weaken.

"I had no idea your parents were doctors," Junie said when she was able to speak. "Let alone volunteering in Darfur."

"They're coming back in four months."

"You're not by yourself, are you?" Mrs. D. gave him a concerned look.

"No." Wade picked up both Tabitha's and Junie's backpacks, which had been slouched against the railing. He slung one on each shoulder. "I'm living with my brother. He's a fourth-year med student."

Not only hadn't Junie known anything about his parents, but she hadn't known this, either. How could he be so exotic and cool and not brag about it all over school? If she'd had anything to brag about, be damned sure she'd have been crowing it from every possible perch. She gave Tabitha a look, eyebrows raised. Tabitha gave her head a little shake in reply, her astonished expression confirming that all of this was news to her, too.

How cool, to be living with your brilliant older brother, temporarily parentless because your equally brilliant parents were overseas doing their best to save the world? Never mind having a crush on him . . . Junie practically wanted to *be* him.

"Well . . ." Mrs. D. was clearly as smitten with him as Junie and Tabitha were. She normally had a lot more to say at this point in any conversation. "Very nice to meet you, Wade. It certainly sounds as though you are quite the young man."

"We should go." Tabitha cut her mother off before Mrs. D. could embarrass them further. Now Junie could see how she herself had ended up saying *okey-dokey* to him. He had a way of making otherwise fairly intelligent people say rather stupid things.

"You come from exceptional stock," Mrs. D.

continued, oblivious to Tabitha's warning. "I'm eager to see what you will make of yourself, young man."

And just like that, it had become another *okey-dokey* moment. *Young man?* Twice? Even Mrs. D. had spiralled down from savvy, hip mom to dotty auntie in one minute flat.

"And what are your plans after you finish high school?" she asked.

"I'm going to go to film school." Suitably cool. "I want to be a documentary filmmaker. I'm hoping my first movie will be about my parents. I want to follow them for a year on one of their overseas trips. Document that. They're okay with it. It took them about five minutes to mourn the fact that I didn't want to be a doctor like them and my brother. Now they're into it."

Junie, Tabitha and Mrs. D. all practically swooned. How very cool was that? They all gazed adoringly at Wade for a long, sighful moment. He was lovely. Dreamy, smart and so handsome. Junie, for one, wanted to reach out and touch his muscular brown arm. And after that she'd have liked to lean on tippy-toe and kiss him on the lips—

"So, ladies . . ." Wade blushed. He must have been used to this, girls and women fawning over him on a regular basis. "I dropped by to see if Junie wanted a ride." He gave Junie an absolutely delicious smile. "So, do you and your sister-in-arms want a lift to school? Because if you do, we should get going."

"Of course." Mrs. D. was the first to recover. She kissed Tabitha on the cheek, then realized her blunder and kissed Junie, too. "Off you go, girls."

"Bye, Mom," Tabitha said, still stunned. Then she realized her own screw-up. "I call her that all the time," she said to Wade with a shrill little laugh. "She's like a mother to me, too."

"See you later," Junie said as she pulled Tabitha down the steps. "We're going to be late, Tab." She wanted her out of there before she ruined her messy little lie. "Let's go."

Junie sat in the front because Tabitha—bless her heart—scooted into the back before Junie could. No one said anything for the first few moments, which felt awkward. But then it got even more awkward, because when they passed Junie's real house, Wade made a comment about Mr. and Mrs. Rawley's little scene.

"Did you tell Tabitha about that man and woman going at each other in their driveway?"

Of course Junie had. "Yeah." Junie was pretty sure that she was, at that very moment, shrivelling into a pile of dried-up humiliation.

"Crazy." Wade glanced in the rear-view mirror. "Both of them yelling at each other like that? In broad daylight? And it was like Jack Sprat, you know? 'Jack Sprat could eat no fat, his wife could eat no lean . . .' He was super-skinny and she was super-fat and she was shaking her finger at him, yelling, and all the while her arm fat was wobbling so hard I thought it was going to throw her off balance. And it was all that much more bizarre because the street is so super-normal and tidy, like they were deviating from some kind of social code, you know? A very filmable moment. Very *American Beauty.*"

He'd got all that, in the few seconds it took to drive

by? With that kind of attention to detail, he really would be a very brilliant filmmaker someday. Junie was as impressed as she was mortified. And she'd never heard of *American Beauty*, which just made her feel stupid.

Tabitha said nothing. Junie turned to look at her.

Say something, she mouthed silently.

What am I supposed to say? Tabitha mouthed back, shrugging.

Tabitha had never bad-mouthed Junie's mother. Not once. So why would Junie expect her to now? Because of the unique and painful situation, that was why. Junie stared at her, pleading silently for her to bend her morals just this once. Tabitha stared back. That girl did not have a mean bone in her body, Junie marvelled, annoyed. Usually she loved that about Tabitha. No judgment. No belittling. But right then, it would have been helpful if Tabitha could have tapped into her inner bitch for just one eensy minute to play along. If she even had an inner bitch. Tabitha shook her head, wordlessly resolute. Junie turned back to the front. If Tabitha wasn't going to say anything, then Junie would have to.

"It was kind of funny." Junie choked out the words. "I guess."

"It wasn't 'kind of' funny," Wade said. "It was very funny. One of those moments I wish I could've caught on film, you know?"

Junie held her breath. She knew that this would make Tabitha mad. She took after her mother that way, always rooting for the underdog. Never making fun of anyone. Always being the advocate. The champion. Junie turned, ready to silently implore her just to play along, but Tabitha would not be stopped.

"I don't think it's particularly funny at all," she said, glaring pointedly at Junie. "I know them. They're going through a rough time. And there's a kid involved. A *friend* of mine. So I don't think it's funny at all. And definitely not something I'd want to see preserved forever on film by you, to do with whatever you want. No thank you."

Awkward silence descended upon the van like an invisible villain. Tabitha was waiting for Junie to agree with her, and for Wade to apologize. He went first.

"Sorry." He raised his eyes to the rear-view mirror again, this time smiling. "I am sorry. *Mea culpa*."

"*Mea culpa* is right," Tabitha continued, while Junie stayed mute. "It's not cool to make fun of people who are going through a hard time."

"You are absolutely right." Wade placed a hand on his chest and bowed his head. "I am sorry. I didn't know."

"You shouldn't have to know. You should just not make assumptions in the first place. You have no idea who they are or what they're going through. What do you know about any of it? Nothing. That's what you know."

"I'm sorry," Wade repeated. "You're absolutely right. I, Wade Jaffre, am a complete and utter asshole." Junie could hear the easy tone in his words, as though he was making fun of himself.

Was he being sincere? Or just saying that to appease Tabitha? And if he was just apologizing for her sake, was that because he was trying to impress her in the first place, and now that it had backfired he was backpedalling to get back into her good books? Or was he apologizing because he really meant it? Tabitha interrupted Junie's bout of over-thinking, which was a good thing, because Junie knew she should care more about the insult to her parents than whether Wade liked her or Tabitha better.

"Junie?" Tabitha glared at her. Waiting for her to come clean and admit that Jack Sprat and his big fat wife were her parents. End the lie. But no way. Not a chance. Junie wasn't going to give up that easily. "We know them, Junie. You're better than that."

Ouch. A punch right into the solar plexus of Junie's guilt. She had to catch her breath before she could respond. Tabitha was worse than a parent when it came to guilt trips.

Junie thought hard about what she would say next. She could hear her father's voice advising her: *Think before you speak.* And she was. Thinking hard. Thinking hard about how she could come clean. How she *should* come clean. How this was the moment, the perfect time to do it. How she could try to work it to be funny. How once she'd told the truth, everything would get easier.

"It *was* kind of funny," Junie finally said, forcing the words out. She'd thought hard, and still she'd come up with something she immediately regretted.

And so the moment passed. She looked over her shoulder, as if she were actually watching the opportunity to tell the truth slip behind her, a shimmering wake, dissolving.

FOUR

:
:
•

Tabitha said nothing for the rest of the ride. Junie could feel her glare of disappointment drilling into her from the back seat. She didn't even have to look back to know that Tabitha was sitting ramrod straight with her arms crossed and her chin jutted out like a pissed off six-year-old. Or a pissed off sixteen-year-old.

Wade and Junie talked about the bottle drive, or he did mostly. Junie responded with appropriate one- or two-word answers while all the while she was wishing he hadn't driven by her parents' house in the first place. She'd have given up her ride home with him if it meant she could erase what had happened along the way. She wished he'd never pulled up beside her. Or she tried to wish that.

"So the money is going to Darfur," he was saying when Junie broke out of her thoughts. "Not because my parents are there. Well, sort of, I guess, if I'm being honest. But more because it's the cause we decided to support."

"Right." Why had he stopped in the first place? What did he really want with her? Or Tab?

"And the teachers' union is going to match whatever we make, so it's double what we can get out of the bottle drive."

"Cool." Junie glanced back at Tabitha. Still with the glare. Tabitha added a cocked eyebrow for good measure. Junie returned her fractured attention to her so-called conversation. Wade didn't seem to notice her lack of attention. He just kept talking.

"You wouldn't believe what we went through to make that happen. Apparently, the teachers' union never does that."

"Really."

It was Tabitha's fault that Junie couldn't talk to Wade like a real, functioning person would. Her glare was so loud that it drowned out everything else. Junie could hardly hear what Wade was saying because of the pounding disapproval coming from the back seat.

When they got to the school, Tabitha slammed out of the van and waited until after Wade said goodbye and went ahead of them into the building before she turned on Junie.

"How could you?"

"You know exactly how." Junie hitched her backpack up on one shoulder and started walking. "You, out of everyone in the whole world, know how."

"Come on, Junie." Tabitha caught up to her. "Your own parents?"

"Exactly."

"You can't just let him go on thinking that you don't know them, that they're not your very own mother and father."

"I don't need a reminder of that fact, thank you." Junie had Art first period, and Tabitha had Physics, so this couldn't go on forever, thankfully.

"Apparently you do. You've got one mother and one father and you just betrayed them both. What have they ever done to you?"

Junie stopped in her tracks and stared at her best friend in disbelief. "Seriously?"

Tabitha gave her head a little shake. "Sorry. Okay. Not fair."

"Thank you."

And then the bell rang. As Junie headed for Art, she heard Tabitha call after her. "We're not done with this, Juniper Rawley."

Junie turned. "You sound like my mother."

"There are worse things!" Tabitha added for good measure.

But were there? Her mother was definitely one of the Worst Things right now. She hadn't always been this bad. Junie remembered when she was little, and her mother would make cupcakes for her whole class on her birthday, and come along on field trips, and help out in her classroom on special days. Sure, it seemed like it cost her way more effort than the average mom, but she did it anyway. She'd make costumes for the school plays and come to all her soccer practices and take her out to lunch for a special mother-daughter day at least once a month. But even while she was busy being Supermom on the outside, everything was piling up at home. Even then. And it had slowly got worse, year by year. And her mother had got fatter, year by year, as if her weight reflected the sheer mass she'd hoarded and collected and squirrelled away since Junie was little. There were pictures from back then, ones where the rooms looked almost normal on Christmas Day or Junie's first few birthdays. The house was cluttered, but in a warm, homey kind of way. Not like now. By the time her fifth birthday rolled around, the house was bad enough that her mother booked the community room at the nearby library and held the party there. Junie had not had a birthday party at home since. After fourth grade, she didn't have a party at all. Just her and Tabitha at Tabitha's house, with pizza and cake and more than a couple of presents from Mrs. D. to make up for the sad state of affairs.

In Art class, Junie glanced down at her sketchbook. Forty-five minutes had passed, and all she had to show for it was an angry-looking mess of charcoal that kind of looked like a monster in a box. Surprise, surprise. Wouldn't want the school psychologist to get a hold of that.

Lulu leaned over. "What is that?"

"I don't know."

"Why not?"

"I don't know." Junie glanced at what Lulu was working on: an elaborate pen-and-ink drawing of a fairy perched gracefully on a toadstool. It might as well have been a self-portrait. Lulu was a tiny, elfin girl, with fine features and big green eyes. Her long, dark brown hair hung halfway down her back, and her flowy skirts and shimmering tops and sandals all year round made her appear altogether otherworldly. "What's yours?" Junie said, hoping to shift the subject off of herself and her disturbing work of art. If you could call it art.

"Your drawing looks very, very angry." Lulu shook her head a little. "That's not healthy, Junie."

"Duly noted, Lulu."

Junie considered Lulu a friend—a really good one, actually—even if she didn't know a thing about her life at home. She was Ollie's girlfriend—if you could believe that a geek like him could find true love in the tenth grade. They were both super-smart, he was dorky, she was whimsical, and together they were sickeningly sweet. Junie considered Ollie a friend too, and he was yet another one who had no idea about the mess she went home to every day.

Junie and Lulu stopped by their lockers and then made their way to the cafeteria, where Tabitha was waiting for Junie just outside the door. Lulu went ahead to join Ollie, leaving Tabitha and Junie behind.

"Look." Tabitha pointed to their usual table through the open doors. There was Lulu, just sitting down beside Ollie, and there was Wade Jaffre, too.

"Wow." This was an interesting new development. Junie didn't know what he'd done during his lunch hour until now, but there he was, in the flesh, at her table. "He must really like you."

"After this morning? Highly doubt it. More likely you. He probably thinks I'm a total goody-goody." Tabitha yanked her arm, forcing Junie's attention back on her. "Either way or neither way, you have to come clean about your parents."

"But you agreed to play along!"

"That was before you were so awful!"

"Tabitha, that isn't fair." Another glance at the table. Wade was looking their way. He waved. Junie and Tabitha both broke from their argument to each give him a flirty little wave back. And then they went back to it.

"Isn't it?"

"Don't go all parental on me, okay? You can't honestly tell me that you wouldn't have done the exact same thing as me."

"I can so."

"Oh yeah?"

He was still looking at them, only now he was waving them over. Tabitha held up a finger, gesturing that they'd be another minute.

"What would you have done, oh Holier Than Thou Tabitha, who is—in fact—a total goody-goody?"

"Told him to stop in front of the house and let me out so I could go referee my deeply embarrassing parents."

Junie thought that that was actually a pretty good response. But then Tabitha had had a long time to come up with it. It was infinitely easier to come up with a witty retort after the fact.

"Well, it's too late. I can't go back in time, as much as I'd like to for a zillion reasons, so here we are. I've got a good little lie going, and don't you go messing it up. Or I'll trump you."

"You would?" She looked genuinely hurt. Since they were old enough to know what "trump" meant they'd had trump power over each other. It was a little like double-dog-dare-you, only it was even more binding. Junie could trump her, and Tabitha could trump Junie, but never at the same time. Whoever got there first. And Junie just had.

"I would. So this is me officially trumping you on this matter, Tabitha Faith Dillard. You have to play along with my lie."

Tabitha clutched her lunch bag to her chest, horrified. "I can't believe that you just did that, Junie."

"Well, I did." Junie headed for the table. "Now come on. Your boyfriend is clearly requesting your company."

"Or your boyfriend," Tabitha said, catching up.

"Or Ollie's," Junie suggested. This sent them into a fit of giggles, just in time for both of them to look like ditzes by the time they got to the table.

Ollie and Lulu and Wade were talking about the bottle drive. Who knew one little charity fundraiser could command such time and attention? Ollie and Lulu were sitting side by side on one side of the table, with Wade all by himself in the middle of the bench on the other side. Tabitha and Junie looked at each other, silently daring the other to sit first. With a defiant arch of her eyebrow—payback for trumping her—Tabitha helped herself to the spot on Wade's left. Not to be outdone, Junie slid in on his right side.

Neither Junie nor Tabitha contributed much to the conversation; they were too busy having their own silent argument with each other. Junie couldn't believe that

Tabitha was acting this way—she might have been the only person who knew the truth about Junie's home and screwed up family, but she didn't actually know what it was like to live there. To have that be her life.

When the bell rang, Junie pulled Tabitha aside. "Listen, don't try to fix this, okay? Sometimes it's okay to lie. Sometimes it's even better to lie. This is one of those times."

"It's never better to lie."

"Yes, it is, Tabitha." Junie squeezed her arm. "You might not have had one of those times yet, but I have. Just trust me on this, okay?"

Tabitha pulled her arm away and held it to her chest, as if Junie's touch had been scalding. "For now. I guess. But I don't like it."

"And I don't like my life, but it is what it is for now. I'll tell him the truth when the time is right. Leave that up to me, okay? You don't have to worry about it. Just play along."

"Fine. I'll play along. But I'll worry about it, too."

⋮

Junie wanted to walk home with Tabitha after school, just to make sure that things were okay between them, but it was Wednesday. Wednesday was her father's night to have her at his place. The current arrangement was that he got her every Wednesday and every other weekend. She usually agreed to hang out with her dad on Wednesdays, though she wouldn't spend the night, and she rarely went otherwise. Partly because of That Woman, but mostly because of her mom. Junie didn't think she should be left alone, and her dad seemed to agree, as he didn't do much to enforce the weekend visits.

Junie went out to the parking lot to wait for her dad and was relieved when Tabitha joined her, sitting beside her on the curb.

"Are we okay?" Tabitha asked.

"Mind-reader freak." Junie leaned against her. "I think we're okay. You think we're okay?"

"I guess. Yeah."

She and Tabitha had to leave it at that, because her dad pulled into the parking lot just then. Even before he stopped, Junie could see that That Woman was sitting in the passenger seat, and Princess Over All III—her prize-winning Weimaraner—was stretched out across the back seat, front paws regally set one atop the other. Junie said goodbye to Tabitha with a tight hug and then approached the car.

"Where am I supposed to sit?"

That Woman—Evelyn St. Claire, if Junie was being polite—turned and gave Princess a look. That was all it took and the dog sat up, now only taking up half the back seat. Evelyn looked at Junie, all smiles.

"There," she said. "Better?"

"*Better* would be the dog in the very back, where dogs are supposed to be." Junie opened the door. "That would be slightly better. Very slightly."

Once Junie was in and the door was closed and they pulled away, Evelyn turned and said, "*Better* is a negotiable quality. We all have our own versions of what is better." Another smile.

"Dad?" Junie put it out there in general, trying to fill that little word with all of her questions *why*. Why was he with That Woman, the life coach he'd hired to help her mom but who had only succeeded in breaking up his marriage and ruining her life even more than it was already? Why had he brought her along today, on *their* day? Why did he like her in the first place?

"I got off early, and Evelyn is done for the day, so we thought we'd go get ice cream before dinner. Live on the wild side. Dessert before the main course."

Evelyn laughed. She turned to Junie again. "Your father is so funny, Juniper."

Junie didn't think it was funny at all.

"What if I don't want ice cream?" This elicited small daggers from her father via the rear-view mirror.

They drove silently for a while. That Woman rested her hand on Junie's father's thigh. Princess Over All III stared at her out of the corner of her eye as she sat facing carefully forward, hardly moving a muscle as the car leaned into the corners and pulled to and from complete stops. That dog was not a dog. That dog was a robotic statue.

And That Woman was not a woman. She was an evil home wrecker. What kind of personal life coach would do that to a client? Especially a client as vulnerable as Junie's mother. She'd lured her father away with her perfect ponytail and tailored suits. She'd charmed him away with her lime-green hybrid car and downtown loft. She'd weaselled her way into their lives by lying, saying that she could make Junie's mom better when all she wanted was to snatch her dad away and make him her love slave.

Junie let her thoughts slide back to ice cream as her dad parked the car. She did not want ice cream. She did not want to be here with That Woman and her dog. She didn't even particularly want to be with her dad. With a sigh, she climbed out of the car and trailed into the ice cream parlour behind her dad. That Woman waited outside. She didn't eat ice cream, and didn't want to leave Princess tied up.

Junie reluctantly ordered chocolate peanut swirl, which was, in fact, her favourite. But all that thinking about the state of her ruined family turned her stomach and she really, honestly, didn't want the ice cream. She waited until her father and Evelyn strolled ahead of her along the river path, away from the ice cream shop, and then she dumped it in the garbage. Princess Over All III looked back just then, from her perfect heel at Evelyn's side, as if to say she knew all, saw all. Which apparently she did. She even slept up in the loft bedroom, where her father and Evelyn slept, which meant that she was watching when they did it. That thought was the one that tipped Junie over the edge. Her stomach swirled and churned. A horrible image invaded her thoughts: her father's naked, hairy butt plunging up and down between That Woman's waxed stick legs. She doubled over and ran for the women's washroom, where she threw up her lunch into the garbage can. Finished, she cupped her hands under the faucet and rinsed out her mouth with water. She spat, and rinsed again, but the taste of bile was still there. Welcome to another fabulous Wednesday night, brought to you by the home wrecker and the oblivious fool and their creepy omniscient dog.

FIVE

On the morning of the bottle drive, Junie woke to the steady patter of rain. She pulled on the outfit she and Tabitha had agreed on the night before and made her way downstairs. Her mother had slept in her chair again, for the seventeenth day in a row.

"Mom."

A line of drool crept down her chin. Her hair was smashed flat on one side and sticking up on the other. She was snoring, her chest rising and falling heavily. Her open laptop was perched on her thighs.

"Mom!"

"Unh?" She opened her eyes. "What?"

"You should sleep in your bed. That's what they're for."

"What?" She blinked, still sleepy.

"Beds are for sleeping. Chairs are not. You should sleep in your *bed*."

"Maybe I did." Her mother sat up a little, set aside the computer and stretched her arms. "Maybe I got up early and came down."

"No. You slept right there. All night. Again." *Like a loser*, she wanted to add. "There's no way you can sleep in your own bed because it's covered in dirty clothes and junk."

"And so what if I did sleep here? What's it to you?"

Junie could think of all kinds of answers to that, but she held her tongue. Her mother stretched again and then pushed herself up out of the chair and headed for the bathroom, leaving a great big sag in the chair in the shape of her butt. Junie shook her head and hurried into the kitchen to get something to eat. She and Tabitha got groceries once a week, so at least she knew there was food. She grabbed the bread and stuck two pieces into the toaster.

On her way back to the chair, her mother passed through the kitchen, where Junie was eating at the table, which was piled high above her head with her mother's crap, except for the tiny wedge Junie kept clear for herself. Her whole family used to eat at this table, but not for many years. At first her mom had used the table just to "organize" her things as she brought them home or they arrived in the mail. And then it became the first dumping ground and they ate dinner in front of the TV in the living room. That's when Junie knew something was wrong. She was old enough to know that good families ate dinner together around the table. Even families of two, like Tabitha and her mom. They still ate dinner together every night at the dining room table, with cloth placemats ironed flat and cloth napkins tucked neatly into carved pewter rings, and smudge-less glasses and cutlery set in the proper place and order.

"Where're you off to so early?" her mother asked the fridge, staring at its insides.

That fridge was actually one of the cleanest spots in the house. About a year ago, the old fridge had gotten so disgusting, with expired tubs of unrecognizable foodstuffs and moulding fruit and soured milk and leaking jars of ancient condiments, that Junie's mother had ordered a new fridge online, and had just abandoned the other one rather than clean it out. The delivery guy had brought it in through the sliding glass door off the dining room, and grudgingly wrestled it along the narrow trail through the detritus to wedge it in beside the old fridge. He'd taken one surreptitious peak into the other one and did not offer to cart it away. So there it stood. Junie had taken ownership of the new fridge, and that's why it was the third-cleanest spot in the house, after her room and the one bathroom she kept spotless too.

"I told you. Today is the bottle drive."

"Right."

"You forgot."

"Right." She took a slice of cold pizza from a greasy box, hesitated, and then helped herself to another one. "But it's all coming back to me now."

"Oh, really?" Junie set her cereal bowl down with a deliberate clatter. "Then tell me, why is this not just a bottle drive? Why is it actually something much more important?"

A piece of pizza in each hand, her mother winked at her. "I believe his name is Wade. Wade Jaffre."

She had remembered. Junie was genuinely surprised. And impressed. She'd told her about him while her mother watched the Shopping Channel. *Superstorage System! Holds up to twelve pairs of shoes and just slides away under the bed! For just $19.95, we'll send you two Superstorage Systems PLUS the Handyman Keychain, with eight different screw heads!* Four of them were on the way. One for her, one for Junie's father—even though he'd left them for That Woman—one for Junie, and one spare in case any of them lost theirs. Just what they needed.

"He's the one you have a crush on, right?" She took a bite of pizza. "And Tabitha too?"

"He's the one that half of the girls at school have a crush on, but yes. Both of us too."

"That's not good." Her mother shook her head. "What are you going to do when he picks one of you over the other?"

"He won't pick either of us, I bet. He's just being nice. Getting us to help him out with the bottle drive. I'm sure that there are plenty of grade eleven girls he could choose from."

"Sounds like he's being more than nice. Sounds like he's courting you. Both of you."

Junie cringed at the word "courting." Who said "courting" any more? And what would her mother know about it anyway? The last time she'd gone on a date was over twenty years ago. And that was with Junie's father, who'd been her first and only boyfriend. So there was no way that Junie would take any so-called "courting" advice from her mother.

Junie brought her bowl to the sink—which she insisted on being kept clear after she'd found a writhing colony of maggots in a heap of unwashed dishes a few months before—and rinsed it.

"Besides, if he picks one of us, he'll pick Tabitha. She's prettier."

"She is not. You're both beautiful."

"You have to say that."

"And I would anyway." She took another bite of pizza.

Junie gave her a long, sad look. This was the mother she missed so much that it actually hurt her, drawing a tightness around her heart that made it hard to breathe. This mother, the one who took an interest in her instead of all the crap she ordered off the Internet and all the sparkling junk from the Shopping Channel. The one who asked questions and was interested in the answers.

"You're beautiful, Junie."

Junie wished she could say the same for her mother. She had been beautiful, back when she was first dating Junie's dad. There were pictures as proof. Snapshots of the two of them going to prom, dressed up in their tragically outdated finery, beaming at each other. But she'd been wearing the same filthy clothes for five days now, and likely hadn't washed in as long either. Junie wanted to shove her mother into the bathroom, make her strip and then force her to get into the shower and actually take care of herself. Where had that polished, slender earlier version of her mom gone?

Her mother turned away, as if she knew what Junie was thinking. They both heard the familiar theme song of the British soap opera her mom watched on the weekend. On Saturday mornings they played all of the week's episodes back to back.

"*Coronation Street* is starting." Her mother hesitated in the doorway, her cold pizza slices drooping. "Don't you even want a plate?" Junie cringed. She didn't mean to sound bitchy, but she did anyway. Junie tried that again. "I mean, can I get you a plate?"

Her mom looked at her, her face blank. "Yes. Please."

Junie got a plate from the cupboard and held it out to her.

"You know, Junie . . . I don't . . . I mean, I never . . ." She took the plate and arranged the pizza on it before wiping her hands on her pants. "I just want to tell you that I don't want to be like this. The hoarding just crept up and now—"

"You don't have to explain—"

"I see the way you look at me. At all of this." She gestured around her with the pizza. "When I was a little girl, I never imagined I'd end up like this. I wanted so much more for myself. And for you, too."

Junie felt a wash of shame flood her veins. "I don't—"

"You *do*. And that's okay. I can't imagine what it's like to be you, Junie. Living with this. With *me*."

The phone rang. Junie lunged for it, so very thankful to have a way to stop the conversation from unravelling even more.

"Hello?"

"Your boyfriend called." Wade had Tabitha's number as Junie's, and vice versa. So far that hadn't been a problem because he hadn't called either of them, but to be on the safe side, they'd both recorded generic messages with no names. Mrs. D. was in on it, and Junie's mom never answered the phone, so it didn't matter on that end. Neither of the girls had cell phones. Not since they'd each been given one for Christmas and the bills were over six hundred dollars by the end of January. And that was just from calling and texting each other. They were still paying them off.

"Or *your* boyfriend. Did you talk to him?"

Tabitha sighed. "No, I saw it was his number, so I had my mom pick it up. I'm not stupid."

Junie's mom was back in the living room, her soap playing loudly, working-class English accents sharp and jangly.

"No, but you *want* him to know the truth, so I could see you 'screwing up' just so my lie would be exposed. I know you're trying to play along . . . but I also know that you don't really want to."

"Good morning, Junie. How are you today?" Tabitha's words were awash in sarcasm. "I, for one, am just peachy. Thanks for asking, rather than launching into a critique of my morals, which are just peachy too, by the way."

"Sorry," Junie said. "Good morning, Tabitha. What did Wade want?"

"He told my mom he was calling to see if you wanted a ride."

As if on cue, the phone beeped. Junie looked at the Caller ID. Jaffre. "He's calling here."

"Offering me a ride, I bet."

"Should I get it?"

"No, because *this* is supposed to be your house."

"Right, well . . . I'll come over there and we can call him back together."

"This is getting ridiculous, Junie."

"Ridiculous or not, Tabitha, I trumped you. And don't you and your peachy morals forget it."

⋮

Junie grabbed an umbrella and made her way through the rain and wind to Tabitha's house. Mrs. D. greeted her at the door with a frown. She was dressed to go out and had a rolled up yoga mat hanging over her shoulder in its own narrow bag.

"You know I don't like all this lying, Junie."

"I know, I know. And I'm sorry, Mrs. D. I promise to set it straight as soon as I can."

"I trust you will." She slipped her water bottle into her purse and collected her keys. "I've set out a box of bottles for the drive. It's in the garage by the recycling."

"Great, thanks."

One step out the door, she turned and said, "I don't like you trumping Tabitha on this one, honey. Just so you know. Think about what you're doing, okay?"

Junie blanched. "Okay, Mrs. D., I will."

Junie stomped up the stairs to Tabitha's room. "You told your mom that I trumped you about Wade?"

"Yep. Unlike some of us, I don't lie."

There wasn't much Junie could say to that. Tabitha

handed her the phone and she called Wade, thanking him for his offer of a ride and explaining that Tabitha was already at her house.

Before he got there, they decided that Tabitha would sit in the front, so she'd have her chance to flirt with him.

"Because the minute he finds out that I've been lying to him, he'll choose you anyway, so what does it matter?"

"I'm lying to him too."

"Not really. You're just playing along with my big fat lie. And no, I'm not calling my mother fat."

"Good."

Wade honked his horn, so they dashed out into the rain, Junie carrying the box of bottles from Tabitha's house.

"Ladies," he said as they shook off the rain and buckled up their seatbelts. He glanced at the box and then turned to Tabitha, "Any from your house?"

"Those are—"

"From both of our houses," Junie finished before Tabitha could barrel forward, being honest without thinking.

Tabitha turned and rolled her eyes at Junie as Wade pulled away from the curb. There were probably more empty bottles in Junie's house than they'd collect for the whole drive, but she wasn't about to admit that.

The bottle drive was in the far corner of the mall parking lot. Lulu and Ollie had beaten them there and were struggling to put up a big white tent to cover the area where they'd be sorting the bottles. Between the five of them, they managed to get it up and set up the tables that Ollie's dad had brought in the back of his truck.

"Who's supposed to do what?" Lulu asked once everything was ready.

"Lulu and Tabitha can greet people and take their bottles," Wade said. "Ollie, Junie and I can sort them out. How does that sound?"

Tabitha shot Junie a look. *See? He likes you best*, she said with her eyes, and for the first time, Junie wondered if she might be right.

⋮

Ollie settled himself at one end of the long table, Wade and Junie at the other. People backed up their cars and unloaded beer bottles and pop cans, and Junie and Wade and Ollie took them and sorted like with like. They had to pack the bottles by dozens. Junie caught Ollie watching her count.

"I can count to twelve," she said. "It's pretty much everything after that that's the problem."

Wade raised an eyebrow. He turned to Ollie, but Ollie just shook his head.

"Math is not my forte," Junie added. "Ollie tutors me."

"Ah." Wade grinned.

"Still want me to count for you?"

"Sure." Wade stacked another box on top of a tower of boxes. His arm muscles firmed up as he did. "Ollie can help you if you get stuck."

"Jerk." Junie punched him in the arm.

Tabitha, having seen the whole exchange, called Junie over.

"For the record, you only punch your crush in the arm

if you are eight years old or younger. Case in point, Nick Gimse in third grade." She accepted a bag of wine bottles from a guy driving a Land Cruiser. "Thank you, sir." She returned her attention to Junie. "If you want Wade Jaffre to take you seriously, you have to act your age."

"Are you giving me boy advice? Do I have to remind you that I've been your date for every high school dance we've ever been to? So much so that I'm sure the whole school population thinks we're lesbians."

"Maybe I am."

"Fine, then me too." Junie glanced back at the sorting table. The bottles were piling up. "Okay, lesbo. Are we finished with this little coaching session?"

She punched Junie in the arm. "No more elementary school dating techniques. Be a woman."

"Maybe Evelyn St. Claire can employ you as a life coach intern for your summer job this year."

"And maybe her Weimaraner will chew off her surgically sculpted nose while she sleeps."

"That's not a very Tabitha thing to say."

"Well, That Woman inspires terribly violent thoughts. Very un-Tabitha-like thoughts. Out of everyone involved in your family's massive meltdown, she's the only one worth blaming anything on."

Wade came up in time to hear the last bit. "Who're we blaming? And for what?"

"No one," Tabitha and Junie said in unison. "Nothing."

"Understood." He helped himself to the wine bottles and took Junie's hand. Tabitha grinned. Junie felt luscious, nervous chills dance up her arms. Wade Jaffre was holding her hand. In his. Their hands were touching. His was warm and dry. Hers felt clammy and sticky from handling the dirty bottles. "Care to join me at the sorting table?"

"Oh, Wade. Are you asking Junie on a date?" Tabitha's tone was cheeky. "Because it kind of looks like it."

Wade blushed—actually blushed, his brown cheeks brimming dark red. "Maybe."

Junie glared at Tabitha. She wanted to both kill her and make her queen of the world. She mouthed over her shoulder, *I hate you*, and then, *I love you!* as Wade dragged her back to the sorting table.

SIX

· · · ·

They raised five hundred and sixteen dollars at the bottle
drive, and so would end up with over a thousand by the
time the teachers' union matched them. At the end of the
day, after they'd made several trips to the bottle depot in
Ollie's dad's truck, Wade suggested they get warm at the
café across the street from the mall.

"What can I get everyone?" he asked as they gathered
at the counter to read the menu. "It's my treat."

"You don't have to do that," Lulu said in her breathy
way.

"She's right," Junie added. "You don't."

"You all helped me out, so let me do this to thank you."

He bought their drinks, and they took a table as the
barista started to make them. Ollie's and Lulu's soy lattes
came up first, and then Tabitha's mocha. When the three
of them had gone to collect their drinks, Wade leaned over

to Junie and said in a low voice, "If I was going to ask you out on a date, you'd know it."

This caught Junie off guard. What was she supposed to say to that? It didn't matter, though, because everyone was back at the table, and Junie's and Wade's drinks were ready. He leapt up. "I'll go get them."

Junie sat back in her chair, stunned. She glanced at Ollie and Lulu and then told Tabitha that she had to go to the bathroom. Which Tabitha understood as code for "come with me."

Once in the privacy of the bathroom, Junie told Tabitha what Wade had said to her.

"Out of nowhere."

"No. Not out of nowhere." Tabitha shook her head. "Like he'd been thinking about it since I mentioned it."

"You think?"

"I know." Tabitha groaned. "Just like I know he's into you. Not me. Way to go, Junie. You're horrible, I hate you, etcetera, etcetera."

Junie was going to argue, but thought better of it. "Want to have a cat fight? Go all scratch-your-face-up-bitch on each other?"

Tabitha shook her head. "Nah."

"Yeah, me either."

But still, a long moment passed, and Junie knew that Tabitha was taking the time to imagine what could have been. At least, that's what she would have been doing if the tables had been turned.

"Just promise me one thing," Tabitha said.

"Anything."

Tabitha pulled the door open. Across the café, Junie could see the others, laughing. Ollie and Lulu tucked into one big easy chair all knotted up with each other, and Wade across from them, his and Junie's drinks on the low table beside him. He glanced up and smiled. Waved.

"Don't gloat. Okay?"

"That's easy. I won't." Junie made her way down the little hall, her eyes on Wade the whole time. At the end of the hall, Tabitha grabbed her.

"You might, though. Even if you don't mean it." Junie could tell by her words and the expression that went along with them that Tabitha was more hurt than she was letting on. Junie would have been too, if it had been her.

She pulled Tabitha into a hug. "I won't. Promise."

"Thanks." Tabitha pulled away, her eyes red around the rims. "You go ahead. I'll be there in a minute."

"Your drink will be cold."

Tabitha shrugged. "Doesn't matter."

"Sorry, Tab."

She shrugged again. "Go on."

But then the weird thing was that once she was back at the table, her drink in hand, Wade hardly said one more word to her. He talked to Ollie, and Lulu, and even Tabitha when she finally came back to the table. But he didn't say much to Junie, hardly even a goodbye when he dropped her and Tab off at Tabitha's/Junie's house.

It had finally stopped raining. Junie and Tabitha stood on the sidewalk watching his van drive away. Tabitha looked at Junie. Junie shook her head.

"Now what am I supposed to think?"

Tabitha draped an arm across Junie's shoulders. "Not sure. Playing hard to get?"

"Here's hoping," Junie said with a shrug.

⋮

As it turned out, Junie didn't have to hope for long. The next Tuesday in World Studies, Wade asked if he could be her partner for the War History trivia game the class was putting together. Of course she said yes. But again, he didn't say much. They were in charge of coming up with ten question cards about the Geneva Convention. They sat side by side at the computer, pulling up bits of the agreement they could use.

"Ever hear of Stanley Kubrick?"

"Sure." Junie hadn't. So why had she said so? Lying was becoming so normal to her that it came as easily as—if not more easily than—the truth. She didn't like that about herself. She had plenty of big lies to take care of. To hell with the small ones. "Actually, no. I haven't," she corrected. "I don't know why I said yes."

"Well, I'm a big fan. He's a filmmaker. *Clockwork Orange, The Shining, Full Metal Jacket*, you know? The conspiracy theorists say he even manufactured the footage of the first moon landing, all on a closed set somewhere outside of London. They say it never happened at all. That it was 'just' a movie."

"Really?" Junie scrolled down to the part where it stated that prisoners of war were entitled to the same quality of health care as their captors. That would make a good question.

"I found some cuttings from *Dr. Strangelove* for sale online."

"Cuttings?"

"The actual bits of film that the editor cut."

"I take it they're pretty rare then." Junie carefully transcribed the text onto an index card. "Right?"

"Very rare. So, the guy who's selling them lives in Chilliwack, if you can believe it. He's that close."

And all of a sudden, Junie realized where this was going. She swallowed. Her hand shook. She had to put her pen down so she wouldn't mess up the rest of the words.

"Yeah?"

"So, I thought I'd drive out after school on Thursday to get them."

"Sounds like a plan." Junie's throat was dry. She needed a glass of water. She wasn't sure if she could bark out even one more word without a drink of water first. She glanced at the water fountain by the door. She coughed. "Excuse me." She got up and crossed to the fountain and took a long drink. He was going to ask her to go with him. Where was Tabitha at a time like this? But, if she'd been here, and Junie asked her for support, would that be gloating? This not-gloating thing might be harder than she thought.

The walk back to the desk was long. Very long. It went on forever, in fact. And the whole while, Wade was looking at her, his face pale. Apparently that was the face of someone about to ask another someone out on a date.

"So, Junie." Wade forced a smile. "Remember when I said you'd know when I asked you out on a date?"

Junie could only nod. She felt like he was asking her

to marry him. She was surprised that he wasn't on one knee, the whole class looking on.

"Will you go with me? To Chilliwack? On a date?"

"Yes."

Wade whistled. The people on either side of them glanced up from their own work. "Phew. Jesus. That was hard."

Junie couldn't have agreed more.

⋮

That afternoon at Tabitha's house, Tab said that telling her a fact was not gloating. It was a fact that Wade had asked her out. It was a fact that Junie had said yes.

"Anything more than that and I might have to cry."

"You just tell me when to shut up."

"I will."

And then Tabitha squealed and bowled Junie over with a great big hug. "Oh my God! You're going on a date! Our first real date! But why Chilliwack? What the heck is out there except farms and smelly cows? And what are you going to *wear*?"

It was funny to hear Tabitha talk like that, but Junie was relieved. She wasn't sure she could stem her excitement, even in the face of Tabitha not being the chosen one.

Tabitha leapt off the bed. "I have the perfect thing."

And it was. A white cotton sundress dotted with small pink flowers. It had dainty straps and a bodice that snugged neatly across Junie's chest. The skirt wasn't too full either. It was exactly right. Junie remembered it from the summer after eighth grade. Tabitha had got it for her uncle's wedding.

"It doesn't fit me any more," Tabitha said by way of explanation. "Boobs got too big."

"It is perfect."

"I think you should wear those pink cowboy boots with it."

"Really?" Junie spun in front of the mirror, trying to picture the boots with it.

"And this." Tab topped the outfit with the straw cowboy hat Junie had brought back for her from the Calgary Stampede, which was also where she'd bought the boots. It was one of those trips that her dad had taken her on last year, while the breakup was in full swing. He called them "distractions." Junie called it guilt.

The hat fit perfectly and was on the smallish side for a cowboy hat. It was more like the ones Hollywood stars and rock idols could get away with wearing. It looked great on Tabitha. But on Junie? Junie tipped it up a bit. That was better. She looked good. She actually looked really good.

"But I'd have to wear it to school because we're going after."

"Right. That. It's too much for school." Tabitha tilted her head, assessing the outfit. "You'll have to change after last period."

"Or skip school altogether." Junie winked at her. "I'll be too nervous to concentrate anyway."

"But if you're 'sick,'" Tabitha quoted with her fingers, "then your mom won't let you out of the house to go on a date."

Junie shrugged. "What do I care?"

"Junie," Tabitha said with a little whine. "Don't become *that* girl. Please don't."

"What girl?" Junie spun again. She was genuinely surprised how her reflection pleased her. As if having been asked out made her suddenly better-looking. Was that possible?"

"The girl from the screwed up home who was the model student until she descended into badass teenage oblivion, ending up a heroin addict on skid row with a pimp for a boyfriend. You know how it goes."

"You should be a writer, Tabitha." Junie took off the hat and shrugged out of the dress. Standing there in her bra and panties, she scowled at Tabitha. "And no. I'm not going to be *that* girl."

⋮

Junie stayed for supper again, and only left for home when Mrs. D. said that her mother would probably like to see the whites of her eyes every now and again, just to know that she was still alive. When Junie opened the door, she heard the theme music for *The Kendra Show*. She glanced at her watch. It was the evening replay of that afternoon's episode. Junie hung the plastic bag with the dress folded up in it on the knob to the closet.

"Junie?"

"Yeah."

"Want to come watch this with me?"

Junie couldn't see her mom for the towers of stuff, so she had to make her way along the dingy trail to get to her. Never, ever, would Wade know about this. Even if they dated through university and got married and had two point five children and a house with a white picket fence and a station wagon, she would never let him into her mother's house. It didn't feel like home, anyway. And hadn't for a long time.

Her mother held up a waxed cardboard box with a plastic fork sticking out of it. "Pad Thai. Want some?"

Junie shook her head.

"You were at Tabitha's?"

"Where else?" Junie leaned against a large box containing the Stairmaster exercise machine that had never been set up.

Her mother paused. Set down the takeout. "I was just asking—"

"And I answered!" Junie sighed. She glanced back in the general direction of the door, which hadn't been visible from the living room for at least five years now. Why was it that she turned into a snarky little bitch when she walked through that front door?

On *The Kendra Show*, a father was weeping, his head in his hands. He'd piled the kids into the minivan one hot, busy weekday morning, dropped the two older ones off at school and then left the baby asleep in the back seat while he took the train to work, mistakenly thinking that the baby had gone with his wife and not with him. He'd forgotten about the baby all day, and when he'd returned to his car that evening, he'd found her dead in her car seat, having died from the heat.

"Why do you watch that stuff?" Junie cringed as a picture of the infant flashed on the screen, chubby cheeks and toothless grin.

"That poor father," her mother answered. "I'll bet he dies over and over every single day, reliving his mistake." Her eyes filled with tears. She lifted the corner of her shirt and wiped them away. Junie caught a glimpse of her mother's pale, fat belly and turned away. "So, so sad."

Junie had nothing to say to that. It was sad. A picture of the baby laid out in a tiny coffin took up the whole screen now. Junie wanted to tell her mom about being asked out for the first time. About the dress. About Wade and Stanley Kubrick and the drive out to Chilliwack. But she couldn't make her mouth open. Instead she mumbled something about having lots of homework and went up to bed, pushing the dead baby out of her mind.

⋮

Junie slept in the next morning, waking to the sound of the front doorbell. She leapt out of bed and threw on the same jeans and T-shirt she'd worn the day before and looked out her window to see Tabitha waving from the sidewalk. Junie waved back, and then hurried downstairs. School started in twenty minutes and it was a good fifteen-minute walk from her house.

Junie stopped short on the bottom step. Her mother had gotten out of her chair and let Tabitha in. And in the few seconds they'd been alone down there, something had happened, because her mother looked wounded. And then it hit Junie. Tabitha had told her. About the date. Wade. Stanley Kubrick.

"I just asked her what she thought of the dress," Tabitha said. "You should've told her, Junie."

Her mother was shaking her head as tears welled up. "No. I get it."

"Mom." Junie's heart sped up. No matter what, no matter anything, she didn't want to make her mother cry. "I was going to. I forgot."

"Your first date?" Her mother choked out a tiny, pathetic laugh. "I don't think so, Junie. A girl's first date is not something you forget."

"Okay, so I didn't tell you. I'm sorry." And she was, even if she didn't sound like it. "Okay? Just stop crying."

But it was too late. Her mother was full-on weeping now. Her cheeks splotchy, her eyes puffed up like dumplings. And as quickly as that, Junie went from sympathetic to mad.

"You wonder why I don't tell you stuff?"

"Junie," Tabitha warned. "Don't."

Junie ignored her. "Because I don't care what you think! Why would I give a shit about what you think? Your life is a disaster! So why would I want anything from you?"

Her mother held up her hands, as if trying to fend off Junie's words.

"We're going to be late, Junie." Tabitha took Junie's arm and squeezed hard. And again, in another split second, the anger abandoned her and she just felt plainly and simply horrible.

"Mom. I'm sorry."

Her mother nodded. "Me too."

Junie pulled away from Tabitha and hugged her mom, ignoring her rank smell. "I'm sorry."

"I know."

"I am. I am sorry."

"I'm sorry too," her mother said through her tears.

"I'll wait outside," Tabitha said.

"No, no. We're okay. It's okay." She pulled away and gave Junie a kiss on the forehead before shoving her gently toward the door. "You girls get off to school or you'll be late."

Junie bent to pick up her backpack, and as she straightened, her mother grabbed her in another hug. "I'm so excited for you! Your first date!"

"Did you see the dress?" Tabitha asked.

It was still hanging on the closet door, so Junie pulled it out and held it against her.

Her mother wiped her face and smiled. "It's very pretty. You'll look wonderful, Junie."

.
.
.

Junie and Tabitha got a few blocks away from home before either of them spoke, and then both of them did at the same time, Junie to scold Tabitha for opening her big mouth, and Tabitha to scold Junie for not telling her mom about the date.

"Truce?" Junie offered when they both stopped to take a breath.

"Truce."

They walked along for another while, quiet again, and then Tabitha stopped walking. "It's getting worse."

Junie knew exactly what she was talking about. She kept walking. She didn't want to have this conversation. Not right now anyway, not while she was still riding the high of being asked out for the first time. But Tabitha caught up to her, and kept talking. "I mean, you'd better keep my mom out of there, because if she saw the state of your house, I wouldn't put it past her to call a social worker and report it as some kind of child abuse or neglect, you know. She has to. As a lawyer."

"I know."

"I saw a rat," Tabitha said.

"What?" Junie's stomach flipped. She hadn't told Tabitha that she'd been setting out traps. She hadn't told her of all the dead rats she'd sprung from them, knotted into a plastic bag and dumped into the garbage can in the alley. She hardly wanted to think about it herself, and she most definitely did not want to be talking about it with Tabitha. Certainly not because Tabitha saw one with her very own eyes.

"In the front hall."

"I'll get some traps. I'll take care of it."

"I saw a trap too, Junie. You didn't tell me."

"Do you blame me?"

"No." Tabitha paused. They were at a light, waiting to cross. When they started walking again, Tabitha said, "It's the smell, too. It smells like someone took a crap and died in there—"

"Yeah, my mother. She's as good as dead."

"We should talk to my mom—"

"No!"

"Junie . . . you can't live in that house like that. It should be condemned."

"So? What's new? Why do you all of a sudden feel compelled to remind me how bad it is?"

"Because it's gotten a lot worse since your dad left."

The school lay ahead of them at the end of the block. Junie wanted to break out in a run and leave Tabitha behind her. Instead, she stopped walking and grabbed Tabitha by the arm. "I know. And I'm trying to fix it. And I'm dealing with the rats. So don't do anything. Don't tell your mom. Everything will be fine. Don't tell her. Okay? Promise?"

Tabitha made a face. Junie knew exactly what that meant. Tabitha didn't want to make a promise she couldn't keep.

"I don't want to have to trump you, Tab."

"You can't always be doing that!"

"Then just promise you won't tell your mom. Not right now. Not yet. Maybe sometime. But not right now."

"I can promise that. I won't tell my mom . . . yet. And if I decide that I have to, then I'll tell you first. Okay? No surprises?"

"Thanks. Sorry about the rat. Did it freak you out?"

"Not really," Tabitha said with a shrug. "I kind of figured they were there."

"How bad is it that you weren't surprised to see a rat?" Junie meant it as kind of a joke, but it wasn't funny. Not at all.

"It's bad," Tabitha said, nodding. "Really bad."

The bell rang for first period, so Junie went one way and Tabitha went the other. Junie's first class was World Studies. Wade would be there, and she would forget about everything else. Her mother and her stinking, festering mountains of garbage. The rats. All of that would disappear for the hour.

SEVEN

⋮

That afternoon Tabitha waited with Junie for her father to pick her up for his usual Wednesday visit.

"I'm sorry about this morning," Tabitha said. "I didn't mean to bring it all up like that."

"You're right to, Tab. I know that."

Junie didn't want to talk about the morning though. She wanted to obsess over her Very First Date. But she couldn't. Her mother and her hoarding and her general decay loomed over everything like an enormous blimp casting a wide, dark shadow. Junie was mad.

"And what I hate the most is that I can't even be a stupid, giggly teenage girl freaking out about tomorrow."

"I know. It sucks."

Junie turned to Tabitha. "And it sucks that you're not going on your Very First Date too. I'm sorry I'm harping

on it. But I really screwed up. With the lie. How am I going
to get out of it without him thinking I'm a jerk?"

But Tabitha didn't have time to answer, because just
then her father's car turned into the parking lot. And he
wasn't alone. That Woman was with him. Again. And her
creepy perfect dog.

"Unbelievable." Junie shook her head in disgust. She
hoped they both saw. "This is supposed to be my time with
him. Not my time with him and *her*."

"Be nice," Tabitha warned. She waved hello as the car
pulled up.

With a roll of her eyes, Junie spun away from the car
without so much as a nod in her father's direction. She pulled
Tabitha close and growled, "I am done with being nice."

"It's not his fault."

"How can you say that, Tab? It is his fault. He could've
fixed it! He had *years* to fix it. And he didn't!"

Junie heard the hum of the window opening behind
her. That Woman's window.

"What?" She turned, her eyes narrowed.

Evelyn St. Claire took a little breath, pulling her chin
back. "And good afternoon to you too, Juniper."

"Call me later." Tabitha gave her a shove toward the
car. She leaned down. "Hi, Mr. Rawley. Hello, Ms. St.
Claire."

That Woman smiled. "Oh, please, call me Evelyn. I've
asked Juniper to and she just won't. Maybe if you do, she
will too."

"Maybe." Tabitha eyed Junie, still standing there,
frozen. "Get in the car, Junie."

With a huff, Junie opened the back door. "Move over," she said, shouldering Princess Over All III to the other side of the back seat. The dog gave her a sniff and tucked herself as far away from Junie as she could get. As her dad eased out of the parking lot, the dog stared at her, never blinking.

"How was school?" Her dad smiled at her in the rear-view mirror.

"Fine."

"Learn anything interesting?"

"No, actually."

"Well, we thought we'd go bowling," he said, ignoring Junie's tone. "Evelyn remembered that you like to bowl."

"When I was eight, maybe."

At this, Evelyn shifted in her seat but didn't turn to look at Junie. She glanced at Junie's father pointedly instead, putting her hand on his thigh as she did. This made Junie's face hot with rage.

"I hate bowling, as a matter of fact."

"You don't hate bowling," her dad said with a laugh. "You're just being difficult."

"Fine. Let's go bowling. What do I care?"

The three of them said nothing. Princess leaned forward a little and licked her lips, as if she might go ahead and bite Junie in the face for being a bitch to Evelyn. The dog was that smart.

After six blocks of saying nothing, the silence piling up in the car like corpses, Evelyn finally turned in her seat, her face set in a careful posture of neutrality.

"I feel compelled to say something—"

"Evelyn," Junie's dad said. "Maybe now isn't the time."

"It's the perfect time, Ron." Evelyn tucked a wave of blond hair behind her ear. "Juniper . . . as you know, I'm a professional life coach. That's what I do. Coach people to reach their full potential."

Junie couldn't believe this. That Woman was going to lecture her. After what she did!

"And I see so much beautiful potential in you," Evelyn continued. "And I want to help you in any way that I can to reach it. You are a smart, savvy, gorgeous young woman. And I know how hard this last year has been for you, and for your family. And I realize that I've had a part to play in that too. And I take responsibility for that. It's up to you to take responsibility for your part in it, as well. As part of your journey to becoming a responsible adult in the world."

Here, she paused.

Junie stared at her. Her mouth opened and shut, and she stared. At first, she had nothing to say to Evelyn St. Claire, and then, like a sudden belch of fury, she had *everything* to say to That Woman.

"Who the hell are you to talk to me about responsibility? When we hired you to help my mom escape from the clutches of her dysfunction, you had a *responsibility* to do your job and leave our family in a better position than when you came. And what did you do? Pulled out a couple of plastic bins, got my mom to barely start sorting out twenty years of junk, and then moved in on my dad and had an affair with him!"

"Junie!" There was panic in her father's voice. "We can talk about this later."

"Not later. Now!" Junie jabbed Evelyn's shoulder.

"You took him away! You stole my dad and left my mom way worse than ever, and you have the balls to sit there and talk to me about responsibility?"

"I'm trained to help—"

"By having sex with your clients?"

"Junie!" Her father pulled the car to the side of the road. "That's enough."

"No, it's not enough. Evelyn, you are a complete and utter bitch. You know that? You're not a professional life coach. You're a total bitch." Finally spent, Junie sat back. Her heart pounded. She looked over at the dog. Princess was emitting a low, menacing growl, her lips curled up ever so slightly.

"Juniper Elspeth Rawley, you apologize this very instant." Her father craned around in his seat, his nose red, which was what always happened when he was mad enough to drag out her whole name like that. "Right now."

Junie shook her head and crossed her arms. "Not a chance."

Evelyn's expression was still parked on neutral. "Ron, never mind." She undid her seatbelt and unfolded herself out of the car. She leaned back in and smiled at Junie's dad. "You two need some time to get things sorted out. I'll take a cab home."

"And take your dog with you," Junie added, surprised at her own gall.

"I will," Evelyn said evenly.

Junie was astounded. Not even that had cracked her shellacked exterior.

"Apologize, Junie. Now."

"No."

"Now!"

Junie shook her head. There was no way on this green earth that any kind of apology or anything that could be mistaken for an apology was going to leave her lips. Not a chance.

Evelyn came around to the other side and let Princess out. Then she leaned into Ron's window and gave him a chaste peck on the check. "I'll see you at home." She straightened and turned her gaze to Junie. "And maybe I'll see you there, too. I hope so, Juniper."

With her trendy little purse tucked under her arm and her dog at a perfect heel, Evelyn St. Claire walked away, tossing a little wave in her wake.

Alone in the car with her dad, still sitting in the back seat like a six-year-old, Junie started to unwind. Her hands shook and her throat constricted. She'd just been horrible. Tabitha would disown her. She might just disown herself. But still, she wasn't sorry.

Her father said nothing. He tipped his head forward until his forehead rested on the steering wheel. He didn't rip into her about being so rude. He didn't tell her to get in the front. He just sat there, with his head down. For a very long time. Cars passed. The traffic light switched four times, and still he sat. Until, at long last, Junie tapped his shoulder and he looked up.

"Dad?"

"Yes."

"I'm sorry." She meant the apology for him, and him alone. And he knew it.

He shook his head. "Not good enough."

"But . . ." A mixture of sadness and frustration and anger tangled Junie's thoughts. She wasn't sure which way to go with everything that was pushing at her head, wanting out. "But I'm not sorry about what I said to her. It's true."

"True or not, that was inexcusable."

"Was it? Don't I get to be honest?"

"No." He shook his head again, slowly. "Not like that."

Anger pushed its way to the front. Junie didn't want it to, but there it was, hot and red. "You're wrong, Dad." As she spoke, her dad pulled the car back into traffic. "You don't get to demand apologies from me. You're the one who should be saying sorry. To me. And Mom. For breaking up our family. For leaving."

"I'm not proud of what I did, Junie." Her dad signalled to turn left, even though Evelyn's place was to the right. "But it's done. And it needed to be done. I was ready to leave, with or without Evelyn's influence."

Junie wasn't sure she wanted to hear this.

"And I think you should leave too."

She absolutely didn't want to hear that. Her dad waited for her to say something, but when she didn't, he kept talking.

"Your mother is an addict. Hoarding is a disease. Your mother needs stuff. Like a drug addict needs a fix, or an alcoholic needs a drink. She's chosen her stuff over her family. I know it's hard to hear it put like that. But that's the truth."

Junie shook her head. She wanted to argue. But she couldn't. Because she knew he was right.

"I'm not going to live with you at That Woman's place, if that's where you're going with this. I belong at home. With Mom. And so do you."

"No, sweetheart. Your mom is sick. She needs to get better. You need to get out of there."

"I can make her better."

"No, you can't. She has to do it herself."

"Is that what Evelyn says?" Her dad made another right turn. He was driving her home. "What about our visit?"

He let out a sad little laugh. "I think you've pretty much put the kibosh on that for today, hon."

Junie's eyes welled with tears. "But I don't want to go home."

"And you don't want to be with me, either. That's clear."

"But I do!" Junie really felt like the six-year-old in the back seat now. Whining. Unsure of what she wanted. Sure that she wanted her dad. And her mom. Together. And not screwed up.

By the time her dad pulled into the driveway, Junie was bawling. It was true; she didn't want to be with her dad right then. Or her mom. So she opened the car door and ran down the street to the only place that felt safe any more. Tabitha's house.

⋮

It took a while, but Tabitha finally calmed Junie down enough that she was ready to go home. It was dark out as they walked the short distance.

"It's not fair," Tabitha said as Junie's house came into sight, the blue flicker of the TV illuminating the living room window. "You should be all giddy and stupid over your date, not worrying about all this mess."

"Tell me about it."

Tabitha hugged her. "See you tomorrow?"

"The big day," Junie said, with a sarcastic edge in her voice. "My Very First Date."

"It'll get your mind off everything else," Tabitha said. "Promise."

⋮

Junie tried to open the front door, but it wouldn't open all the way. Two large garbage cans were shoved against the closet. They were the big plastic kind with wheels and lids, and both of them were filled with bits and bobs of junk. More junk. New junk. Junie squeezed inside, then shut the door and leaned against it. She wasn't sure she could handle any more today.

"Mom? What's with the garbage cans?"

"You'll be very proud to know that I left the house today," her mother called from the living room. "I went to get groceries."

"That's great!" And it was. But not if it meant what Junie thought it meant.

"And the garbage cans?"

"They were in the alley behind the Quikmart. With 'free' signs on them. Perfectly good except the handles on the lids are broken."

There was no point in going into all the reasons

why they did not need two broken garbage bins. Or the crap inside of them. Junie didn't have to ask about that. She knew exactly what had happened. Her mother had gone alley-shopping, helping herself to all the crap people had put out for the garbage. It was the end of the month, so people were on the move from one house to another and would put out what her mother called "perfectly good and useful items" rather than cart them to the new place.

She hadn't left the house to go grocery shopping. She'd left to go alley-shopping. Junie lifted one of the lids. A rusty toaster sat on top of a damp stuffed penguin. Below that she could see a jumble of plastic containers, no lids.

Junie sighed. "You didn't get any actual groceries, did you?"

"I did!" Her mother laughed. She was in a good mood, having brought even more dirty junk home. "I even put them away. After I had a shower. That's right. A shower. So you can stop counting the days. Set your counter back to zero, kid."

"I wasn't counting."

"Oh, come on. I know you were."

"Either way, that is very cool." And it was, but something suddenly occurred to Junie, and now she wasn't thinking about her mother at all. She was thinking about the dress.

The dress Tabitha had given her. Where was the dress? Junie hadn't brought it upstairs yet. The last time she'd seen the dress it had still been hanging on the closet door. She pushed aside a garbage bag full of Styrofoam balls her

mother was keeping for a craft project that never happened. Her mom had rearranged all the crap to fit the garbage bins in. Of course they wouldn't fit in the garage. Nothing had for a good five years. They couldn't even open those doors any more.

The bag wasn't there. The bag with Tabitha's perfect white dress folded neatly inside of it was not there.

"Where's the dress?" Junie hollered. "It's not here!"

"I didn't see it."

"You moved all this shit around to get the stupid garbage cans in the door, so you must've seen it. It was right here!"

Junie heard her mother push out of her chair and make her way to the hall. When she was standing beside her, she asked again, her voice a low growl, "Where the hell is the dress?"

"I didn't see it when I was organizing—"

"You were *not* organizing, Mom! You were adding to the disaster! Can't you see what's happening? Why can't you just *stop*?"

"I didn't see your dress."

"Of course you didn't." Junie put her hands on her hips and shook her head. "Because you can't see anything any more! You're sick! When are you going to get it into your thick skull that you've ruined everything? You drove Dad away, and pretty soon you're going to lose me, too, when a social worker comes and takes me away."

"That won't happen. It's not that bad."

"It is, Mom. It's that bad, and worse." Junie pushed past her and fought her way through the maze of crap to the stairs. Once inside the sanctuary of her room, she slammed the door.

That's when she saw it.

The dress.

Right where Junie had left it that morning. After she'd shown her mom, after her mom had shuffled back to her chair and just as the girls were about to leave, Junie had remembered that she hadn't brushed her teeth. She'd grabbed the dress and brought it upstairs on her way to the bathroom.

In that moment, it didn't occur to Junie to go down and apologize to her mother, but it did occur to her that she should call Wade and just cancel the date. She was that much of a mess.

EIGHT

But, of course, Junie didn't cancel the date.

When she woke up the next morning, there were a few brief moments during which she forgot the horrible day before and all its wretched awfulness. But it all came flooding back when she sat up to get out of bed and saw the dress hanging there. The one she'd accused her mom of losing.

She still wasn't ready to apologize to her mother, though. She was feeling pretty righteous in her careful and emphatic placement of blame. Junie stretched and yawned. This was a new day. The best day. The day of her Very First Date. This would be a better day than the one that came before it. It had to be. If this day went south, then Junie would just curl up under her covers and never get out of bed again. Ever.

She didn't have World Studies that day, so she only saw

Wade at lunch, when he came to sit with her and Tabitha and Ollie and Lulu at their table. Junie had asked him to pick her up at "her" house (Tabitha's) at four o'clock, so that she could have time to get ready and not have to wear the outfit to school.

When the last bell rang and Junie filed out of English, there was Wade, waiting in the hallway.

"I thought I'd give you a ride home. That way we can get out of the city faster."

"Sure!"

Junie fell into step beside him. His locker was at the far end of the same hall as hers, so he went ahead to get his things while Junie sorted herself out at her locker. Tabitha joined her, and when Wade came back, he extended the offer to her, too. They followed him out to the van, and as Wade walked around to the driver's side, Tabitha yanked on Junie's arm.

"Junie, the dress is still at your house. Your *real* house. So, do you see a problem here?"

"I know. What are we going to do?"

Tabitha rolled her eyes. "I'll come up with something."

"Will you?"

"Yeah. Just follow my lead. When the time comes."

The whole ride "home," Junie worried about how she was going to get the dress. This date was not getting off to a good start, and it was just another big fat reminder of her big fat lie and how deeply she was mired in it. And sinking fast.

But when they arrived, Tabitha slipped Junie the front door key as they got out of the van, so that Junie could let them in.

"Do you want a soda, Wade? While Junie's getting ready?" Tabitha eyed Junie as she said it.

"Sure." Wade flopped down on the sofa in the living room. "Thanks."

Junie followed Tabitha into the kitchen.

"Go out the back, and be fast! I'll keep him occupied. Girls are supposed to take forever to get ready. Use it to your advantage. Go!"

Junie sprinted down the back steps and through the back gate, running down the alley to her own back yard. She let herself in the back door and slammed it shut.

"Junie?" her mother called from her television throne. "Why are you coming in the back?"

"I need to get something. Wade's at Tabitha's, waiting. I've got to hurry."

"Well come in here real quick and let me give you a kiss for good luck."

It was as if last night had never happened. As if Junie hadn't said what she'd said. Her mother was acting like the proud parent seeing her lovely daughter off on her first date. Like she wasn't a compulsive hoarder on the brink of losing her only child, either by will or forceful removal. But as Junie made her way into the living room, she had to pass the two garbage bins, which only reminded her of it all again.

"When do you think you'll be back?" her mom asked as *The Kendra Show* went to commercial break.

"Wade figures by eight, nine at the latest."

"No later than nine."

"Okay." Junie let her mom hug her. "I'll tell him the carriage turns back into a pumpkin at nine."

"Wear your seatbelt."

"Of course."

"Did you find the dress?"

Junie wasn't ready to admit that she had, so she shook her head. "No. But that's okay." Part of her wanted her mother to feel bad. It wasn't nice, but it satisfied that part of her nonetheless. "I've got something else in mind. I've got to go."

"I didn't see it. I swear I didn't."

"Never mind. It's okay."

"Well, if I moved it . . . I'm sorry. Truly, Junie." *The Kendra Show* was back on. Sex addicts who had become celibate. Junie's mom hugged her again, and then settled back in her chair to watch the show.

Junie took the stairs two at a time, grabbed the dress, boots and hat and ran out the back door and up the alley to Tabitha's. Tabitha wasn't in the kitchen. She was in the living room with Wade. Junie peeked in on her way upstairs. Wade was looking at Mrs. D.'s movie collection. He had her 70ᵗʰ Anniversary Edition of *Gone with the Wind* in his hands and was reading the back. He didn't see Junie. Junie caught Tabitha's attention and pointed up.

As Junie hurried up the stairs, Tabitha said to Wade, "I'm going to go see how long Junie's going to be. Be right back."

"Sure. Can I put this on?"

"Yeah, go for it." Tabitha pointed out the remote and then followed Junie upstairs.

Junie got dressed in record time. Tabitha was sorting through her makeup and pulling out the colours she thought best. "Here." She dumped the small handful in Junie's lap. "I'm going back downstairs to stall for you. Be quick."

Junie did the best she could with the mascara and lipstick, but decided not to bother with anything else. She rarely wore makeup, and so the more she put on, the faker she looked. She decided she looked better with less. Or she looked less desperate, anyway. She took a good look at herself in Tabitha's full-length mirror one last time. She corrected her slouch and put her hands on her hips, one leg in front of the other. That was better. The dress clung to her in all the right places, and the boots did look really good with it. She tried the hat on and decided it was a bit too much, considering. It wasn't like they were going out to dinner and a movie. This was just a ride in the country. But then, she reconsidered; a ride in the country was the perfect occasion to wear a cowboy hat, wasn't it? So she took it along anyway, not sure if she could pull it off, but willing to try.

As she came down the stairs, Wade gave a little whistle.

"Wow." He grinned. "You look great. Really great."

"Thanks." Junie blushed. She fingered the dress awkwardly. "It's Tabitha's dress, actually."

"It's yours now, Junie." Tabitha nodded. "It looks way better on you than it ever did on me."

"Doesn't matter whose it is." Wade's eyes were locked on Junie's. "It looks incredible on you. And I love the boots. Not every girl can pull off wearing such excellent boots. But you can."

Junie didn't know what to say, so she murmured another "Thanks," and moved closer to the door. "Should we go?"

"Yeah. Absolutely." Wade handed the DVD back to Tabitha. "See you later, Tab. Don't worry about your Siamese twin."

"I'll try not to." Tabitha waited until Wade wasn't looking, and then did a silent, ridiculous victory dance that made Junie laugh out loud. Wade turned, but by then Tabitha had composed herself, except for the enormous grin on her face. "Have fun, kids! Drive safe."

⋮

Junie and Wade didn't talk much as they made their way out of the city. Junie wondered if it was nerves, or if he was just concentrating on not getting them killed. There was a lot of traffic. The afternoon commute was gearing up.

"Sorry I took so long," Junie said. "We'd have beaten the traffic if we'd left earlier."

"It's all right," Wade said with a shrug. "You don't have anywhere else to be, do you?"

"Not at all."

"Good then." Wade winked at her. He reached for the radio and turned it up. He had it on the same oldies station it'd been on when she'd got that first ride from him. Frank Sinatra was crooning about flying to the moon. Junie could completely relate. She was on the moon. Her Very First Date! She grinned. And kept grinning. She hoped Wade wouldn't choose that moment to look over and see her silly smile. But then, maybe that would be okay. She didn't know what to do with her hands, so she fussed with the brim of her cowboy hat.

"What's the story behind the hat?"

"This?" Junie tipped it toward him. "My dad took me to the Calgary Stampede last year."

"Yeah? You into rodeos?" Wade looked surprised. "Didn't figure you for a rodeo fan."

"Oh, I'm not. Not at all." Junie shook her head. "I could hardly stand it, all the bulls and cows and horses being forced to do all that stuff. No way."

"Your dad made you go?"

"Sort of." Junie turned the hat in her hands. She remembered the flight, sitting beside her father, hating him. He'd just left them and moved in with That Woman. "He won the trip at work. Some bonus incentive thing. He was going to take . . ." Did Junie really want to get into this? Was this when she was supposed to come clean? Tell him about her father, and then spill it about her mother too? No. Not yet. She could be careful. Not tell any more lies, but not undo the ones that already existed. Not yet. Junie shook her head, arguing with herself. He'd find out soon enough that she'd been lying to him all this time. And he would dump her then, so she might as well enjoy herself now, because this might be the one and only date she'd ever go on. "He was going to take a friend, but his friend bailed. So I went instead." There. She'd leave it at that.

In truth, her dad had been going to take Evelyn St. Claire. And Junie had had a fit. So he'd told Evelyn that it was too soon, and too painful for Junie (entirely true), and that Junie had begged to go instead (also true), and that Junie really wanted to go to the rodeo and would be devastated if she didn't (categorically untrue). Junie had insisted that she'd always wanted to go to the rodeo, just to wreck it for That

Woman. The punishment for succeeding at that was actually having to endure the rodeo and hang out with her dad for the better part of a week, during which he plied her with guilt presents in between long, awkward silences and equally awkward attempts at conversation. Hence, the hat.

They were on the freeway now, cruising along in the commuter lane. Wade had his window rolled down, and the wind rushed in, crisp and cool. On either side of the freeway, trees were newly green, and above, the sky stretched out blue for as far as Junie could see. The mountains in the distance still had a lot of snow on them, but it was definitely spring. It was the perfect day for a Very First Date.

She and Wade talked about school, his parents' work, his brother, Wade's plans for film school after graduation. They drove farther and farther out into the valley, and the farther Junie got from home, the farther away all her troubles seemed. By the time they saw the sign welcoming them to Chilliwack, she felt halfway normal. Like a regular teenager on a regular date, and not a liar trying to maintain a shaky façade.

Wade checked the directions, and then pulled off the highway and headed down a long, flat road that cut through farmland.

"What if this guy isn't a film buff at all, but some psycho who's lured you out here only to hack you into bits and feed you to his pigs?" Junie said as the farms grew more derelict the farther they drove along the road.

"This is possible." Wade nodded. "Entirely possible. And if that's the case, you're in trouble too, sweetheart."

Junie flushed when he called her "sweetheart." It

sounded so casual and absolutely right. She could get used to that. But she couldn't, she reminded herself. Because soon enough he'd be calling her "liar" instead. She slumped in her seat. No matter how far she got from her mother and her mess, it was always right there with her. Looming large and smelly alongside her heaps of garbage, as if Junie were towing her along behind her.

They found the address, wrought-iron numbers sitting atop a neat split-rail fence. They couldn't see the house from the road. The driveway wound down toward the river, and only when they were halfway down could they see it. Small, painted bright purple with black trim. A crumbling old red barn leaned toward the river behind the house.

Wade made pig noises.

"Funny," Junie said.

More pig noises.

"Hysterical."

Wade stopped the van in front of the house. "Do you want to wait here?"

"If they're going to hack us up, I'd just as soon go first, so no." Junie undid her seatbelt and got out of the van. It was cool by the river, so she pulled on the sweater she'd brought and pulled it tight across her chest. The wind chilled her bare legs and pushed the dress against her thighs, and her hair over her shoulders. She was cold, but she felt beautiful. Like a girl in a famous photograph.

She wasn't the only one who thought so. When she turned to see where Wade was, he was aiming his video camera at her.

"Do you mind?"

Junie felt her cheeks flush red. "No. Go ahead." She racked her brain for something witty to say. "That way, if we get fed to the pigs, it can be evidence."

"Put the hat on," Wade said from behind the camera.

Junie reached into the van for it and placed it on her head, feeling at once both silly and star-like. "Ta da," she said, doing a pirouette.

On the porch, the front door opened, and an older man came out. "You Wade?" he said, none too politely.

"Yeah, hi." Wade lowered the camera. "Sorry. You've just got an awesome place here. Add a pretty girl, and I couldn't resist."

Junie wished she could collect his words and tuck them in her pocket so that she could hold them in the palm of her hand much, much later and still feel the warm heat of them deep in her belly.

"And it's not available for film shoots, so come get the celluloid and get out of here." With that, he turned back inside, letting a big Rottweiler out as he did. The dog sat at the top of the steps, staring at them with dark, wet eyes.

"Okay then." Wade turned the camera off and put it back in the van. "Perhaps the feeding-us-to-the-pigs story isn't so far off the mark."

Junie backed up to the van, keeping the dog in her sights. "Only maybe he'll feed us to the canine beast of doom instead."

The man came back with a shallow, round silver box, just like the film canisters Junie's grandma had kept the really old home movies in. Wade pulled a few crumpled bills out of his pocket. "Do you think I'm supposed to go up there?" he whispered as he counted the money.

"He did say to come and get it," Junie whispered back. She smiled at the man. He did not smile back. "Just go get it and let's get out of here."

Wade approached the steps. The dog stood up, hackles rising too, and growled.

"She friendly?" Wade asked as he took the first step.

"She look friendly to you?"

Wade glanced back at Junie and mouthed *Help me*, making a desperate face. Junie stifled a laugh. Wade got to the top of the steps, and the dog bared her teeth. He and the man made their exchange and Wade backed down the steps and cleared the distance to the van in a hurry.

"Film shoot's over," he said as he turned the key in the ignition. The engine was silent. He turned the key again. It spluttered, and then nothing. It wouldn't turn over. "Shit."

"This is the part in the movie where we get stranded for the night on a dark country road and are forced to take shelter with a crazed madman and he holds us captive in his elaborate dungeon for several years and our families are overwrought with grief and never stop looking for us."

"'Wrought with grief.'" Wade turned the key again, to no avail. "That's good."

NINE

.
.
.

Wade waited a few minutes, explaining with a nervous catch in his voice that he'd probably flooded the engine and just needed to give it a chance to empty. Junie nodded, eyes locked on the man and his dog, still standing on the front step. Watching them.

"Here goes." Wade gave the van a little pat. "Come on, Victor. Take us home."

He turned the key. There was a tiny chug deep in the engine, which set Junie's heart alight with hope.

"Yes!"

The chug spluttered into silence.

Wade turned the key again. And again.

"Mister Victor Van Go-Go is dead," he finally announced after a dozen or more tries.

"Mister Victor Van Go-Go?" Junie tried to keep her

tone light, when in fact she was actually quite panicked. How were they going to get out of there?

"Victor for short." Wade sat back in his seat and pulled out his cellphone. "I'll call my brother. He'll come get us."

Junie nodded. But what she was thinking was that if his brother came to get them, they'd still be stuck there for a good hour and a half, if not more. His brother would be coming out in the thick of rush hour traffic. This was not good. Not good at all. Junie could feel a nervous sweat dampen her pits and brow. She was very glad she hadn't put on any more makeup than she had.

She listened to Wade's side of the conversation. By the sound of it, his brother had to write an exam. That was also not good. Wade got off the phone.

"He can come get us, but he can't leave Vancouver until eight o'clock." He held the phone out to Junie. "How about your people? Anyone who can come get us?"

Junie took the phone, thinking fast. Not her mom or dad. That would blow her lie out of the water, and she wasn't ready for that. Not just yet. Mrs. D. was the only one. Junie wasn't sure how to make the phone call without giving herself up. She turned the phone over in her hand, puzzling out how best to do it.

"You going to make a call?" Wade was sitting sideways in his seat, watching her.

"Sure." Junie dialled Tabitha's house. It rang several times and then went to voice mail. She hung up without leaving a message. "Not home."

"Who're you calling? Your mom?"

Junie nodded. She tried again and got the message again.

"Try her cell."

But Junie didn't know Mrs. D.'s cell number. "That was her cell," she said. Another lie. She should start collecting points for them, she had so many going.

"But you said she wasn't home. Didn't you phone the house first?"

"Yeah. The second time was her cell."

"Ah." Wade sat back and folded his arms behind his head. "So here we are. In the middle of nowhere. Here's hoping you have a pretty good sense of humour. And a decent sense of adventure to go with it."

"Sure I do." Yet another lie. Junie liked things to be somewhat predictable. This, to her tastes, was far too much excitement. The thrill of her Very First Date was one thing. Being stranded with no hope of rescue was another.

The man and his dog were coming down the steps.

Wade made more pig noises, only not so loudly or enthusiastically.

"Really, not funny," Junie said. "Not at all."

The man came around to Wade's side and leaned in the window. "Think you flooded it with all that business?"

"No, sir." Wade shook his head. "I was careful not to."

"Hmph." The man patted the van, almost tenderly. "You got to treat these old ladies with kid gloves, you know."

"It's a man," Junie blurted, victim to her nerves.

"What's that?" The man scowled.

Junie withered. "It's a male van. His name is Victor."

The man squinted at her and made a sort of grumble in his throat. "Well. Suppose you two should come inside. Make whatever phone calls you need to. Get yourselves organized. Might be able to help you."

Wade held up his cellphone. "We're good. Thanks."

But Junie had to pee and she wasn't about to squat behind the van or traipse off to the bushes. "Actually, I'd love it if I could use your washroom. Sir," she added, taking Wade's lead.

The man nodded and made his way back to the steps, implying that they should follow.

"Now there's a good sense of adventure." Wade grinned at her. "I like it. A lot. My kind of woman."

Junie didn't tell him that she really did have to pee. She hopped out of the van, and the two of them climbed the steps. They waited at the top, even though the man had left the front door open. The dog was sitting in the doorway, growling. The man returned.

"Out of the way, Lucy."

The dog trotted inside, casting one more casual growl over her shoulder as she did.

The house was filled with art. Paintings hung in groups on every wall. Small sculptures lined the surface of the long dresser in the front hall. The art was the first surprise. The next was that the home was extremely neat. Even tidier than Tabitha's. Junie had thought the man would live like a typical bachelor, in a kind of comfortable mess. But the house was clean, and bright, with skylights letting in the sunshine.

"Phone's in there." The man pointed in the same

direction and then went in ahead of them. There was another man. Older, by the looks of it. Bundled in a quilt, sitting at one end of the couch, watching an old black-and-white movie on a large flat-screen television.

"Mister movie buff, I presume." He muted the movie and then lifted a hand in a half-wave. "I hear you're having some engine trouble." He had a British accent, and a pronounced wheeze.

"Yes, sir." Wade pointed to the TV. "And that's *Double Indemnity*, right?"

"Very good. I'm impressed. I like a bit of Barbara Stanwyck on a regular basis."

Junie had no idea what they were talking about.

"1945?" Wade ventured.

"Close. 1944." The man sat up a little straighter and shrugged off the quilt. "And your microbus?" He was very thin, his shoulders bony through his sweater. He struggled to stand and get a look at the van through the window. "What is she, a '78?"

"Yes, sir." Wade elbowed Junie and gave her a look. This guy knew his stuff. Junie hoped Wade was right and the old fellow could get them on their way.

"I'm Royce." The man held out a shrivelled hand. Wade took it, shaking it lightly. Junie followed suit. "And I don't suppose Jeremy has properly introduced himself." He held out a hand, ushering Jeremy into the introduction. "Shake hands, Jeremy. Don't be a dragon."

"I'm Wade. And this is Junie." More handshaking. Now Junie really had to pee.

"Excuse me, but could I please use your bathroom?"

"Down the hall, on the left," Jeremy said.

June found the bathroom easily. It was filled with art too, and it had one of those fabulous claw-foot bathtubs. Above the toilet was a black-and-white photo of a much younger Royce and Jeremy outside, sitting naked in what looked like a homemade hot tub, which was really only a big wooden barrel filled with water, sitting atop a rock perch above a fire. Their arms were slung around each other. Big grins on their faces. Royce had a beard and looked a lot more robust, but you could still tell it was him.

As Junie peed, she realized that Royce and Jeremy were gay, of course. What an odd couple.

After she washed her hands, she opened the door to find the dog sitting there, staring at her, growling again.

"Good girl, Lucy," Junie murmured, looking down the hall to see if Jeremy was there to call her off. The front door was open. Beyond it, she could see all three of them bending over the back of the van where the engine was. Junie held out a hand, hoping to make friends with the enormous dog. Lucy growled louder, baring her teeth. "Help?" Junie said quietly. She took a step to move past the dog, but Lucy stood, and up went the hackles again.

"Okay. I get it." Junie backed up, and sat on the edge of the bathtub. Lucy didn't budge, until quite a while later, when Junie heard footsteps, and then Jeremy's voice.

"You caught me a girl? Good dog, Lucy." And then, "It's okay. I got her."

"Thanks," Junie said. Although she wasn't sure she should be thanking Jeremy. He shouldn't have had such a vicious dog.

"She's a good guard dog," Jeremy said. "We like it like that."

"She *is* a good guard dog." Junie pointed to the front door. "Will she let me go now?"

"Sure." Jeremy stepped aside and kept a hand on Lucy's collar as she passed. "They're trying to get the van fixed. She's got a lot going on under the hood."

Junie didn't bother to remind him again that it was a male van.

⋮

Not even twenty minutes later, the van started, and sounded even better than it had before.

Royce wiped his hands on a rag and smiled proudly. "Never met a microbus who didn't like me." He closed the engine hood and grabbed the cane that had been resting against the van. "Now, can I invite you two in for a beverage before you get back on the road? Seeing as how Jeremy here hasn't exactly been the best of hosts. Not his forte."

Jeremy shrugged. Lucy sat at his side, her tongue lolling out. With a canine sigh, she rolled her shoulders back in what looked very much like a shrug too.

"What do you say, Junie? Should we get going?" Wade looked at her, and she could tell by his expression that he was letting her decide if they'd stay or go. She had no idea what he'd had in mind to do after they'd done the "quick" errand of picking up the movie. All she knew was that, as weird as the afternoon had been so far, she didn't want it to end.

"Sure, we can stay." Junie looked at her watch. "For a while. I turn into a pumpkin at nine, though."

Royce looked at his watch, and Wade checked his cell. "I'll call my brother and tell him we don't need a ride. Thanks so much, sir. We've got about an hour before we should start heading back."

"Exactly enough time for soup and biscuits," Royce said. "And please, call me Royce. And don't call Jeremy 'sir,' either. Neither of us have been knighted by the Queen. Yet."

The sun had slipped behind the hill on the far side of the river, and any warmth had gone with it. Soup would be perfect. And Junie was hungry, she realized. She had hardly eaten lunch, she'd been so nervous about the date.

"If you want to shoot your movie or what have you," Jeremy mumbled, "go ahead."

"Thank you, sir. I mean, Jeremy." Wade winked at Junie as the two men went back inside, Lucy following them. He grabbed the camera from the van and set her in his sights. "I need some footage for my English term project and I've just had the best idea. Want to be a star, Junie?"

Junie did a little curtsey. "Sure. Why not?"

He filmed her walking from the porch, around back, along the lopsided barn wall and down to the river. She picked up rocks along the way, as per his direction, and put them into her sweater pockets.

"Like Virginia Woolf," he explained, telling her that that was how she'd committed suicide, by loading herself down with rocks and then walking into the river.

"I'm not walking into the river," Junie said. "It's bad enough that the rocks are stretching my sweater."

"Not today. But before it's due? For the sake of art," Wade said. "And an A in English."

It was growing dark as they made their way back to the house and knocked on the front door. Lucy barked on the other side, only settling when Jeremy let them in.

"In the kitchen," he said, and then headed there himself.

Royce was standing at the oven, his cane leaning on the counter beside him. He slipped his hands into a pair of oven mitts before removing a tray of hot biscuits from the oven.

"Sit," he said as he brought the tray to a small table under a window overlooking the river, almost black in the dusk. "I have borscht, with sour cream to put on top. And great big slabs of butter and chunks of nice sharp cheese for the biscuits. Heavenly, if I do say so myself."

Not surprisingly, Jeremy didn't say much while they ate, leaving all the talking to Royce, who was obviously the more social of the two. Over dinner, he told them how he and Jeremy had met back in the '60s when Jeremy had come to London to intern at the movie studio where Royce had already worked on three of Stanley Kubrick's movies, as a production assistant at first, and then as assistant director.

"Jeremy was a scenic artist. Doing the sets." He pointed to an arrangement of framed art hanging on the wall above the table. "He did those, too. A very talented man indeed, my Jeremy."

"It's an honour to meet you guys," Wade said. "Honestly. I have a million questions."

"Ask away. And if not today, then you're welcome to

come back." Royce coughed, and then struggled to catch his breath. "Anytime. Really. I love company."

"You want your oxygen?" Jeremy grumbled, his mouth full of biscuit.

"No, ta." Royce sat back, a hand on his chest. "I'm good."

Junie studied the men's faces while Jeremy scrutinized Royce, clearly not believing him. She was curious about them both, and the life they lived there at the edge of the river, in such an unlikely little town. She would like to come back, she thought. And if Wade's awed expression was anything to go by, he was thinking the same thing.

Jeremy got up from the table and came back with a bottle of wine. "Helps with the breathing, sometimes," he said by way of explanation.

Royce smiled as Jeremy poured him a glass of the crimson liquid. "Especially if it's a good vintage."

Without asking, Jeremy got two more wine glasses, filled them a quarter full and set one each in front of Wade and Junie.

"Jeremy," Royce scolded, "they're children."

"Old enough to drive," Jeremy said as he filled his own glass nearly to the brim. "Old enough to drink responsibly. I only gave them a wee bit. No harm."

"And I won't even finish it, but thank you." Wade raised his glass, readying for a toast. Junie marvelled at his ease, at his smooth ability to go along with whatever came at him. If it was possible, he was even more attractive to her now than he had been just hours earlier. "To Jeremy, and Royce. And Lucy—" Here he bobbed his glass in her direction, where she lay on a dog bed by the back door. "Thank you for your hospitality and mad skills with a wrench. Cheers." They all clinked glasses.

"*Slainte!*" Royce said and took a swig. Jeremy took a sip too, and so did Wade.

Junie brought the glass to her lips and took the tiniest of sips. She'd tried red wine before, but hadn't liked it. She fully expected not to like it now, either. But maybe it was the kind of wine, or the day in general, but it was lovely. Tasted like smoked cherries, and warmed her throat as it went down.

"Cheers!" she said. Her cheeks felt warm. And her belly full with the fragrant soup and warm biscuits. She grinned. She couldn't help it. This Very First Date had been nothing like she'd expected. And yet it had been perfect. Absolutely perfect.

TEN

:
:

It was dark by the time they left, the lights streaking by at the highway exits as they drove back to the city. Junie and Wade talked about Jeremy and Royce almost all the way home. Sharing their assumptions that they were gay, trying to figure out how they'd got from London to Chilliwack, what made Royce so frail. Wade, the child of doctors, suggested congestive heart failure, while Junie placed her bet on AIDS. Then it seemed suddenly very sad to be discussing his health so lightly, and Junie said so, so they changed the subject. Wade talked about his English term project due at the end of the school year, a short biopic of Virginia Woolf.

"You're my muse now," he said as they pulled off the highway, back in the city. "I didn't even know that I was looking for one until today. But you're it. Definitely."

Junie didn't know what to say. She loved the idea of

being his muse but was too shy to say so. "But I don't look anything like Virginia Woolf," she said instead, thinking of the poster in her English classroom, the dour-looking woman with the horsey face and plain hair.

"No, you're far, far more beautiful than she was."

Junie leaned forward and gasped silently, the wind knocked out of her by what he'd just said. She was thankful for the dark covering her reaction.

"You are," Wade continued, a hint of nerves in his voice now. "She was gangly and plain, with those buggy, uneven eyes."

But Junie was gangly and plain too. Although her eyes were just fine. Still, she couldn't think of anything to say. Not one thing.

Sensing her unease, Wade babbled on, getting more and more nervous himself, judging by how fast he was talking, and how much.

"She was mentally ill. Definitely. A genius. But tortured. Did you know that on the day she died she wrote a note to her husband, and one to her sister, too? Her sister's name was Vanessa. I was thinking I could use Tabitha as Vanessa, if you think she'd go along with it. They were really close. Vanessa and Virginia, I mean. I don't know why I want to do Virginia Woolf. I mean, she's on the list that Mrs. Hooper put up of writers we could choose, but I totally thought I was going to do Jack Kerouac. You know, *On The Road*. Which has got to be one of the best books ever."

Junie knew she should try to say something, if only to knock him out of his nervous babbling. She opened her mouth. Closed it. Tried again.

"All I know about Virginia Woolf is that she killed herself." That would do. And it did. Wade shut up. "But I didn't even know how until you told me."

"So you'll do it?" Wade turned to her in the dark. They passed a streetlight. Then another. She could see him grinning at her. "You'll be my Virginia Woolf?"

"Wade," Junie said, quite seriously amazed at herself, "I'd pretty much be your anything."

Silence.

Junie's gut churned with regret.

Seconds dragged themselves by, like war casualties. They came to a red light. Wade slowed the van to a stop. It was a bright intersection, not far from their school. Junie was afraid to look at him. She'd blown it. Too much. Too soon.

But then Wade reached for her hand, took it gently in his and turned it over. He kissed it. A sweet, slow kiss on the palm of her hand, which seemed so much more intimate than if he'd kissed her anywhere else, even her lips. That one kiss set off a cascade of delicious shocks that zinged up her arm and radiated through her whole body.

"Perfect," Wade said. "Perfect."

⋮

As far as Very First Dates go, Junie couldn't think how it could have been any better. It had been perfect. Absolutely perfect.

Until Wade turned onto her street, and Junie saw her house. Her real house. With the blue light of the television shimmering behind the living room curtains, the rest of the house dark. It was almost nine. She'd gone several hours without thinking about home. About her mother. Her father and That Woman. And the big fat lie she'd told Wade.

She should tell him. Right now. Junie could practically hear Tabitha ordering her to get Wade to stop at her real house. The house of doom and decay. The house of a compulsive hoarder and superior slob. The house so full of junk and crap that you had to make your way from room to room along narrow trails burrowed out of the heaps of debris, like a rat living in the city dump.

She couldn't tell him. Not yet. Not after such a perfect Very First Date.

Wade stopped the van in front of Tabitha's house. The living room was brightly lit behind the curtains. Mrs. D. didn't allow TV in the living room. She said it had nothing to do with living. It was down in the basement. But the basement windows were dark. Junie glanced up. The light in Tabitha's room was on. The curtains parted, and there was Mrs. D., looking out for just a moment before tugging the curtains closed again.

"Making sure we're not making out," Wade blurted into the dark.

Junie sucked in her breath. "Guess so." She put her hand on the door handle, all of a sudden desperate to get out of the van. But she didn't know how to exactly end the date, so she just sat there. She wanted to make out with him. Sure she did. But she thought if she did, she might shatter into a million pieces of crush and never be put back together again. Considering the shock of just the kiss on the palm of her hand, she doubted that she was ready for his tongue down her throat. Her face flushed at the thought. She turned the door handle. "I should go."

"Wait." Wade threw off his seatbelt. "Let me."

Junie watched him get out and come around to her side of the van. She felt like a girl out of the '50s, out of one of Wade's beloved black-and-white films, as though she should be wearing bobby socks and a poodle skirt. She didn't know guys still did that stuff—hold doors, stand up when girls came into the room. But then Wade was cut from a different cloth than most guys. Which was why she liked him.

He opened the door and offered her a hand. "Virginia." She took his hand and let him help her down. "It has been a pleasure."

"I had a really good time too." Junie felt an *okey-dokey* moment coming on. As though she might burst into a fit of giggles, or trip on the step up to the walk. Wade kept holding her hand as they walked up to the front door.

Junie desperately hoped that Tabitha had told Mrs. D. to expect Junie to come "home" that night. The porch light was on. Junie glanced at her watch. It was five minutes after nine. She was supposed to be at her own home five minutes ago. She heard the phone ring inside. That would be her mom, looking for her.

"I'd better get inside." Junie took her hand back, but then wasn't sure what to do with it. She dropped it to her side, but then thought better of that and put it on the door handle. "It's after nine."

"Okay. Thanks for coming with me." Wade stepped

backwards, nearly toppling off the stoop. Junie laughed, and immediately felt bad for doing so. Wade bowed. "And for tonight's finale . . ." He took a step forward and kissed Junie on the lips. It lasted long enough that Junie blinked several times, surprised. Wade's eyes were closed. And then he pulled away, eyes wide open. "See ya."

And he sprinted back to his van, got in and drove away. Just like that.

Junie turned in a dazed little circle. Her skin felt loose, as if it might slide off and pool around her ankles. Her mouth felt tingly. She put her fingers to her lips, wondering if they would feel any different now.

The door opened, and Mrs. D. appraised her with a stern look.

"Your mother is looking for you."

"Can I come in?" Junie heard Tabitha thundering down the stairs. "Just for a minute."

Mrs. D. opened the door wider. "If you call your mother."

"I saw!" Tabitha screeched. She grabbed Junie and yanked her inside. "Oh my God, I saw! He kissed you!"

Mrs. D. handed Junie the phone. "Call your mother. Now."

⋮

Her mother wanted Junie home immediately. Tabitha walked her there so Junie could tell her the short version of her Very First Date along the way. They said goodbye, and Junie went inside, still floating from everything that had happened. She found her mom in the living room, of course, where no doubt she'd been all day.

"I am in love," she announced, sliding to the floor at her mother's feet. "I am absolutely in love."

"You had a good time, then," her mother said with a chuckle as she muted the Shopping Channel. The woman selling the Miracle Scissors fell silent, but still her collagen-plumped lips kept flapping.

"I had a great time." Junie and Tabitha had decided not to tell either of their moms about Jeremy and Royce. Neither of them would be okay with Junie having spent several hours at a strange house in the middle of nowhere with strange men. Her mom might not let her see Wade again. And there *would* be a next time. Junie could feel it in her bones. "The best time ever, actually."

"I'm glad." Junie could hear something else in her mother's voice. A coolness that shouldn't have been there, considering.

"You could be a little more excited for me, Mom." Junie stood up. She kicked off her boots and picked one up in each hand. If she left them down there, there was no telling if she'd ever find them again.

That was when she realized that she was wearing the same dress that she'd accused her mom of losing.

"I found it," Junie said as a sheepish lump formed in her throat. "Just before I left."

"Clearly."

Junie wished that she wanted to apologize to her mom. But she didn't. She really didn't. But she should. Even if she didn't want to. "I'm sorry."

"Mm-hmm." Her mom turned her eyes back to the TV.

Junie had apologized, but it hadn't sounded genuine. Not at all. She didn't blame her mom for brushing it off.

"I *am* sorry." That was better. "I jumped to conclusions. When, really, I'd brought it upstairs this morning, when I brushed my teeth."

"And you didn't think to tell me that this afternoon, when you came home?"

Junie just stood there, feeling like an ass.

"It would've been nice to know. Instead of sitting here all this time, thinking that I'd ruined your date."

"You didn't ruin it."

"But I thought I had."

Junie felt the elation of the day slip away, and in its place came the steady anxiety she usually felt. Her constant undercurrent of unease. Her miserable, exhausting normal. "That was crappy of me. Sorry."

"Apology accepted." Her mother looked as though she was about to cry. Great. "And I'm sorry too. For being the kind of mom you feel the need to lie to."

If she only knew. Junie was pretty sure that she'd just shrunk a few inches. She looked down at the white dress, a pink cowboy boot in each hand. It felt stupid all of a sudden. Like she'd been trying too hard, and Wade knew it. The whole world knew it. Like she should just forget about being anyone's "anything" and go back to being a liar. It was what she was best at, after all.

Junie pursed her lips shut, trapping all of the ugly things she could say to her mother. Leave it to her to wreck

Junie's Very First Date. Instead, and wisely, she pinched out an icy "Good night" and then went upstairs to bed.

⋮

Junie woke up the next day to the sound of the phone ringing. Her mom never answered it, so Junie leapt out of bed and grabbed the one in the hall.

"Better get over here," Tabitha said. "Lover-boy just called and left a message saying that he's going to stop by on his way to school to see if you want a ride."

"Crap!" Junie knocked herself on the forehead with the phone. "I'll be right there."

"This has got to stop, Junie." Junie could practically hear Tabitha shaking her head with disapproval. "Really." And then she hung up.

Junie got dressed as fast as she could, washed her face and brushed her teeth, grabbed her backpack and slammed out the front door without so much as a "good morning" or "goodbye" to her mother.

The phone was ringing when Junie walked into Tabitha's house, breathless. Mrs. D. handed it to her. "Your mother."

"Good morning, Juniper."

"Sorry, Mom. I was in a rush."

"That's no excuse." Her mother sighed. "I'm of half a mind to make you come back here and try that again, with manners this time."

"I'm sorry. It won't happen again."

"I certainly hope not. You're getting pretty stroppy, young lady. Maybe this Wade business is going to your head."

Oh how Junie wanted to tell her that *she* was the root of all of this. But there was no time. Outside, a horn honked. "That's Victor, I've got to go."

"Who's Victor? I thought we were all about Wade?"

Not *we*. Not ever *we* when it came to her and her mother. Junie bit her lip. Stay civil. Get off the phone.

"Victor is what he calls his van. Victor Van Go-Go. Get it?"

"That's cute." Her mother laughed. "I'm looking forward to meeting this Wade character."

Not on your life. Not a chance in hell. Never in a million years. Hell would have to freeze, thaw and freeze again several times before that would happen.

"Gotta go, Mom. That's my ride." Junie hung up.

Mrs. D. and Tabitha stared at her, both of them with their arms crossed and frowning.

"I know, I know."

But she didn't know. Didn't know how to get out of it. Didn't know how to fix her mom. Didn't know how to bring her dad back home. Didn't know how to act around Wade. Didn't know what to do next, about anything at all.

ELEVEN

:

One thing was for sure, Junie thought: life was better when you were in love. Everything was shinier. Prettier. Easier. At least some things were, anyway. Junie's lie was still dull and ugly and difficult. She worked hard at hiding it, like a big nasty zit.

Two whole weeks went by with the new normal: starting the day at Tabitha's, getting dropped off at Tabitha's, letting the phone go to voice mail whenever Wade called. The façade was so well maintained that it started to feel real. As though Junie could live like that forever.

And that wouldn't have been so bad. She and Wade were an acknowledged item now. Like Ollie and Lulu. As a result, Junie's status at school had skyrocketed. To be a part of a couple was a big deal. And to be Wade's girlfriend was an even bigger deal. Not that he was the coolest guy in school in the traditional sense. He didn't play sports or host kegger parties or drive a hot car or strut around being the reigning class asshole. But he was the guy that the girls actually liked. Smart and artistic. Funny. And handsome. There was very clearly something about him, a charisma that no one could resist. Even the guys wanted to be his friend. Even the ones who made misanthropy a part of their image, along with death metal and a matching pallor.

And he was Junie's. And she was his. Or would have been wholeheartedly so, if it hadn't been for the lie that kept her holding back. It kept her on her toes, never able to relax. As if she'd done three shots of espresso before getting out of bed every day. Sometimes she woke up with her heart racing, panic souring her throat like vomit.

Despite her own belief that all that was good (she and Wade) would come to a horrible, all-revealing, screeching halt . . . it didn't. Each day, she was amazed that her lie held. Every time he appeared outside of class, waiting for her, she was surprised. And he noticed. One day, she actually jumped at the sight of him. It was after Art class, and there he was when she and Lulu turned the corner out of the room.

"You always look like you're shocked to see me." He slung an arm across Junie's shoulder. "Hey, Lulu."

"Hi, Wade." Lulu glanced at Junie, and then added, "Don't mind Junie's nerves. She's always been highly excitable that way."

Junie had not. She didn't meet Lulu's eyes, because she sensed that Lulu was making a friendly effort of shoring up something she didn't entirely understand, but was keenly aware of.

"If every crow you see is black, wouldn't you think the next one would be black too? I always come meet you after class."

Junie laughed, her nerves jangling her voice into a cackle. "But isn't the other part of that theory that you shouldn't be surprised if one day you see a white crow?"

Lulu, with her infinite intuition, took her leave, flapping her wings and cawing down the hall, which only she could make look graceful and theatrical rather than goofy.

Both Wade and Junie had a spare next, and then lunch. They were going to meet Jeremy and Royce at the Buckled Star. They were in town for a doctor's appointment for Royce. And Wade had been right. It was congestive heart failure. He'd figured it out based on the specialist's clinic the appointment was at. Junie had looked it up. Not good.

With congestive heart failure, Wade explained, the heart became too weak to pump blood throughout the body. When the blood didn't circulate properly, fluid would build up. For Royce, if fluid filled his lungs, it would feel like drowning on the inside.

So Junie was surprised that Royce looked a bit better that day. He was ashen still, and wheezing, but he was dressed in a sharply pressed dress shirt and slacks, with his hair combed back and a fresh shave. He beamed when Wade and Junie entered the café, and struggled to stand to greet them.

"Don't get up, please," Wade said. "Don't get up."

Junie loved that he always knew what to say, when Junie was typically left with her words making macramé in her head and never making it out of her mouth.

Royce stood up anyway. "I'll stand if I wish. I won't be bossed around by a choirboy. Lovely to see you two." Then he sat again, relaxing back into his seat, one of the comfy armchairs by the window. Junie imagined that if he hadn't already been sitting there, or had been suffering on one of the awful, hard, ladder-back chairs, Wade would have easily asked someone to give up the chair for Royce. It was things like that that endeared him to everyone.

"Did you get a chance to screen the footage?"

"I'm nervous to. I don't want to ruin it." Wade took the chair across from him and set down his movie camera, which he took everywhere. Junie sat in the chair beside his. "I started to thread it into my projector, but then I wasn't sure if I should."

"Of course you should," Jeremy said. "You want to see the treasure you hunted down, don't you?"

"Indeed," Royce said. "Meant to be watched. No use sticking it in a box in the attic like we did."

"I'll do it, then," Wade promised. "Tonight. For sure."

"What can we get you?" Junie asked, having finally found her voice.

"Oh, no need to treat us." Royce waved away the idea.

"Definitely," Junie said. "After you fixed Victor, and gave us supper—"

"It's the least we can do," Wade finished.

Junie grinned. She loved it when he finished her sentences, or vice versa. As if they'd been together forever. And it felt like that, too. She was honestly the luckiest girl in the world.

Wade went to order, then brought back the drinks and a plate-sized chocolate chip cookie for each of them.

Junie didn't say much over the next hour. She listened to Wade ask questions about the movie industry in the '60s and '70s, and Royce answer with elaborate detail about this camera and that director and this location and that actor, while Jeremy grunted his reluctant replies, albeit with a not-so-reluctant smile.

After they'd said goodbye and were on their way back to school, Wade announced that he wanted to make a movie about Jeremy and Royce. "Can't you see it? One of those quirky documentaries that all the film festivals love. Great characters, interesting story. Shot grainy and cheap, which ends up lending it a convincing air of authenticity."

"Shot and directed by the world's next great filmmaker," Junie added.

"Hardly." Wade laughed. "But I do like the sound of that."

"They might not want to. They're so private."

"No they're not. They love us!"

"You, Wade. They love *you*," Junie said.

"I love *them*! They're great. You can't make that stuff up, you know? I feel like I stumbled onto a gold mine."

"True."

"So you're in?" Wade held out his hand for a handshake. "Want to be my crew?"

"Absolutely." Junie shook his hand. He took the other as they walked. "Although I'm not so sure how Jeremy's going to like the idea. He might like you, but I don't think he likes the world all that much."

"I'm not worried," Wade said. "I think Royce could get him to do pretty much anything he wanted. Besides, he can appreciate a young filmmaker finding his feet. And I can be sensitive. There's an art to being a doc filmmaker. You don't want to hit people over the head. And you don't want to force a fake relationship between you and the camera and them. You want a real relationship, brought to the screen intact."

Junie loved hearing him talk about something he so clearly loved and knew a lot about. She wanted him to go on and on, but then a car honked near them. And then again, closer. Junie didn't think anything of it, until it honked for a third time. Much to her horror and surprise, her father had pulled to the side of the road up ahead and was getting out. That Woman was with him, but she was staying in the car. And then Junie saw Princess Over All III lift her head up in the back seat. The happy family. This was not good.

Junie hadn't told Wade much about her dad, other than the snippet about the rodeo trip. She hadn't told him about the divorce, or That Woman. She hadn't even told him about the obligatory visits. And he hadn't pushed. Thank God he wasn't making a documentary about her, or else he'd have been grilling her the way he did Royce and Jeremy. Thankfully, he'd just assumed Mrs. D. was the one and only parent, and Junie had been going along with that. Until now.

"Junie!" Her dad opened his arms for a hug. Junie had no choice but to oblige. She hadn't seen him since that day they'd fought. At first she'd been giving it some time, and then she'd been busy with Wade. And ultimately, she'd figured if her dad couldn't be bothered to enforce her visits, what did she care? Screw him. That's what she'd been thinking lately. But seeing him in real life changed all that. She'd missed him. She hadn't known it until now, but she'd missed him.

"You never return my calls."

"Sorry, Dad. I've been super-busy with school and everything. This is Wade." Of course Junie had to introduce them. She had no choice. She could only hope that Wade wouldn't recognize her father from the spectacle in the driveway. "Wade, this is my father, Ron."

"Good to meet you, Mr. Rawley." Wade held out his hand. Nothing in his expression suggested that Wade remembered him. Thank God.

"Call me Ron." Ron pumped Wade's hand, all the while grinning at Junie. "You didn't tell me you had a special friend, Junie!"

Junie wanted to lift up the sidewalk and crawl underneath. *Special friend*? No wonder her dad was such a loser.

Out of the corner of her eye, Junie saw That Woman getting out of the car. Junie put a hand to her forehead. Why was this happening? She wished they'd stayed another few minutes at the café. She wished her dad had kept driving. Now she just hoped that this little interaction wouldn't blow her cover. She silently willed her father and That Woman not to mention anything about the house, or her mother. Or anything at all, really. She silently willed them both to vanish immediately, but that didn't work.

Evelyn St. Claire strutted over with her runway

walk, her dog at her side like an accessory. She held out her hand, big clunky bracelets jumbling down to her thin wrist.

"Evelyn St. Claire," she announced. "And you are?"

"Wade." Wade glanced at Junie. "Junie's boyfriend."

Boyfriend! That was the first time he'd ever said that. All of a sudden, Junie didn't hate That Woman so much. How could she hate anyone when she had a boyfriend? She couldn't wait to tell Tabitha. As soon as she could extricate herself and Wade from this shaky situation.

Evelyn took her cellphone out of her purse and looked at the time. "Shouldn't you be in school?"

"We're skipping," Junie said with a straight face. "I do it all the time. That's how I keep getting straight As." Apparently her newfound affection for That Woman had only lasted those few seconds.

Wade angled a look at her out of the corner of his eye. Junie sounded ugly, and she knew it. She took a breath and explained. "We had a spare before lunch. We went out for coffee."

"Good! Good." Her dad beamed at her and Wade. "Can we give you kids a ride back to school?"

"Sure," Wade said. "Thank you. That'd be great."

Junie couldn't think of anything worse.

Wade and Junie sat in the back, with Princess between them like a chaperone.

"How's your mother doing?" her father asked as they turned the corner.

No way was Junie going to have a conversation about her mother. Not with Wade in the car. And besides, what did her father care? Junie had to literally bite her tongue so she wouldn't ask him that exactly.

"Fine."

"I thought we'd come by on the weekend. Maybe mow the lawn."

Was he actually having this conversation with her? And this was okay with That Woman? Apparently so, because That Woman smiled at Ron and slipped her hand onto his knee. "We could bring Junie's mom one of those gift baskets I'm having made." She turned in her seat and graced Junie with a wide, fake smile. "For my clients."

"She's not your client," Junie said through gritted teeth. "Not any more."

"She might like it anyway, don't you think?" The smile got wider. "She likes that sort of thing."

Junie wanted to gouge out Evelyn St. Claire's eyes with her bare hands and feed them to her godforsaken dog. That Woman was baiting her. Taunting her. Of course her mother "liked" that sort of thing. She was a compulsive hoarder! You could bring her an old garden hose and a loaf of mouldy bread and she'd think it was Christmas! Evelyn was goading her. Punishing Junie for treating Evelyn the way she had that last time in the car. Junie sank into her seat, fuming. She would not take the bait. Not with Wade in the car.

Junie didn't say another word until they said goodbye at the school, and even then, she only offered the goodbye to her father, promising him that she'd see him on the weekend sometime.

"Maybe we could do something together," her dad said. "Bring Wade along, too. The four of us."

Junie thought not. She waved as the car disappeared. That had been unbearable, to say the least. But at least it was over, and Wade hadn't recognized her father, and neither her dad nor That Woman had given anything away. Or it didn't seem like it, anyway.

Out of the car, Wade looked at her funny. "So. Your dad."

Junie nodded, not sure where this was going to go. "My dad."

"You seem kind of—"

"Awful to him. I know." Junie shrugged. "I'm not all that fond of him right now."

"Yeah. I got that. And I take it that you're even less fond of his girlfriend."

"Ugh." Junie cringed. "Don't call her that. Tabitha and I refer to her as That Woman."

"And she is. . . ?"

"Satan in heels? Beelzebub in haute couture? The Wicked Witch of the West?" Junie's shoulders slumped. She was tired of all of this. She should tell him everything. Right then. Just get it over with. But then it *would* be over. And she wasn't ready for that. She'd give him a little. Just a little. "Evelyn St. Claire. She was sort of working for my mom, and ended up dragging my dad into an affair. My parents are getting a divorce, thanks to her. He lives with her in her snotty loft downtown. With her stupid snotty dog. Or, I guess she's not stupid. She's actually pretty smart. For a dog."

"What does she do?"

"The dog, or That Woman?" Junie didn't want to

tell him that Evelyn was a life coach. Then he'd wonder why her mom had needed one of those. "The dog lies around looking royal. That Woman does project management or something. I don't know exactly. And I don't care at all."

Lulu and Ollie and Tabitha came around the side of the school just then, saving Junie from herself.

"We all have our fair share of family drama. My mom was married before she met my dad and was still married when they moved in together. Big scandal. I can relate." Wade pulled her to him and kissed her. Junie leaned against him, her cheek resting on his chest. It was warm. She could hear his heartbeat. Forget that he couldn't really relate because he didn't know the half of it. Forget the rest of the day. The rest of her life. She could stay right there forever. Truly. "We all have a bit of mystery. And besides, I like that in a girl."

Junie could only hope that that was true, and wonder if her particular mysteriousness would be all that attractive to him when the big lie finally unravelled. She doubted it. But for now, here she was. In the arms of her boyfriend. And that was just about as good as it got.

⋮

Tabitha and Junie walked home together after school because Wade was staying behind to work on a project with his Physics study group. Junie told Tabitha about Wade meeting her father, and how Wade hadn't realized who he really was.

"Maybe it would've been better if he had," Tabitha

said gently. "That way, everything would be out in the open. Where it has to be. Eventually."

"I can't carry this on forever," Junie said. "That's what you mean?"

"Uh-huh."

"How about just for now, though? Everything is perfect. Right now."

"It only seems perfect, Junie."

"Gee thanks, counsellor."

"Speaking of," Tabitha said, "it's that day of the month again."

Once a month Tabitha and her mother met with a family therapist. Not for any reason in particular. "Just to keep the gears oiled," as Mrs. D. often said. Mrs. D. had given Junie the card of the therapist at least four times, urging her to give it to her parents. This was even before they'd broken up. But Junie couldn't imagine being stuck in some therapist's office with her parents, talking about their feelings. She'd rather have drunk rat poison and died a slow, agonizing death.

⋮

It was another gorgeous spring afternoon, but inside Junie's house it might as well have been the middle of the night. Usually Junie drew open the drapes and lifted the blinds before she left for school in the morning, but that morning she'd been rushing to get to Tabitha's in time for Wade to pick them up, so now the house was even more dank and depressing than usual.

From the living room, the theme song to *The Kendra Show* announced a commercial break.

"You're home early," her mother called over an ad for stain remover.

"Everyone's busy." Junie kicked aside a dusty salad of plastic fruit that had tumbled out of a basket perched on top of a pile of junk and made her way to the living room. Was it possible that the trails weaving through the crap had gotten narrower, or did it just seem that way with the house being so dark? She climbed atop a hill of clothes that hadn't fit her since grade three and were "awaiting sorting" and reached past another shelf ("Somewhere to keep my clock collection") to yank open the living room curtains, letting in the sunlight. They always left the sheers closed, though, just so no one could actually see in and get a good look at the teetering stacks of useless crap, piles of old science fiction books her father used to read but her mother refused to get rid of, broken laundry baskets full of puzzles with missing pieces, mismatched containers and craft supplies that had never been opened. Wade drove by the house every day. Usually twice a day, at least. With that thought chilling her to the core, Junie rearranged the sheers, making sure there was no gap whatsoever.

"So when am I going to meet this boy of yours?" Her mother sat forward in her chair, trying to look interested.

Junie was going to say, "Not until the house burns down and you take a shower," but *Kendra* was back on, and her mother was only half paying attention to Junie.

"I don't know," Junie said, holding back the barbs.

On *The Kendra Show* that day, Kendra was touring the poorest parts of Harlem, bringing party dresses to little girls. Like they needed party dresses. They needed shoes maybe, food definitely. A little help with the rent for sure. Junie sat at her mother's feet on the tiny clear patch of filthy carpet there and watched.

Kendra, in her high-heeled shoes and tailored suit clinging to her generous curves, climbed the graffiti-filled stairwell in a rundown tenement because the elevator wasn't working. She was out of breath by the third floor, where she was headed to give a Haitian immigrant family with seven girls seven glittery dresses with matching handbags and princess slippers covered in sequins.

The family's tiny two-bedroom apartment was as neat as any sprawling home bragging in a home décor magazine, only without the décor.

Junie glanced up at her mom. "Our place could be that neat," she mumbled. "They can manage it and they have nothing."

Her mother didn't respond. The chair rocked back a little, but that was it.

The girls squealed with delight but politely waited their turn to get their party dresses. They put them on, and Kendra's hair and makeup people did the girls up for a photo shoot. The father stood quietly in the doorway, wearing worn-out slippers and a suit that was several sizes too big for him, and shiny with wear at the elbows and knees. Then Kendra mentioned that the mother had died, and that he was raising the girls by himself on his meagre wage as a worker in a factory that manufactured parts for dishwashers.

"They keep that place neat and tidy and they don't even have a mom," Junie said. She knew she'd gone too far as soon as she'd said it. Her mother actually got out of her chair.

"Maybe you'd be better off if I died, too," she said as she headed for the kitchen. "Then you could do whatever you wanted."

On the television, the seven girls were swirling their shiny skirts, dancing with each other, great big smiles on their faces. Later, they'd get together with all the other girls who got new dresses and they'd have a tea party.

Junie had been wrong. Turned out, party dresses were exactly what those little girls needed.

TWELVE

. . . .

On the weekend, Wade reminded Junie that she'd promised to hang out with her dad. Junie had conveniently forgotten that, and now there was plenty else that she'd rather have done. Including nothing at all.

"It'll be fun," he said. "I'll come with you."

He and Junie, along with Tabitha and Lulu and Ollie, were sitting around a big table at the Buckled Star on Saturday morning.

"I think your definition of fun and mine are totally different." Junie looked to Tabitha for support, but she wasn't giving it.

"You've been ignoring him," Tabitha said. "He misses you."

"Can I just say that ganging up on me isn't going to make me want to do what you guys want me to do?" Junie tried to keep her tone light, but the truth was, she was more than slightly irked.

Lulu reached out and patted Junie's arm. "You can do whatever you want, Junie."

"Thanks, Lulu," Junie said pointedly.

"Actually," Ollie lifted a finger to object, "not true. You're still a minor. You can do whatever your parents want you to. But you can't do whatever you want. Not so."

"Your mom doesn't seem the type to force," Wade said. "Maybe debate you in a lawyerly fashion. I could see that."

"Lawyerly?" Ollie said. "What do you mean?"

"Never mind," Junie said quickly. "I'll call my dad."

Junie wanted to get off the topic of her parents. She didn't like where this was going. Ollie and Lulu hadn't met her mom, just her dad, in the school parking lot. But they knew she didn't work. They thought she was a stay-at-home mom. Like Ollie's. One who kept a tidy house and made something interesting for dinner every night and packed her child a nutritious sandwich on whole wheat bread for lunch every day. Plus, they knew which house was hers, even if Junie had never invited them in. They also knew that Tabitha's mom was a lawyer.

Wade handed her his cellphone. "Go ahead."

Junie dialled her dad's cell. Unfortunately, he picked up on the second ring.

"I'm so glad you called," he said, after she fumbled through a hello. "What's the plan? I've left the day open for you. And the lawn."

"Is Evelyn working?"

"No. We're just finishing a late brunch here at home and then we're all yours."

Junie brought the phone away from her ear and scowled at it before bringing it back. "Oh."

"So, what do you want to do, kiddo?" Her dad's tone was bright. Oblivious. How could he not know that she didn't want to be anywhere near Evelyn St. Claire? That she'd rather shove That Woman into moving traffic and watch a semi truck roll over her head than spend the afternoon with her.

"Wade thought I should call you." Junie got up from the table and went to the back of the café where the others couldn't hear her. She wasn't sure if she was going to spontaneously turn bitchy, and if so, she didn't need Wade to overhear.

"And he's absolutely right."

Had her father taken happy pills since he'd left them? He never used to be so chipper. He was always sort of mopey, following behind her mother, trying to corral her mess. And failing. Clearly. Junie resented him for that. He could have tried harder.

"What do you say? Matinee? Go-karts?"

Junie tried to picture Evelyn St. Claire driving a go-kart. She couldn't. Maybe that meant she wouldn't come along. It was worth a shot.

"Go-karts sound good," Junie said. "Can Wade come too?"

"Sure. The more the merrier."

Junie pulled the phone away again and looked at it. Who was this version of her father? Maybe he was on drugs. Antidepressants. That would have explained a lot. He couldn't be this happy naturally. Not having to endure That Woman day in and day out. Or maybe—Junie cringed at the thought—she did make him happy. And that was worse. Far worse. Because that would mean he was never coming home.

"Okay. I guess."

"I'll come by first and mow the lawn. Pick you guys up at the house?"

"No! No. We'll come to your—" She was going to say *your house.* "We'll meet you at Evelyn's place. I did the lawn yesterday." She hadn't, of course.

That Woman answered the intercom, and Junie didn't even say hello. Just, "Is my dad there?"

In reply, Evelyn buzzed them in without a word.

"I guess that means, 'Good morning, Come on in!' For both of you." Wade held open the door. "Now be nice."

"Do I have to?" Junie glanced up. That Woman lived on the eighth floor. Junie saw her jump from the window and hurtle to her death, landing with a splat on the pavement at her feet. Maybe that was a little over the top, in terms of wishful thinking. But part of her hoped. She'd keep that macabre little daydream to herself. Wade would think she was awful for even having the notion.

"Yes, you have to." Wade gave her a gentle push through the doorway.

In the elevator, he pushed her again. This time, toward

the polished steel wall, where he pressed himself against her ever so slightly, the wall cool on Junie's back. "They do this in all the movies. Sometimes the elevator gets stuck," he murmured. "That could happen."

"Best idea ever," Junie managed to say between kisses. His fingertips felt electric on her skin.

Alas, the floors dinged by quickly, and soon they were at the eighth.

"Let's just keep riding the elevator. All day." Junie held onto Wade's jacket when he tried to lead her out of the elevator. The doors closed, and he kissed her again. Junie reached out to press the button to take them back down to the lobby, but the doors opened suddenly, and a woman got on pulling a suitcase behind her.

Junie and Wade broke apart, both of them blushing. "Sorry, excuse us." Wade blocked the door from shutting. "This is our floor."

The woman pursed her lips and glared at them as they got off. The elevator doors closed and Wade gave them a little bow and the tip of an imaginary hat. "And a good day to you too, madam. Many happy returns."

"I told you. The whole building is snotty. Come on," Junie said. "It's this way. The sooner we do this the sooner we get it over with."

⋮

Evelyn St. Claire and her dog both came along. So Wade and Junie were stuck in the back seat with Princess between them again. Halfway to the track, Princess farted, a quiet, prim little wheeze of gas. But it stank. Wade peered over the slope of the dog's back and made a face. Junie laughed. She pinched her nose.

"Your dog just let one rip," she announced.

"A little one," Wade said.

"Silent but violent."

"Open a window, then," her dad said. "Here." He used his buttons to lower both Wade's and Junie's window a little. "That better?"

"Better would be no dog at all," Junie said through her plugged nose, by which she meant no Evelyn St. Claire either. Wade and her dad didn't pick up on it, but the sentiment wasn't lost on That Woman. After not having said much more than hello, now she spun and glared at Junie.

"I won't have it, Junie. Not any more."

"What?" Junie knew what, though.

"You know perfectly well what." Evelyn pointed a finger at her. "I've been nothing but pleasant to you, and you've been nothing but horrid. Is that fair?"

"Ladies, please," Ron pleaded. "Let's just have a nice day together, okay?"

Wade took Junie's hand and gave it a squeeze. "Sounds like a great idea, sir."

"Ron." Junie's father sounded relieved to have someone on his side for once. "Call me Ron."

But still, Evelyn glared at Junie. "I won't have it. Not any more. You treat me with respect, and I will do the same. Understood?"

Junie glared right back at her. "Understood."

"Good." With that, Evelyn turned in her seat and settled back.

In the back seat, Junie fumed. She murmured, "Bitch," under her breath. She could feel that her cheeks were red. If Evelyn St. Claire wanted to have a conversation about respect, she'd get one. Not right this minute. Not with Wade beside her. But soon. Junie had a thing or two to say to That Woman about respect.

.
.
.

As Junie guessed, Evelyn took a pass on the karts. She had put on a big floppy hat once they'd gotten out of the car and wound a long, pink chiffon scarf around her neck, as if she were spending the day at the horse races and not some rundown go-kart track in the middle of the burbs. Ron paid for Wade and Junie, and said he'd join them on the second go-round. Evelyn sat in the bleachers that rose off to one side, with Princess lying at her feet.

"So much for quality time with my dad," Junie muttered as he went to join Evelyn there.

"Don't be so hard on him," Wade said. "He's trying."

Junie felt a pang of anger toward Wade. He didn't know the half of it, and shouldn't pretend to. But then she reasoned herself away from the anger. She hadn't told him the whole story, so it wasn't fair to expect him to know.

Before they were let out to choose their karts, the guy working there told them no bumping, no cutting each other off and no erratic steering.

"But that's what makes it fun," Wade said as he lowered himself into his kart. "See you on the dark side, babe." He winked at Junie and pulled his helmet on.

"Not before I kick your ass," Junie said.

Wade took off with his tires squealing. Junie stepped on the gas and tried to catch up, but he was going super-fast. She finally caught up to him when he took the first corner. He slowed down for it and she didn't. Junie bumped into the rubber guardrail and careened back into the middle of the lane, knocking Wade's rear end, sending him into a spin.

"That's my girl!" he hollered as he wrangled the steering wheel to regain control of his car.

Over the loudspeaker, the guy reminded them of the rules.

"Can't hear him over the engine!" Wade cranked his wheel to the right and drifted sidelong into Junie.

"Oh, that was dirty!" She laughed, gripping her wheel to stay on course. She stepped on the gas and passed Wade, pulling in front of him and slamming on her brakes. He bashed into her, jolting them both.

"Payback, mothertrucker." He gunned it until he was alongside her.

She grinned and gave him the finger. He returned it twofold, taking both hands off the wheel to do it.

The loudspeaker crackled on again: *Please return to the garage immediately.*

"Now you've done it," Wade said. "Way to go."

They were both laughing when they pulled into the garage. The guy from the track stood there, hands on his hips.

"You heard the rules."

"Sorry," Wade said.

"Yeah. Sorry."

"Yeah, well, you've lost your second and third laps. You want to go again, you pay again, plus a charge for abusing the karts."

Junie felt bad, but not *that* bad. She'd had a blast. And so had Wade.

"You're a vixen on wheels, Junie." Wade set his helmet aside and helped her out of her kart. "That's hot."

"You're not so bad yourself."

Junie's dad was waiting for them on the other side of the fence.

"Was that necessary?"

"Yes, Dad. Deeply, deeply necessary."

"Sorry, sir." Wade ducked his head.

"It's Ron." Her dad tried not to smile, but he was failing at it. "It did look like fun. Hard to resist. I get it. I was sixteen once too, you know."

Junie couldn't imagine it. And didn't want to, truth be told.

"Want to go again?" her dad asked.

"How about you and Wade go?" Junie suggested. "I'll sit this one out."

"That's all right, Ron." Wade explained about the lost laps and the fine. "We should take the punch on the chin."

"Ah, never mind," her dad said. And again, Junie wondered who this happier version of her father was. "I'll pay for it. I need someone to race with. I'm not going by myself. Junie, you're sure you want to sit this one out?"

Junie nodded. As much as she'd have loved to go again, she had a few things to say to Evelyn, and now was the perfect time to do it.

She joined Evelyn on the bleachers and watched as Wade and her dad got into their karts. The two took off, much more tamely this time, racing each other around the track. Evelyn watched for a few moments and then took a book out of her large purse and began to read. *The Power of Now: A Guide to Spiritual Enlightenment.*

"Good book?" Junie laughed to herself. Of course that would be the kind of book That Woman would read.

"Not that you particularly care," Evelyn said. "But yes. It's one everyone should read."

Which Junie took to mean her mother.

"I was just asking."

Evelyn didn't look up from the page. "And I was just saying."

Junie watched Wade and her dad start their second lap. She was running out of time to say her piece. She forced herself to say the words that she'd rehearsed.

"I don't like you and you don't like me—"

That made Evelyn look up. "Not true."

"Come on, you know it's true."

"I hardly *know* you." Evelyn touched the scarf at her throat. "And that's because you haven't let me get to know you."

"And I won't anytime soon." That wasn't part of what Junie had prepared to say.

The guys started the third lap, with Wade in the lead by far.

"Your point?" Evelyn took off her sunglasses and fixed Junie with the first real expression Junie had ever seen on her. Annoyance. That was more like it. Now they were getting somewhere.

"My point is that I don't like you. And I won't. I hate you for what you did to my family."

"We can work through those feelings." Back to her façade. Always the life coach. "I can help you overcome your negativity."

"Well, the thing is, Ms. St. Claire, 'life coach' . . ." Junie put air quotes around that, ". . . I don't want to overcome my negativity toward you." What Junie wanted to do was tighten that pink scarf around Evelyn's neck until she choked. Whatever she'd rehearsed had been lost. She was making it up as she went along now. "I hate you. It's pretty simple. I'm not looking to change that anytime soon."

"I see," Evelyn said quietly. "I'm sorry you feel that way."

"And one more thing," Junie said as Wade and her dad pulled into the garage. She hadn't even seen who'd come in first. "Don't ever talk to me about respect. You clearly don't know the first thing about it, judging by what you did to my family."

"Perhaps you should be having this conversation with your father. He's a grown man. An adult who makes mature, grown-up decisions for himself, and his family." Evelyn set her bookmark in her place and closed her book. "I, for one, am done with this little chat."

"So am I."

"Good, then."

"Good."

Only now, Junie didn't know what to do with herself. Stay? Get up and leave? Evelyn made the decision for her by leaving first. She stood, replaced her sunglasses and then made her way down the steps to the asphalt, Princess at her heels. That left Junie alone on the bleachers, feeling at once relieved to have said what she'd wanted to say and ashamed for having said it.

If either her father or Wade noticed the chill between Evelyn and Junie, neither of them showed it or said anything about it. They went for an early dinner, and then back to Evelyn's, where Wade had parked the van. When they got out of her father's car, Junie made some lame excuse about homework and not having time to go up. Evelyn helped her along by saying that she had to prepare for a client meeting and didn't have the time to hang out either.

"Do you really have homework?" Wade asked as they pulled away.

"Not that I need to do tonight."

"Good." He grinned at her. "*The Big Lebowski* is playing at the drive-in. Want to?"

"Absolutely."

Wade parked the van at an angle, so that they could sit together on the back bench and still see the screen. It didn't matter, though. They hardly watched the movie at all.

THIRTEEN

•
•
•
•

On Sunday morning Junie awoke to her mother calling for her from downstairs, and by her tone, Junie knew that something was very wrong. She leapt out of bed and bounded down the stairs to find her mother at the door that led to the basement. The door was closed. Her mom held the doorknob so tightly her knuckles were white.

"What is it?" Junie asked, breathless.

"The bathroom down there backed up." Her mother started crying. "There's water everywhere!"

Junie tried to think of the last time she'd gone down to the basement. Maybe two years ago? It was the last time her father had brought in help before That Woman. A professional organizer called Harold, who'd acted like a drill sergeant, yelling orders and chucking stuff away behind her mother's back until she'd ended up going to the hospital in the back of an ambulance with chest pains. Turned out it was only a panic attack, but her dad had sent Harold away, after he'd tackled only a small portion of the basement. There'd been no reason for Junie to go down there. It was floor-to-ceiling packed with her mother's junk.

"What were you doing down there?" Junie headed for the basement door, but her mother stopped her.

"Wait!" Her mother sucked back a sob. "I went down to get that floor lamp we brought from Grandma's. The one by my chair isn't working any more."

Junie couldn't remember a particular floor lamp out of the two moving truck loads her mother had jammed into the house after her own mother had died a year ago. It was remarkable that her mother could find anything specific amidst the ruins.

"I don't know if you should go down there."

"Why not?" Junie pushed past her and opened the door. That was when the smell hit her.

"It's not just water," her mother cried behind her. "It's raw sewage, Junie!"

So that explained why the house had smelled even worse lately, despite the candles and incense. Junie clamped a hand over her mouth and went down a couple of steps until she could peek around the corner and see the bathroom. The door was open, and even in the dim light Junie could see brown sludge oozing out of the bathroom and seeping into boxes and bags and broken furniture.

This was bad. Very bad.

Junie glanced at her watch. She was supposed to meet Wade in an hour. She'd have to go to Tabitha's to call and cancel.

Junie backed up the stairs, stifling a gag. She closed the door behind her and took a steadying breath. "We have to call a plumber."

"I don't want anyone coming in here," her mother said.

"You don't have a choice. It's toxic down there!"

"You and I can clean it up." Her mother grabbed Junie's wrists. "Please! I can't bear the thought of someone coming in here." She started to hyperventilate—the precursor to a panic attack.

"Calm down, Mom." Junie pulled her hands free and set them firmly on her mother's shoulders.

"I can't! I can't!" Her mother shook her head. "All of my things are down there! Ruined! All of my Mother's things. Ruined!"

"That should be the least of your worries, Mom!" Junie couldn't believe it. Even with their basement brimming with shit, her mom was worried about her stuff. "We have to get a plumber in here to fix it. And then we have to get a cleanup crew. A real one. Not just us. Professionals. Biohazard professionals. Seriously."

"No. No, no, no." Her mother groaned as if she'd been kicked in the gut. "Please, Junie. No. Please just help me clean it up. We can do it. It's probably not as bad as it looks. Right? It's never as bad as it looks. It just smells bad."

"Mom, you have no idea how long it's been like this. It might be dangerous down there."

"No, no it's not." Her mother rallied, wiping the tears from her cheeks. "It's not that bad. We can do it."

"We can't." Addicts were supposed to hit rock bottom

before they could admit they needed help. Junie had read about that. Seen it on TV. This, she thought, was her mother's rock bottom. But no. She was going to try to brush it off. "We need help, Mom. You need help. We can't do this by ourselves."

Junie wasn't just referring to the basement. She was referring to her mother's entire life. Her body, her mind, her soul. And her home. "Give up, Mom. Please. Isn't this bad enough?"

Her mother fixed Junie with a determined gaze, as if Junie hadn't just said what she'd said. "We can do it. The Rawley girls to the rescue. We'll get cleaning supplies and go down there and tackle it. Good as new."

"No, Mom." Junie shook her head. She raised her hands in a truce. "You're on your own this time." One thing that Evelyn St. Claire had said, when she'd still been pretending to be a responsible life coach, was that Junie and her dad were enabling her mother. By keeping her secrets and not saying no. By not giving her difficult ultimatums. That Woman might have been a bitch, but she wasn't entirely stupid. "I can't help you any more. I'm sorry."

"Don't do this to me now, sweetheart." Her mother's tears were back. "I know what you're trying to do, and I appreciate it. I do. But not today, okay? Don't abandon me today."

"I'm not abandoning you. I'm trying to do what's right. For both of us." Junie dropped her hands to her sides, defeated. Evelyn had said her mother would plead and cajole. And it was working. Junie felt the familiar tugs of guilt pulling at her gut. But along with that was anger.

"You'd leave me alone to deal with this by myself?" Her mother's voice quavered.

Junie sighed. "Emotional blackmail. Do you remember? That's exactly what Evelyn St. Claire said you would do if we set limits."

Her mother reeled back as if she'd been slapped. "I can't believe you're bringing up that woman. Now, of all times."

"*That Woman* knows a thing or two about your sickness."

"I'm not sick."

"You are!"

"I am not *sick*. I need help getting myself sorted out. I have a severe organizational problem. I'm a collector whose collections have gotten the better of her. But I am not sick."

"You are so, Mom. You're a compulsive hoarder. You know that, I know that. Dad knows it. And That Woman knows it too."

"Please don't talk about her, Junie. Please. Not in my house."

"Evelyn said you would do whatever it took to hold onto all your crap, even if you had to emotionally black-mail us into going along with you, and that is exactly what you're doing now. It has to stop, Mom."

"What has to stop is you mentioning her!" Her mother covered her ears with her hands.

The day before, Junie had told Evelyn how much she hated her. And here she was now, touting her advice. The irony was not lost on her.

"She said you would use guilt to keep us under your thumb. And she was right."

Her mother sank to the floor and leaned her head against the wall. Her breathing quickened again. She banged her head, so hard that a pile of papers on a shelf above slipped, sliding in a cascade of sheets to her side. Her mother hit her head again, harder.

"Don't do this to me today! Give me more time! Not today!" She banged her head again, and again. "Not today! Not today! Not today!"

"Mom!" Junie grabbed her mother's arm, alarmed. "Stop it!"

Her mother looked up, her eyes suddenly clear. Manipulative. "*You* stop it." She said it quietly, emphasizing each word carefully. "Don't abandon me. Not now. I don't think I could take it. I know I can't. I would die, Junie. I would die here. Is that what you want?"

⋮

Junie went in search of usable cleaning supplies, looking throughout the house and garage. She found eight mops, but only one that still had a sponge attached that wasn't mouldy. She found four brooms, but they wouldn't be much help. She also found three large packages of paper towels, each with twenty-four rolls. She didn't have to search for bleach or bathroom cleanser. Junie kept those things upstairs in her own bathroom, the one that was spotless. She knew there wasn't enough of either, though, to tackle this mess. There were as many empty bleach bottles as you could ever possibly need, though—enough to build a raft, and even more empty cleanser bottles of other varieties. They were all strung up through the handles with twine, hanging from a rafter in the garage, waiting to be turned into bird feeders for the local bird rescue centre. But one thing was for sure, there was not enough bleach in the house to deal with a mess of that magnitude. A trip to the store was in order.

Her mother put together a list while Junie went upstairs to get dressed. She couldn't believe she was doing this. She'd tried to be strong. She'd try to call her mom on her shit, as Evelyn had advised—not in those words, maybe. But Junie had been listening. As much as she didn't want to admit it, those two weeks that Evelyn had been in their home, working with her mother, Junie had learned a lot. Everything was to go into one of three bins: keep, toss, donate. Sort like with like—that was when all the bleach bottles got strung up, because her mother refused to part with them—and then find a home for each item. No home, it goes. And the biggest rule: be firm with the hoarder. Keep your boundaries.

Junie wondered if today's disaster was karmic payback for having been such a bitch to Evelyn the day before. "I'm not apologizing," Junie grumbled to herself as she made her way back downstairs. "Not a chance."

"Take a taxi." Her mother held out a wad of cash. "It'll be easier with all the stuff to carry."

Junie gawked at her. "There is NO WAY that I'm going to get all this cleaning stuff by MYSELF."

"But—"

"No!" Junie threw the money at her. "You might've

guilted me into helping you clean up this mess, but there is no effin' way that I'm doing any part of it by myself. Get some clean clothes on, wash your face and get your purse. You are coming with me."

"Watch your tone with me, Junie." Her mother squatted and retrieved the money with a wheeze. "I'm still your mother. All right. I'll come."

Junie took a step back, she was surprised that her mother had given in so easily. Maybe being firm was the way to go. It wasn't going to get her mother to agree to bring in professionals to fix the disaster downstairs, but it had accomplished this one small victory of getting her mother out the front door.

They got a taxi to the hardware store, but had to wait twenty minutes until it opened at ten. Her mother sat on the curb outside, working on keeping her breathing from heading toward panic, while Junie went across the road to the gas station and got them both mochas from the coffee machine. They were sickly sweet and on the watery side, but Junie was a firm believer that a hot drink was a ready balm. Her grandma had taught her that. Her mother's mother, dead now just over a year.

Junie waited at the crosswalk for the light to change, a cup in each hand and an oily muffin wrapped in plastic wrap in each pocket. She thought about her grandma. She was probably wringing her hands in the afterlife to see all of her possessions carelessly crammed into a basement afloat with crap. When she'd been alive she'd come over once a week or more, with occasional hand-wringing and the odd jag of tears when Junie's mother wasn't looking.

It had upset her no end, but she'd tried not to let her own daughter see that. Instead, she and Junie and her mother would play cards and have tea and homemade cookies that her grandma had brought, after her mother had stopped baking.

When Junie was ten, her grandmother had pulled her aside, while she was getting her coat on to leave, and told Junie that she'd have to keep an eye on her mother.

"You'll have to see that it doesn't get any worse than it is." Her grandma shook her head, her eyes getting moist. "She wasn't the neatest of children either. But I'd always hoped once she had—" Her voice caught. She cleared her throat. "I'd hoped that she would pull up her socks for you. She has her reasons, sure. But it's gotten worse since—"

Junie gave her a hug. "It's okay. I can take care of her."

"No, no." Her grandma shook her head. "It shouldn't be like that. She should be taking care of you."

Junie knew that was true. But it wasn't happening. And hadn't for a long time. Even then.

"I worry about you. I worry about *her*. I know she's suffering—"

Junie never knew what had made her grandmother bring it up that day, but that was the first and last time that she ever said anything in reference to the growing piles of junk, the haphazard collections, the filth. Shortly after that, she'd stopped coming by the house altogether. For a while, Junie and her mother had gone over to her small apartment for cards and tea, but then her mother had stopped visiting, sensing the judgment, wincing at the critical tone in her own mother's voice. The shame stopped her from talking to her mother, and pride stopped Junie's grandma from reaching out. Junie's mother and grandma hadn't spoken for months when Junie's grandma died suddenly of a stroke. It was very sad, and made everything even worse after.

Junie missed her grandmother. Very much. Sometimes, not often any more, she picked up the phone and dialled her grandma's number, just to hear it ring once before she hung up. Just on the off chance that she might pick up.

The light changed and Junie crossed the road, keeping her mother in her sights all the while. She'd put on a clean pair of black sweatpants and a brand new red cardigan overtop of the matching sweatshirt, but she still looked dishevelled. As though she were a homeless person begging for change outside the hardware store, who had been given a new sweater by a good Samaritan. Especially sitting on the curb like that. Junie was embarrassed for her. For herself, too.

She offered her mother one of the cups and wondered if anyone watching would think she was being kind to a bag lady, if she was the one who'd given her the sweater. She sat beside her and unwrapped the muffins and offered her mother one.

"Carrot," she said. "With walnuts."

"Thank you, honey." Her mother sipped the coffee and then picked at the muffin, not really eating it.

"If you're going to have the energy to clean up down there, you'll need to eat." Junie took a bite of her own muffin and chewed. Once again, she felt like the mother. "Eat!" she said again as her mother stared at the muffin, not touching it.

The store opened, and they got a cart. They collected several bottles of bleach, a jumbo pack of mop heads, a large box of heavy-duty garbage bags, five different kinds of antibacterial bathroom cleansers and several pairs of rubber gloves.

"We've got buckets at home," her mother said as they passed them. "And lots of rags, too."

"What rags?"

"I've got a few boxes of your father's old T-shirts. We can use those."

Junie marvelled at the thought that her mother would get rid of those. Even to use to clean up the mess.

"Is that what happens when you break up? All of a sudden you don't care what happens to his stuff?" It came out snarkier than she'd meant, but her mother didn't seem to notice.

"He's taken what he wants, if that's what you're asking. These are really old, from when you were little is my guess."

"Then why not get rid of them before?" It was worth a shot.

"And if I had," her mother reasoned, "we'd be spending money on a box of rags instead. I just saved us five bucks."

Junie stopped in her tracks and rolled her eyes. She would never get her mother's logic. Ever.

Before they went to the till, they asked one of the salespeople if they had disposable coveralls and masks.

"Sure do," he said and led them to the back of the store. "What sort of mask are you looking for?"

"We're cleaning up raw sewage," Junie said, not willing to bother with niceties.

"Ah, right." The guy took down a heavy-duty mask with two can-shaped filters and a box of paper masks. "The big one would be the best, but it's pricey. It'll keep you safe from the nasties. This little one here will do the trick too, but obviously not as well as the more expensive one. Depends how much poop you're looking at."

"A lot of poop," Junie said.

"The sewer just backed up into the bathroom," her mother explained. "It's not that bad."

"Oh, yes it is." Junie glared at her mother, and then flashed a smile at the guy. "It's as bad as you can imagine, actually."

"Sorry to hear it," the guy said. He dropped two of the heavy-duty masks into the cart. "You should get the professionals in, but if you're going to tackle it on your own, I'd go with these. If money's not an issue."

Money was always an issue. Junie looked to her mother, eyes narrowed. If she dared to say that they couldn't afford the better masks, Junie would rip into her right there in the hardware store. If her mother could order four identical porcelain miniature Doberman Pinscher figurines from the Shopping Channel, she could damn well buy the better masks.

Her mother said nothing, just pushed the cart along to where the coveralls were stacked on the shelf and added four of them to the cart, along with a pair of safety goggles each, which had also been recommended by the sales guy.

Back home, they wrestled their way into the coveralls and found gumboots amidst the mess in the garage. Junie's mother found a pair with the tags still on and steel toes that made the boots extra heavy, and Junie found a red boot one size too small and a black one that was one size too big, but they'd do.

Junie and her mother stood at the top of the basement stairs and pulled on the masks. It was like wearing some space alien mask, with each breath clicking through the vents. Junie was pretty sure that if they ever had to endure nuclear fallout, these masks would keep them safe.

They each grabbed two handfuls of cleaning supplies and went down the stairs. Junie went first, and when she stepped off the bottom step, she knew at once that it was far worse than she'd first imagined. Her feet were stuck in shitty muck, all the way over by the stairs, which was a good long way from the bathroom. She turned to her mom, who was still halfway down the stairs.

"This is impossible, Mom. Look!" Junie sloshed her boot through the wet slime.

"It's okay." Her mother pushed past her. "Let's start in the bathroom."

Her mom went ahead and turned on the light, illuminating the mess all the better. They hadn't used this bathroom as a bathroom for over a decade, so her mother had stacked boxes of stuff in the bathtub, which was now brimming with raw sewage, dark brown soup with bits of toilet paper and food floating in it. Junie had to turn away as she retched behind her mask.

"I don't know if I can do this, Mom."

Her mother stood in the doorway, staring. The sink was also brimming with shit soup, as was the toilet. Flies were everywhere.

Junie set her supplies on a stack of boxes by the door and pulled up the hood on her coveralls, cinching it tight under her chin. Her mother did the same.

"I'm glad he suggested the safety goggles," her mother said as she waded into the bathroom, plunger in hand.

Five minutes later, using the plunger hadn't accomplished anything except sending more shit soup spilling over the edge of the toilet bowl.

"I'm telling you, Mom, we need a plumber," Junie wheezed from behind her mask. "With one of those snake things."

"I think there's one in the garage. I'll go look." Her mom left.

Junie stood there, having absolutely no idea where to start. She was still standing there when her mother came back ten minutes later.

"Found it!" Her mother sounded almost cheerful.

Junie had hoped that she wouldn't be able to find it, but she hadn't hoped too hard. She was always astounded at how easily her mother could find exactly what she was looking for, despite the chaotic mess.

Junie stood back while her mother stabbed the metal coil down the toilet. She jabbed it in hand over hand until she hit a block.

"That'd be it," she said as if she had a clue about what she was doing. She cranked it around and around, forcing it in farther as she did.

Junie crossed her fingers, praying that it wouldn't work. Praying that her mother would give up and call a plumber. But to her great horror, the toilet made a terrific *glug glug* sound, and the shit soup started draining. Not only from the toilet, but from the sink and bathtub as well.

"Well, how about that?" Her mother collected the snake in big, filthy, dripping coils. "Aren't you proud of me?"

Junie offered her a terse nod in reply. Truly, though, she was appalled. Her mother was on her knees in a shallow sea of crap, her coveralls already split over her fat ass, the front splattered with feces. She was not proud of her. Not one bit. She was ashamed. Deeply, irreparably ashamed.

With the shit soup gone, they still had to get rid of the boxes from the bathtub and then mop up everything off of the floor, and wipe out the dregs from the toilet bowl, sink and bathtub. Junie and her mom put the ruined boxes straight into the garbage bags. Junie was thankful that her mother didn't insist on trying to salvage any of it. By the looks of it, it was all the decorations from the Hawaiian luau party Junie had had for her seventh birthday. Paper palm trees and hula skirts, piles of plastic leis and tiki torches. Junie hiked the fetid trash up the stairs and out the back door to the alley, hoping the neighbours weren't watching.

It took about an hour before it started to look normal again. It took another two hours before they'd cleaned a path to the stairs, and that was without removing any of the contaminated junk. By then, Junie and her mother were exhausted.

"I need a shower," Junie said. "And then we need to eat something before we keep going."

She and her mom stripped off the coveralls and boots and gloves and each had a shower in the upstairs bathroom. Junie made them grilled cheese sandwiches, which they ate on the back step, drinking in the sunshine.

Fortified by the fresh air and food, they pulled on clean coveralls, rinsed off the boots with the garden hose and headed back downstairs. By six o'clock, they'd made some serious progress. But not enough. Junie had another shower, during which she tried to think of how she could convince her mother that everything that had come in contact with the shit soup had to go.

While her mom had her second shower, Junie put on clean clothes and went downstairs. The door to the basement was closed, but it still reeked. It was worse now, actually. Whether because Junie knew what was down there, or because all of their cleaning had stirred it up. Her mother joined her, her hair wrapped in a towel turban, her housecoat knotted over her girth.

"Good job today, Junie." Her mother pulled her into a hug, but Junie resisted.

"Everything that's come anywhere close to that mess has to go, Mom."

"We can sort through it." Her mother undid the towel and tousled her hair. "Bit by bit."

"It's got to go in the garbage! We need to rent a bin. Get rid of everything that got the raw sewage on it."

"Relax, Junie." Her mother patted her arm. "We've done enough for today."

And that's when it hit Junie. She hadn't called Wade to say she couldn't hang out. She'd stood him up.

"We'll talk about this later. I've got to go to Tabitha's." She shoved her feet into her sneakers and slammed out the door.

FOURTEEN

⋮

Tabitha opened the door with a frown. "Where have you been?"

"I had to help my mom with something." Junie wasn't about to tell Tabitha about the shit soup. It was too humiliating. She couldn't quite imagine keeping a secret from Tabitha, but she would try. For the first time ever, she would try. After all, what was one more lie?

"Help her with what?" Tabitha pulled her into the house. "I came by, there was no answer. I called, there was no answer. Where were you all day?"

"I was—" This secret was going to last all of about two minutes. Junie couldn't think of what to tell her. "I was with my dad."

"You weren't," Tabitha said with a snort. "I called him. Why are you lying to me?"

"I'm not. My mom and I—" What? Went shopping? Not likely. "My mom and I . . ."

"Look, while you try to come up with some excuse for dropping off the planet, a certain someone is desperate for you to call him back." Tabitha dragged her toward the phone. "He left six messages, and a note on the door."

"He came here?"

Tabitha thrust the phone at her. "Call him. And you'd better have a good story. He thinks you're lying mortally wounded in the hospital."

Without having a clue as to what she was about to say, Junie dialled Wade's number.

"Junie!" Wade said when he picked up. "What's going on? I was worried."

"I was with my dad." Junie turned away from Tabitha. She didn't want to see her disproval. "I am so sorry. He dropped by this morning to take me out to breakfast and then we went shopping and I just totally blanked. I'm an idiot. I am so sorry."

"Oh." There was a pause on Wade's end. "Okay."

"I'm a space cadet, honestly. Tabitha will tell you." She glanced at Tabitha, eyebrows raised. *Sorry,* she mouthed. "How can I make it up to you?"

"I thought something bad had happened," Wade said flatly. "I was really worried, Junie."

"Wade, I am so sorry. It will never happen again."

"It's okay, I guess."

"No, no it's not." Junie's heart raced. He sounded so disappointed in her.

"I managed to get Royce and Jeremy to agree to my documentary," Wade said. Junie pounced on the new subject with enormous relief.

"Yeah? When do we get started?"

"I was going to pick you up so we could go out there today, but . . ." Wade sighed. "I'm just glad that you're okay."

"I'm an ass who is okay."

"This is true."

"So sorry."

"Apology accepted." Wade laughed. "Do you think now might be a good time to get a cellphone?"

"I've told you, my parents agree on one or two things and me not having a cellphone is one of them."

Tabitha poked her shoulder and said, loudly enough for Wade to hear, "Hi, Wade."

"Hi, Tabitha," Wade said.

"She came over to check on me," Junie said. "I hadn't told her where I was going either, if it's any consolation."

"I called her house too, but there was no answer."

"Church day," Junie said.

Tabitha grabbed the phone. "It does not appear to have been an alien abduction. At least, I haven't noticed any indicators."

Junie could hear Wade laughing. Everything was going to be okay. With him, anyway. For the time being.

They said goodbye to Wade, and then Tabitha turned on Junie. "Tell me."

"I really don't want to."

"It's about your mom."

Junie nodded.

"Are you going to make me play Twenty Questions about this or are you going to give up and tell me what made you disappear all day?"

Junie pursed her lips and tried to think of an excuse. She just couldn't. "All right. Apparently, I cannot lie to you. Even when I really, really want to."

"Spill it, sister."

Junie laughed. "You have no idea how fitting that is!" So Junie told her, sparing no detail.

By the end of the story, they were both in tears, laughing. Now, being removed from the situation, Junie could see how it was kind of funny. Not funny ha-ha, but sick funny. Too-crazy-to-be-true kind of funny.

"And you can never, ever tell Wade," Junie said. "Promise?"

"I wouldn't think of it," Tabitha said solemnly. "Truly. It's that gross."

‧
‧
⦿

All the next day at school, Junie worried that she still smelled like shit, even though she knew better. Even still, she asked Tabitha, who insisted that all she could smell on her was her apple shampoo, but Junie still thought she could catch a whiff of her day down in the basement, slogging through the crap stew. Wade scooped her up in a hug when she got to World Studies. He kissed her on the lips, too. And without a grimace, so she was sure that Tabitha was right, but she still couldn't shake the feeling that she was wafting a wake of poo perfume behind her wherever she went.

She'd surveyed the basement before leaving for school that morning and was still convinced that they needed a professional crew in there to decontaminate. Her mother wouldn't hear anything about it, though, no matter how Junie pleaded with her. Sure, she and Tabitha had been laughing about it the night before, but if Tab saw the basement, she'd call Social Services for sure. It was definitely not a safe home for a minor – or for anyone for that matter.

In Math, Mr. Benson sprung a pop quiz on them and announced that it would count for 10 percent of their overall grade. Everyone groaned—even Ollie—but Junie panicked.

"You'll do fine," Ollie whispered as Benson handed around the quiz.

"No talking!" he barked, dropping a quiz on Ollie's desk. But Ollie, bless his little rebel heart, ignored him.

"Just stay calm and don't over-think it. Go with your first answer."

"Ollie, I'm warning you." Benson retrieved Ollie's quiz. "Your straight-A status does not mean you can break the rules. Go sit at the back, where I'll be sure you're not aiding and abetting in Miss Rawley's demise here."

Ollie winked at her as he made his way to the back. He mimed taking a slow, deep breath and letting it go.

Junie turned to her quiz. There had been hints that this might have been coming. On Friday, Benson had given them a chapter of homework, emphasizing that it would be wise to have the material under their belts by Monday. But Junie had been so busy being angry with That Woman on Saturday, and then dealing with the shit soup all day

Sunday, that she'd only glanced at the chapter before she'd collapsed, exhausted, into bed on Sunday night.

A right triangular prism has edges in the ratio 3:4:5:10. If the volume is 202.5 units find the actual length of the longest side.

The first question would be her last question. She set her head on the desk and squeezed her eyes shut. She would not cry. She would have to redo grade ten Math. This was no surprise. It was just a fact. Ollie had done his best, but this was beyond help. This was simply beyond Junie, period.

She didn't even bother trying. There was no use. She was going to get a zero anyway, so why make herself crazy trying to figure out questions she would never get right?

Mr. Benson gave them half an hour for the quiz, during which Junie doodled on the piece of scrap paper they were allowed to have during tests. When he called for pencils down, Junie was almost calm. Not quite, but almost. Mr. Benson collected the quizzes and then gave them a textbook assignment to do while he marked them. Junie would rather have put off the inevitable until the next class, but Benson thought otherwise. Just five minutes before the bell, he handed them back.

Junie did not get a zero. She got minus five.

"For not even trying," Mr. Benson said with a shake of his head. "Minus five, class. I can't say that I've ever given a negative mark before." He frowned at Junie. "Ever. And that's in fifteen years of teaching. Congratulations on being the first."

When the bell rang, Ollie put an arm across her

shoulders and led her to the cafeteria, where her friends—
and Wade—were suitably sympathetic.

⋮

After school Wade asked if Junie wanted to go get a coffee.

"Something with lots of whipped cream," he said. "To
make your Math mark feel better."

"Thanks, but no." Junie shook her head. "If my mom
finds out that I went out after school after getting a *minus
five* mark, she'd kill me. I should go home and study today.
Or pretend to, anyway. No studying in the world is going
to help me at this point."

"Rain check, then. We can stop for coffee on our
way out of town tomorrow." They were going to go out to
Chilliwack to start filming. Both she and Wade had a spare
period after lunch, so they were going to skip Art and Gym
respectively to get the whole afternoon free.

"Sounds brilliant."

"I'll drive you and Tabitha home."

Junie sat in front as usual, while Tabitha sat in the
back, making plans to salvage Junie's Math grade.

"We could do a math-athon," she said. "Like a
marathon, but with math. Spend next weekend totally
immersed. Ollie can be in charge. All math, all the time.
Try to soak it into you. Math by osmosis."

"Wow," Junie said. "Does that ever sound like fun."

"Might work," Tabitha said as Wade turned onto
Lambert. "It's worth a shot."

"Whoa," Wade said, pointing down the street. "What
the hell is going on? Someone get murdered or something?"

He was pointing at Junie's house. Her real house. The driveway was full of those TV vans with the big satellite dishes on top. Two cop cars sat at the bottom of the driveway, lights flashing.

"Oh my God." Junie's breath got stuck in her throat. "My mom!"

"What?" Wade turned to her.

"Stop the van!" In that moment, Junie didn't care about her lie or that it was about to get blown out of the water, she had to get to her mother. "Let me out!"

"But—"

"Stop the van!" Junie banged on the window, desperate. A collection of official-looking people stood on her front lawn, heads together, talking quietly. "Let me out now!"

Bewildered, Wade stopped the van in front of Junie's real house. Junie flung open her door and raced across the lawn. The front door was wide open, and there was her mother, standing in the cluttered hall, talking to Kendra. Kendra, of *The Kendra Show*. In her house. In real life. In front of her. In person. Not on TV, in person. Right there. It was so strange, so out of context, that Junie had trouble processing the tableau in front of her.

"Mom?" Junie stood frozen, uncomprehending. "What's going on?"

"Hi, I'm Kendra." As if an introduction was necessary. Kendra was smaller in person, shorter than Junie would have imagined. Heavily made up, and in heels, her coiffure shaped and sprayed so that not one hair was out of place, she looked like a life-sized living doll. A very, very famous doll. Junie spun around, spotting a boom and mic, and a guy with an enormous camera on his shoulder. "You must be Juniper," Kendra purred, arm elegantly outstretched, waiting for Junie to grasp it in return.

"Mom?" Junie backed toward the door. This was the very definition of surreal. Why was Kendra, world-famous host and creator of *The Kendra Show* empire, in her horrible house?

"This must be a big shock, honey." Kendra smiled widely, her teeth blazingly white. She gestured at the camera guy. "Turn on her, Jake. Let's get a shot of her reaction. This is good."

The camera guy aimed the camera at her, just as Wade and Tabitha came up the walk behind her.

"What's going on?" Wade asked. "Junie? What is all this?"

"I don't know. Mom? What's going on?"

"Junie, it's *The Kendra Show*! And Kendra herself! They've come to help us."

Kendra smiled at Tabitha and Wade. "And who have we got here?" Neither Wade nor Tabitha offered introductions, and Junie couldn't bring herself to. Junie's mother—summoning a sense of propriety from somewhere deep within, for the sole benefit of the celebrity standing in front of her—did the honours.

"This is Tabitha, Junie's best friend—" Junie's mother pointed to Tabitha, and then Wade. "And this . . . this . . ." Junie's mother suddenly put it all together, despite the chaos. "And this must be Wade! Of course!"

Junie's mother thrust her hand out, and Wade shook it obligingly, his eyes on Junie, questioning.

"I'm Junie's mom. Marla. I've heard a lot about you."
She dropped Wade's hand and grabbed Junie's. "This is
crazy. Crazy, crazy, crazy. Junie, can you believe it? Kendra
is here. She's here at our *house*! In person! For real!"

This was not how it was supposed to happen. Junie
wasn't sure what she'd had in mind, but not this. That
much was for sure. This was not how Wade was supposed
to find out that Junie had been lying to him. He was never
supposed to find out. Not ever.

Wade looked Junie's mother up and down. "You're
Junie's mom? But—"

"This isn't live, is it?" Junie's stomach lurched into
her throat. She wondered if she was about to throw up on
national television. "Please, please tell me that we are not
on TV right now."

"No, honey," Kendra assured her. "We just came
today to get things started."

"What the hell are you talking about?" Junie glared
at her, not caring one iota that she was back-talking one of
the richest, most famous, most highly respected women in
the entire world. "What the hell are you doing here?"

"What are *you* doing here?" Wade asked Junie as he
looked around, taking in the mess. "I don't get it. I don't
understand, Junie. And why does it smell like shit?"

"Let me explain," Junie begged. But she couldn't. She
couldn't explain any of this. "What's happening, Mom?"

"I applied! You know at the end of the show when
they're rolling the credits and they post those little invita-
tions for people to contact the show if they should be on
one of her shows? Well, I did it!"

Junie remembered then her mother saying something about writing to Kendra, but Junie hadn't given it a second thought. "You invited her ... here?"

"Yes! I never thought she'd come in a million years, but it was worth a shot, you know?"

"For a show about. . . ?" But Junie knew. Of course she knew.

"Hoarding," her mother said simply, even though it was anything but simple.

"It was a total long shot. But can you believe it! Kendra herself is right here! In real life! I would never have bet she'd actually pick us, not in a million years. And if they did, I thought they'd call first. And then I was going to tell you. Of course I would've!"

"We typically don't call first," Kendra interrupted. "We like to get gut reactions to our arrival, and we can't get that if you know we're coming."

"And now they're here! They picked *us*!"

It was embarrassing that her mother was ecstatic about being picked when they were picking extreme hoarders. That was nothing to be proud about. Not at all.

And now Kendra, world-famous celebrity and interloper, was in her house. Her horrible, awful, no good, rotten, shit-stink-hole of a house. And so was Wade. This was all wrong. So very wrong. If only she could take it all back, start all over, and make something different out of it. Something better than this current state of emergency in the nation of her miserable self.

Junie forced herself to look at Wade. His arms were folded tightly across his chest, and his eyes were piercingly dark. "So it was all a lie." His words all had edges, each and every one of them cutting into her, drawing blood. "You've been lying to me this whole time."

"She can explain," Tabitha blurted.

"Wade, please, I can explain everything," Junie said. The camera swung slowly from her to Wade and back while he glared at her, two red slashes of anger high on his cheeks. "Turn it off."

"No can do, kid." The cameraman peeked out from behind the camera. "Part of the deal."

"What deal?" Junie held up her hands in front of her face, blocking the shot. "Wade, wait! I can explain."

Wade was backing out of the house, his hands up too, but palms outward in resignation. Disgusted resignation.

"Forget it. I'm out of here."

"No! Don't go!"

"I'll talk to you later," Wade said with a dismissive little wave. "Maybe then you can take a few minutes and tell me the truth."

Junie was frozen. Tabitha shoved her, "Go after him!"

"I'll tell you now!" Junie ran after him. The cameraman followed her. "Please don't go. I'm sorry I lied. I just didn't want you to see my house. And after you saw my parents that day—"

"Save it." Wade shook his head. "I don't want to be on *The Kendra Show*, thanks. I wouldn't even watch that crap, let alone be on it."

Junie took a step back, defeated. "Oh," she bleated, the tiny, useless word all that she could think of. "Oh."

"Yeah. Right. 'Oh.' That's a wicked explanation, Junie.

A simple 'oh' will take care of a month of lies. Sure." With that Wade got into his van and took off, gears grinding angrily, leaving Junie stranded in the three-ring circus going on in her front yard.

Tabitha gently tugged her back toward the house, which was the last place Junie wanted to go.

FIFTEEN

Inside, Junie and Tabitha found Junie's mother giving Kendra a tour of the house. Kendra took mincing steps over the garbage-strewn floor and between the heaps of junk. One cameraman filmed them from the front, walking backwards and tripping often. Another cameraman followed alongside.

"This must be very, very hard for you," Kendra said, her slight Southern drawl sweetening her words, one arm across her mother's shoulders. "To have us in here after keeping it a secret for so long."

Junie's mom nodded, tears streaming down her face. This was the stuff *The Kendra Show* was made of, emotional breakdowns and televised rock bottoms. It was awful. Junie had to stop it.

"Get out!" she shouted suddenly.

Kendra turned, her rock-solid hair hardly moving. "Honey?"

"Get out of my house right this minute!" Junie grabbed the boom operator and shoved him outside. She reached for the first cameraman, but he dodged out of her way.

"You getting this, Bob?" Kendra pointed at Junie.

"Yes, ma'am." Bob aimed his camera in her face.

"Get out," Junie growled. She covered the lens with her hand and then said it again, as menacingly as she could. "Get the hell out of my house. Now."

"Honey, let me talk to you, one on one." Kendra picked her way back to Junie and put a hand on each of her shoulders, ignoring Tabitha. Junie could smell her perfume, something flowery and subtle. Kendra gave her a warm smile. "Now, we both want the same thing here, I'm pretty sure. You want your mama to get better, right?"

"Of course, but not like this—"

"Well now, you don't even know what 'this' is yet, do you, hon?"

Junie shook her head.

"So how about I tell you what we've got going on? Okay?"

Her voice was low, almost hypnotic. Junie could see how she made a living from talking. Junie had to admit that she did want to hear more. Especially if it meant fixing her mom.

"This is an intervention. You know what that is?" Kendra turned Junie around and steered her outside and into the fresh air, where she set her arm across Junie's shoulders as she had with her mom. Tabitha followed, and so did the cameraman, and the boom guy right behind him. "You've seen my show?"

Junie nodded. "Of course. Who hasn't?"

"Then you've seen us do these before for people in trouble. With alcohol, or gambling. There was that one woman who hoarded cats. Did you see that one?"

Junie had. They'd removed seventy-six cats from her crumbling double-wide, along with twenty-two dead ones in various state of decay. Hazmat suits all around.

"My mom's not that bad."

"She is, honey." Kendra gave her a squeeze. "She is. And you know it. And if I know anything about anything at all, you know it better than she does, I bet. Right?"

Junie didn't answer. Until Kendra gave her a tight little hug across the shoulders.

"Maybe," Junie admitted with a whisper. "But that doesn't mean that it's okay for the whole world to know it too."

"And I understand that. I do. But you've got to think about it this way," Kendra said. "This way, we help a whole lot of people just like your mom. And as for your family, we'll take care of everything. We pay for the after-care therapy, the organizers and the trash removers. We do it all. Now, why don't you go on down to catering and get yourself a hot drink and a sandwich? Give it all a big think." Kendra pointed to a shiny black food truck on the street with a silver awning sticking out. "We're going to send a camera with you, understand, but try to act like he's not there, okay? Take Tabitha with you. I know how important a best friend can be at a time like this. I'm going to go back and visit with your mama. Okay?"

Was it okay? Junie wasn't sure. But there was little else

to do in that exact moment. Either she could run screaming down the middle of the street in a panic, or do just what Kendra had suggested.

"Okay."

"All right, then. I like a girl with a head on her shoulders." With that, Kendra went back inside, while Junie slumped onto the top step, her legs suddenly weak. Tabitha sat beside her, leaning her head in close.

"Junie, this is a good thing. Right?"

"No, it's not good! Everyone will know, Tabitha! Everyone at school." Junie couldn't look at Tabitha or she'd cry. She didn't want to cry. Not with cameras everywhere. "Everyone in the whole wide world will know how bad it is. Absolutely everyone."

"Look at me, Juniebean."

Junie shook her head. "Can't."

"Then just listen." Tabitha grabbed Junie's hand. "This is a chance to make your mom better. How can that be a bad thing? Kendra's got millions and millions of dollars. She's got millions and millions of people who can help. You've seen the show. She actually does make a difference. You've got to admit that much, right?"

"But what's the price?" Junie shook her head. "It's not worth it, is it? What if my mom can't handle it? What if she ends up locked in the loony bin? And what about Wade? What if he never talks to me again? And what if everyone laughs at me? I never wanted anyone to know, and now the whole world will see it all. Everyone will know!"

"But maybe it will get better. Maybe the price is worth it? For your mom? For you?" Junie could hear the kindness in Tabitha's voice, and she knew there was some truth in there too, but she didn't want to listen. "You and Wade have been together for a month. You and your mom will be together forever. And you would've had to tell Wade sometime, right? Right, Junie?"

"But not like this." Junie's head thumped angrily, trying to sort out what exactly was happening. She glanced up, seeing the media trucks, the police, the curious onlookers gathering like flies to the carcass that was her house. It was real. No hope that it had all been a terrible daydream. It was fact. *The Kendra Show* was doing an intervention on her mom. Was this a good thing? Or a bad thing? Wade had discovered her lies. Was this a good thing? Or a bad thing? Junie wasn't sure. It just was what it was, and as it was, Junie had no idea what to make of it all. "I screwed up. I've never screwed up so bad in my life."

"Junie?"

Junie looked up. Her mouth felt pasty and thick and the thumping in her head was shaping up into a wicked headache. "Yeah?"

"It's not your fault that your mom is the way she is."

"But it is my fault that I lied to Wade."

"But life goes on. You know that, right?"

"Does it? Or does it all freeze and stay stuck on this horrible day forever?"

"You're going to be okay. I promise."

Junie scowled. Laughed. "You really think so?"

"I know so. This is going to be a good thing in the long run. Maybe even the short run. I promise." Tabitha fell into step beside her as Junie got up and aimed for the catering truck. It wasn't that she was hungry or thirsty, but it was what Kendra had told her to do, and Junie had no idea what else to do other than slash her wrists or run away, so she was doing what she was told until she could think of a better idea. The cameraman and mic guy followed them across the lawn.

"This'll make everything better," Tabitha urged. "Your mom will get help. They'll clean up your house. It will be normal again, like when we were little."

"But what if she doesn't change?" Junie stopped short. "What if all of this happens and the house is cleaned and my mom gets help, but then it all goes back to the way it was?" When Tabitha didn't answer, Junie kept voicing her worries, and there were a lot of them. "What if she can't do it? What if she has a meltdown and ends up in a strait-jacket? Everyone is going to find out. Everyone! And Wade! He's totally going to hate me. What if he never wants to talk to me ever again because of how I lied to him?"

"The truth had to come out somehow," Tabitha said gently.

"Oh my God." All of a sudden, Junie remembered the camera. "Can you guys go away? Please? Just for a few minutes?"

Behind the camera, Bob shook his head. "No can do, kiddo. You know the rules."

"Fine." Junie clamped her mouth shut. And she'd keep it that way. She strode the rest of the way to the catering truck and asked for a hot chocolate. It came heaped with whipped cream, which only reminded her of the coffee date she was supposed to have with Wade tomorrow, on their way out of town. Would he still want her to go with him? Not likely.

Tabitha thrust a ham sandwich into her hands and the two girls sat at one of the tables set out in front of the truck, the feet of the moulded plastic chairs sinking into the lawn. They munched slowly and sipped from their drinks. They didn't talk at all, each of them casting occasional defiant glances at the crew standing off to one side, filming them.

"I get it," Bob said after filming nothing but belligerent silence for several minutes. "You're playing hardball. That's fine. I'll go get some exterior footage of the house, some shots of the garage. Leave you two girls alone for a few minutes. Okay?"

"That would be great," Tabitha said on behalf of them both. "Thank you."

The men turned their cameras back to the house and wandered off.

Junie took a deep breath and took in the spectacle before them. There were the trucks with *The Kendra Show* in tall, glittery vinyl letters on the side, and then the equipment trucks that weren't marked. Then the seven vehicles from local TV stations, there to capture the event. The police cars, Junie figured, were there to manage traffic and fans. And it was a good thing, too, because in the time they'd been sitting there, the crowd had doubled. There had to be at least a hundred people there, gawking, cellphones to their ears, parasitically informing everyone they knew.

"I can't believe this." Junie set her sandwich down beside her. There was no way that she could eat anything at a time like this. The few bites she'd taken were sitting like rocks in her stomach. "I cannot believe this."

An excited murmur rustled through the people gathered on the street. Junie scanned the people for anyone she knew and didn't, thankfully, see anyone. The crowd was made up of mostly older women with homemade signs that said things like *Make me beautiful, Kendra!* and *Your #1 Fan!* and lots of *I ♥ you, Kendra!* Junie glanced back at the house. The living room curtains had been opened for the first time in years, and there stood Kendra and her mother, looking out. Kendra lifted a hand to give the crowd a royal wave. That's when the screaming started.

"Kendra! Kendra!" the crowd chanted. "Kendra!"

"This isn't happening." Junie felt like she was going to puke. She wanted to go back just a little bit, maybe an hour. Just long enough to refuse the ride home from Wade. But that wouldn't have worked, because the whole city was going to know as soon as they turned on the TV, if not sooner. She'd have to go way back in time, to when it was still possible to avert all of this. Back to when her mom was healthy. How far back was that?

"Come on," Tabitha said firmly. "Let's get out of here."

"Are we allowed?" Junie felt as if Kendra had to approve it, as if Kendra was in charge of everything now, including her.

"Who cares? Come on." Tabitha pulled Junie up. "We'll go through the alley."

At Tabitha's house, the girls sat in the middle of the floor in the living room with the curtains drawn, talking in whispers, as if that mattered.

"I can't believe that she did this. I cannot believe that my own mother invited Kendra to come and do this. It's insane. I can't believe it."

"I can."

"What?"

"Do you know how many times I came *this* close—" Tabitha held a finger and thumb barely touching—"this close to calling Social Services on your mom? And the only reason I never did is because you trumped me on it. And you know how much I lied to my own mom about how bad it is over there?" Tabitha's eyes filled with tears.

"Not lies, really."

"But not telling, either." Tabitha sat back a little, covering her face with her hands.

"I'm sorry, Tab."

"Are you?" Tabitha pressed. "Really, Junie?"

"I am." Junie's voice hitched in her throat. She flopped back until she was splayed on the floor, staring at the dim ceiling. "What am I going to do about Wade?"

"I don't know if there is anything you can do." Tabitha wiped her tears. "You could try calling him. See if he'll let you explain."

Junie shook her head. "I doubt he wants to talk to me right now."

"Probably not." Tabitha scooted around the table and flopped down beside her. "Maybe it'll blow over, though. You think?"

"No. Not a chance." Tears slid down Junie's cheeks. "I screwed it up. It's all my fault, Tab. He's never going to talk to me again. My mom and my house might be better after all of this, but Wade isn't going to ever want anything to do with me ever again. That's going to be the cost of all of this. And that's not fair."

Tabitha caught her eye, the two of them paused a beat and then said in unison, "Whoever said life was fair!" They laughed, half-heartedly, but at least the tears had stopped.

Just then there was a knock on the front door. Junie—thinking it was Wade for some hopeful, inexplicable reason—leapt up to answer it. It wasn't Wade. It was a shiny-looking man with slicked-back hair and a microphone.

"Juniper Rawley? Daughter of Marla Rawley?" He thrust the microphone in her face. "I'm Jerrod Campbell, KELB *News Eleven*. How do you feel about the world's most famous talk show host coming to your house to fix your mother's hoarding addiction?"

Junie stared at him, and then at the cameraman behind him, and then at the station's news van behind him, and then at the three other news vans that were pulling up from three other channels, two of which Junie had never heard of. She opened her mouth to tell him to piss off, but before she could, Tabitha yanked her away from the door.

"No comment." She slammed the door shut.

The two girls stood in the hallway as Jerrod Campbell from KELB *News Eleven* banged on the door with his fist.

"A few questions, that's all."

And then there were several more reporters banging on the door.

"What do we do?" Junie wanted to crawl into the closet and not come out until it was all over.

"We call our lawyer, that's what." Tabitha grabbed the phone and called her mother, who was already on her way.

"How did she know?" Junie asked, not sure if she wanted to know the answer.

"Everyone is talking about it downtown," Tabitha said with a grimace. "It's all over the place."

"Not good." Every drop of Junie's blood flooded to her feet and she swayed, suddenly light-headed. "Not good."

"Come sit down." Tabitha steered her into the kitchen, as far away as they could get from the pounding on the front door. She sat Junie at the table and then dug in the freezer until she found cookie dough ice cream. She brought it and two spoons back to the table, but Junie couldn't even look at it. She was so close to throwing up that she was keeping her eye on the door to the bathroom in case she had to beeline.

The phone rang.

"You think they have my number?" Tabitha stared at the phone as it rang. "Can they get it even if it's unlisted?"

Junie was only able to shrug. All of this was way out of her depth. She honestly had no idea.

"I'll go see if we know the number." Tabitha picked up the phone and checked the number on the call display. "It's Wade!" Before Junie could tell her not to, Tabitha answered the phone. "Hi! Wade! We're so glad it's you! It's insanity over—" Tabitha stopped talking, her face falling into a frown. "Of course," she said during a pause. "I understand," she said during another. "Totally."

From Tabitha's expression, Junie knew it wasn't good.

"Let me talk to him." Junie held out her hand for the phone, but Tabitha was shaking her head.

"I'll tell her."

Junie waved her hand. "Give me the phone, Tab."

"I'm sorry, Wade," Tabitha said. She paused while he said something on the other end. "But it is partly my fault too, for going along with it." Another pause. "I'll tell her. She's right here. She wants to talk to you."

All of the blood surged up from her feet and flooded straight to Junie's head. She was dizzy in a whole different way. What would she say to him? How could she make it better? But she wasn't going to have the chance. Tabitha said goodbye to Wade and hung up the phone. She bit her bottom lip. "You were right. He doesn't want to talk to you."

Junie's heart bucked against her chest. Of course he didn't want to talk to her. If she'd been him, she wouldn't have wanted to either. She was a liar. And her lies were big ones. Nothing little, like padding her bra or smoking the odd cigarette in secret, but great big lies that cast shadows the size of mountains. She was a fraud. And her house smelled like shit. And her mother was so screwed up that she was going to be on *The Kendra Show*. These were not little white lies. Not in the least.

"What did he want you to tell me?"

Tabitha stared at the floor.

"Go ahead," Junie said. "Whatever it is, I deserve it."

Tabitha was just about to tell her, but the front door

was flung open, and there was Mrs. D., backing into the house while telling off the reporters. Junie and Tabitha ran to the front hall to watch.

"If you are not off my property within the next sixty seconds, I will sue all of you for trespassing, and you can be sure that I mean it!"

Jerrod Campbell was not deterred. "And your relation-ship to the hoarder is—?"

"You're wasting precious time," Mrs. D. growled. "I'd get moving if I were you."

"We're not intimidated by empty threats, lady."

"She's not just any lady," a reporter from a local station said as he gave up and turned away. "That's Georgia Dillard, Crown prosecutor. Keep talking and you'll end up in court, still talking. And then you'll lose. Like everyone else who goes up against her."

Jerrod smiled at her, but lowered his mic. "Hey, it's a free world."

"You Americans. Those of us from here know better."

Jerrod tipped an imaginary hat to her. "See you next time."

He was the last to go, sauntering casually down the sidewalk. Mrs. D. called after him, "Your sixty seconds are long gone, sir. You can expect the litigation papers within the week."

He kept walking, not turning back, and just lifted a hand and gave her a careless wave before getting into his van.

The scrum gone, Mrs. D. turned to her daughter and Junie. "Now. Tell me exactly what is going on here."

Tabitha and Junie explained everything, and when they were done, Mrs. D. put a hand on Junie's shoulder, her eyes moist.

"Why didn't you tell me, sweetheart?"

"You would've called a social worker." Junie felt tears dampen her own eyes. "You would've had to, right?"

Mrs. D. paused before she eventually nodded. "You're probably right. I almost did that one time, but you managed to explain it away enough that I guess I was content to ignore it then. I wish I'd persisted. I wish I'd checked up on you. I wish I'd known. We could've helped. I'm sorry."

This made Junie cry all the harder. Mrs. D. pulled her into a tight hug. "From this minute on, it's going to get better. I promise. Okay?"

Junie nodded, hoping that she was right. And then Mrs. D. pulled away and headed for the door.

"Where are you going?" Tabitha asked.

"I'm going to Junie's house to see Marla," she said. "I'm not sure if this is the most ridiculous thing she's ever done, or the smartest, but either way, she's going to need me. Either as a lawyer or a friend. Come on, Junie." Mrs. D. waggled a hand at her as if she was a toddler. "You come too. It's time to face the music."

But Tabitha held Junie back. "We'll come in a minute, Mom."

Mrs. D. angled a severe look at the two girls. "See that you do. Promptly."

"We will," Tabitha promised her.

So Mrs. D. left without them. Tabitha turned to Junie. "I'll tell you what Wade said."

Junie groaned. "I don't know if I want to know."

"He asked me to tell you and I told him I would, so I'm going to tell you. You can plug your ears and sing 'Mary Had a Little Lamb' as loud as you want to if that'll make it any easier."

"Speak." Junie hung her head, preparing for the onslaught. "I can take it."

"He said that your date tomorrow is off, and that he's going to start the filming by himself. And that he doesn't want to talk to you right now."

"He's breaking up with me." Junie's stomach lurched up into her throat. She was sure she was going to vomit. She put a hand to her mouth. "Isn't he?"

"He didn't say that."

"He might as well have."

Tabitha repeated what he'd said. "That doesn't mean that he won't want to talk to you when things cool down."

"Cool down? When is that going to happen?" Junie stalked to the living room window, yanked the curtain, and pointed down the street to the circus in front of her house. There had to be at least five hundred fans gathered now. There were two more police cars and three more media vans, from international stations by the looks of it. One van's signage was in Spanish.

"When, exactly, will things cool down?" Junie backed away from the window as a cameraman waiting in the street—off the property—turned his camera on her. She pulled the drapes closed. This was her life crumbling into ruins, and it was going to be televised. Nationally and internationally televised.

SIXTEEN

⋮

Junie and Tabitha took the back way to Junie's house and found Mrs. D. talking with Marla, the cameras nowhere nearby.

"Only your mother could accomplish that," Junie said. She could tell by the expression on Mrs. D.'s face that the house had taken her by surprise.

"You have choices, Marla," Mrs. D. continued as Junie and Tabitha joined them. "You can do this if you want, but you can also change your mind and not do it this way. I can help. If only you'd let me know how bad it had gotten."

"I do want to do it this way," Junie's mother said. "I do. I really do. I think this is the way that will work for me. Nothing else has."

Kendra approached the small group. "Marla? Junie? You girls ready to tackle this?"

"Kendra, pleased to meet you. Georgia Dillard.

Could I have a word? I'm Marla's attorney." Mrs. D. ushered Kendra to one side, and both Junie and Tabitha were impressed that Kendra actually went with her.

While Mrs. D. conferred with Kendra, Junie's mother went back to what she'd been doing before Mrs. D. had arrived: showing Bob how her "system" worked.

"See, I can find pretty much anything I'm looking for. Try me."

"Can opener," he suggested.

Junie watched as her mother beelined for two heaps of dirty, mouldy dishes balancing precariously on the counter. She reached between them and pulled out the can opener.

"See?" Junie's mother held it up like a trophy. "Not so bad, eh?"

Behind the camera, Bob gave her a thumbs-up. Then he turned the camera to Junie, who was feeling so embarrassed for her mother that she wanted to bury her in her pile of Shopping Channel purchases and tell everyone that the intervention was off.

The front door slammed, and a minute later a tiny woman barged into the kitchen, holding her hands up to keep them from touching any of the garbage.

"Oh my God, my flight was so late I thought it was going to be next year before I landed!" She spoke with a nasally New York accent and didn't make eye contact with anyone except Kendra, who gave her a big hug. Beside her, the woman looked even smaller, birdlike. But her voice was bigger than anyone's in the room. "Where do you need me, what can I do, where do we start, hopefully with the awful shit smell if we're going to be here for the week."

A week? Junie grabbed Tabitha's sleeve and eyeballed her.

Kendra, not missing a thing, patted her shoulder. "Deep breaths, hon."

The small woman spun and thrust out her hand. "Your hands clean?"

"Yes."

"Then I'll shake." The woman grabbed Junie's hand and pumped it. "Charlotte Falconetti. Call me Charlie. Assistant producer."

"In other words," Kendra explained, "this is me when I'm not able to be me, only with an A cup rather than a double-D, and not black, and considerably younger."

"B cup, I'll thank you very much." Charlie gave Kendra a friendly smack on the arm. Junie couldn't imagine being so familiar with Kendra that you could slap her. "I'll be here for the week. Miss Thang here will come back to shoot some more on the last couple of days." She gave Kendra a stern look. "But you're getting footage now, right? From the storyboard we worked on back in L.A.?"

"Of course, Charlie." Kendra introduced Junie's mother, and Tabitha and Mrs. D. "Our key players. There's a boy, too. What's his name, hon?"

Junie opened her mouth, but nothing came out.

"Wade," Tabitha said.

"Who very well may not be interested in participating in this adventure," added Mrs. D. "And the same might be said for Junie, and Tabitha, too."

"I sense drama here." Charlie churned her hands in front of her. "We like drama. Drama makes great television."

But Junie didn't want her drama televised. She didn't want her drama at all, and she certainly didn't want to offer it to the millions of people who were devoted fans of *The Kendra Show*. "So what if I say I don't want to do this?"

Junie's mother blanched. "But they want you in the show, Junie."

Mrs. D. put a protective arm across Junie's shoulders. "Marla, Junie is going to have to make that choice for herself. She has to want to do this. You can't force her."

"But I don't have to force you, do I, Junie?"

Junie glanced at Mrs. D. At Kendra. At her mother. Her mother was the odd one out, of course. She was wearing another one of her colour-coordinated sweatsuits, red this time, with tartan Scotty dogs marching down the sleeves. What was Junie supposed to say? She glanced at Bob, too. He had the camera pointed right at her.

"I don't know."

"Whoa, whoa, whoa." Charlie waved her hands. "No kid, no deal, Kendra. Come on. That's the heartstring-tugger, and you know it."

"Give them a minute," Kendra said with a confident nod. "Let Junie make up her mind. We can go. We can clear out right now if that's what she wants. This is her home too."

Mrs. D. let out a scoff. "So, in essence, you're blackmailing her to be involved."

"No, no." Kendra shook her head. "Not at all. But we do want Junie in the show. She's the reason why we picked Marla's story over the other ones. Because she has a child. Who is old enough to understand the impact. The daily impact. Of all of this." She swept an arm, indicating everything in the room.

As much as Junie didn't want her very private mess aired on international television, she also didn't want them to just leave. Her mother would never forgive her. And she might not forgive herself. What if this was her mom's only chance?

"I'll do it." Junie felt the familiar pressure of tears pushing behind her eyes.

"Good to hear, honey." Kendra patted her arm. "Good to hear."

Junie's skin crawled and her eyes pounded. She pressed her fingers against them and tried to stop it, but it was no use. Junie choked back a sob and fled, heading for the sanctuary of her bedroom.

"Where you going?" Charlie hollered after her. "You better not think you can just agree and then disappear, kid!"

Behind her, she heard Mrs. D. growl, "Don't push it, Ms. Falconetti."

And then Charlie replied with a barking laugh, "Give me a few more minutes and you'll see that I'm all push all the time!"

⋮

Junie locked the door, flung herself on her bed and wept until she heard someone on the stairs. Tabitha knocked their secret knock and Junie let her in. Without a word, the two girls lay side by side on Junie's bed as it grew dark and Junie cried, with her stereo on a classic rock station so that The Beatles and The Rolling Stones drowned out the commotion downstairs. When Junie stopped crying, they still didn't talk. They just lay there with their arms behind their heads, staring at the glow-in-the-dark star stickers they'd put up in the shape of constellations ages ago.

"I think we were ten," Tabitha finally said. "When we put up those stars. Remember?"

Junie did. They'd bought six packages of star stickers at the Science World gift shop after spending a Saturday morning there with Mrs. D. Junie's father had brought up the step-ladder from the garage, and she and Tabitha had carefully stuck each one up there, checking the astronomy books they'd gotten out of the library. And then they'd carried the ladder down the street and done the same to Tabitha's ceiling. But that's where the similarities between the two girls' bedrooms ended. While Junie's was always as neat as it could possibly be, Tabitha's was more like a normal teenager's room, with laundry on the floor and sometimes a few dirty dishes perched on her desk, her bed strewn with the sheets and duvet she hadn't bothered to straighten.

"Let's trade," Junie said. "I'll be you and you be me. Just one week."

Tabitha pushed herself up onto her elbows. "It won't be as bad as you think. It can't be."

"In this case, I'm not so sure about that."

"Well, you and your mom got into this mess. Now's your chance to get out."

"Me? What did I ever do?"

"What did you ever do?" Tabitha stared at her, eyes wide. "It's what you *didn't* do. You didn't let anyone in. You didn't tell anyone what was really going on. You kept all those secrets. You lied. And sure, this mess is mostly your mom's fault, but some of it is your dad's fault for giving up, and your fault, too."

"Ouch."

"You've been letting her get away with it! Keeping secrets. Covering for her." Tabitha sat upright now, pointing at Junie. "You, and me, and my mom, and your dad and even That Woman have been enabling her. Making it worse. We all should've put a stop to it sooner. Gotten her real help."

"But now we've got Kendra." Junie pulled a pillow over her head and groaned. "And now my mother will be world famous as a compulsive hoarder whose house smells like shit."

"Junie." Tabitha tapped the pillow. "Just think. When this is all over, your mother will be normal. And your house will be normal."

"But everyone will know me as the daughter of the compulsive hoarder whose house smelled like shit. Tell me I'm wrong. Am I wrong?"

There was a long pause before Tabitha answered. "That won't last forever."

"See?" Junie flung the pillow to the floor. "You agree! That's how everyone will see me!"

"I'll admit it's possible," Tabitha allowed. "And that that part will suck. But it's going to be better in the long run. And that's what's important, right?"

Junie nodded. She could only hope so. She could only desperately hope so.

⋮

Kendra had left not long after Junie stormed upstairs. Charlie stayed behind with the film crew until Mrs. D. kicked them out at around nine o'clock and then went home herself, dragging Tabitha with her. Junie stayed up in her room. She thought her mother would come up to check in on her, but she didn't. She thought her father must have heard and would call or come over, but he didn't. Well, Junie couldn't be bothered to go check on her mom if she couldn't be bothered to check on her, and the same went for her father, so she just crawled under the covers and went to sleep. Blissful, blank, deep sleep.

Hunger woke her up well after dawn, thankfully. She realized she hadn't eaten anything since that couple of bites of sandwich the afternoon before. She had a shower, got dressed and went downstairs.

The house looked exactly the same as it always had. She wasn't sure what she'd expected, but she'd thought for sure it should be different somehow, even just by virtue of Kendra having been there. But all the junk was still piled high, the stacks of boxes full of useless stuff still teetered dangerously, and the funk of crap still permeated from the basement. What good was Kendra if she couldn't fix things magically? On her show everything happened so fast, neatly solved by the end of the hour, the "before" shots surrendering to the "after" shots with plenty of time left over for Kendra to do her end-of-show "life moment" spiel as the credits rolled. But in real life things went a lot slower.

Of course they did. Junie knew this logically, but clearly, her inner kindergartner had been hoping for a magic-wand effect. Kendra was no fairy godmother, despite her loyal following. She was more a master puppeteer. And of course her show was edited, Junie told herself. She was stupid to think things could change overnight. This would take time. A lot of time.

Junie checked the refrigerator—nothing but a cucumber and bottles and jars of condiments and some coffee cream. And a couple of apples in the crisper. Junie's stomach growled as she helped herself to the fruit.

Junie wondered what would become of the old fridge, the one her mother had abandoned, full to nearly bursting with rotting food. Neither she nor her mother had dared open its door since the new fridge came, about a year ago. Junie imagined that the best thing would be to duct-tape it shut for all eternity, and roll it out the front door and straight into one of the bins. She didn't want anyone to find out what was inside—a refrigerated year-old science experiment gone wrong. Disgusting.

Junie went into the living room and peeked outside. It was just seven now, so there were only two media vans, and no spectators. Yet. Kendra's trucks were still there, or there again, and her crew of mostly men wandered around laying out cables and checking equipment and drinking steaming coffee from paper cups. Coffee that they'd got from the catering truck, which was what Junie had been hoping to see.

She pulled on a coat and went outside, where Bob hollered good morning and waved her over to where he was fiddling with his camera, which was in pieces on a folding table beside the camera truck.

"You're up early," he said as she wandered over. His words made clouds in the cold spring morning. "Sleep okay?"

"Yeah, actually. Surprisingly." Junie gestured at the bustle happening around them. "Were you guys here all night?"

"Nope." Bob wiped the camera lens with a special cloth. Junie thought of Wade, and how he did the same. With the same kind of blue cloth. There was no doubt at all that he still wouldn't want to talk to her this morning. A simple "sleep on it" was not going to suffice in this instance.

"We're at the Sheraton downtown," Bob said. "Nice place. Big pool. Has a slide."

Junie laughed at the thought of Bob going down a water slide with his great big belly—hairy more than likely—spilling over his shorts and his beard flung over his shoulder.

"What?" Bob gave her a wink. "Can't picture me in my Speedo?"

Junie laughed again.

"You're in better spirits this morning." Bob glanced at the driveway as a black SUV pulled up. "Oh, that'll be the Falcon. Gotta look busy."

Charlie hopped out of the passenger side, wearing great big sunglasses that made her look like an insect. Her hair was in one of those expensive-looking ponytails, with a chunk of long bangs angling neatly across her face.

"Good morning, my little minions!" She minced across the lawn in her high heels. "Where the hell are the

Got Junk guys?" She flung her arms open, a large travel mug in one hand, her phone in the other. "They were supposed to be here seven minutes ago!" She made her way to a trailer at the top of the driveway and disappeared inside after hollering hello to Junie and Bob as she passed. After a minute she opened the door and leaned out to add, "I want you to go to school today, okay? We're going to go with you. Film some footage. I've already got the okay from your principal. And that Tabitha's rabid mother already looked over the contract, so don't try to get out of it. Awesome, Junie, thanks."

"What? No way," Junie protested, but Charlie had ducked back inside, the door slamming behind her. She addressed Bob instead. "No friggin' way in hell are you guys coming to my school."

"Oh yes we are."

"Oh hell no you are not."

Bob gave her another wink. "You'll live."

"No, actually. I won't. Because I'll see to it that I jump off the bridge. Mid-span, where it's highest. At night, so no one will see. Then you can have the pleasure of knowing that it's your fault that I committed suicide." Junie wasn't hungry any more, but she didn't want to talk to Bob any more either, so she headed for the catering truck.

"Bring me back a cinnamon bun, will ya?" Bob called after her. "Before you jump off the bridge."

⋮

When it was her usual time to leave for school, Tabitha showed up to find Junie sitting on the front step, staring miserably at the convoy of Got Junk trucks lined up at the street.

"You staying home today?" She hefted her backpack over one shoulder. "Man, I was getting used to catching a ride with Wade."

"Wade would probably be more than happy to give you a ride. He broke up with me, not you."

"Oh please, don't be stupid. We're a package deal."

"Well, this part of the package would rather stay home. But I can't. I have to go to school, so that *The Kendra Show* can film me in full humiliation mode. Yes, that's right. I'm going to school today, and so is Bob. To film me."

As if on cue, Bob emerged from the camera truck, camera in hand. He waved. "You ready to go?"

"We're getting a ride?" Tabitha asked.

"Did you hear a word I said?" Junie stood, hands on her hips. "Any of it?"

"What am I supposed to say?" Tabitha shrugged. "This is happening, Junie. You had your chance to say no. Now it's being fixed, and if they want to film you walking down the hall to English, what do you care, if it's going to make your mom better?"

"Wow." Junie reached inside for her backpack. "It's kind of early in the day for emotional blackmail, don't you think?"

"It's never too early." Tabitha grinned. "Come on."

They didn't get a ride in a limo, much to Tabitha's dismay, but in the same black SUV that had dropped Charlie off earlier. It had leather seats and tinted windows and made Junie feel like someone a sniper would be interested in. Despite Junie's protests that the driver—an oddly silent, clean-cut man with a Bluetooth piece in his ear—drop them a couple of blocks away from the school, he pulled right up to the main door and cut the engine.

"I don't think I can do this," Junie said as her breath quickened. "Can we just go home, Bob? Please? I can pay you. I've got almost a thousand dollars in my bank account. It's yours if you just go away."

"Ah, go on," Bob said gently. "What doesn't kill you makes you stronger, right? You'll be fine, kid."

"Fine or not." Tabitha hopped out and leaned back in to grab Junie. "Let's go. The sooner you get it over with the sooner it'll get easier."

"Not likely." With a monumental groan, Junie climbed out of the SUV. She stood on the sidewalk, backpack on her shoulder, staring up at the main doors. "This is so lame. I never even go in the main doors."

Bob gave her a little shove. "Today you do. I want the effect."

"Fine." Junie started up the steps, but Bob called for her to stop.

"Gimme a sec to get set up here, will you?"

The boom guy, who'd been in the back seat, snoring on the ride to the school, set up his gear and hovered over Junie with the big boom, furry like a gigantic bee. A school bus pulled up, and a stream of students filed off, staring and murmuring. No one asked what was going on, and it didn't take Junie long to figure out why. Everyone knew.

Word had already spread. The humiliation would be swift and powerful and exceedingly painful. Jumping off the bridge was beginning to look like a truly viable option.

"What are you looking at?" she asked one of the gawkers. He was no one she knew, just a grade nine kid. He looked away, whispering to his friends. Damon Fielder didn't look away, though. Always the bully, he was not going to let the opportunity pass.

"Hey, Rawley, I need two hundred mouldy old stuffed animals for a science experiment. Think your hoarder— oops, I mean your mother—can help me out with that?"

"Hey, smartass." Bob lowered his camera. "Come closer and say that. I want a nice close-up of your ugly face."

Damon held up his hands and shook his head with a smile. "Thanks, but I'm already famous, man."

"I'm sure you are," Bob growled. "Now buzz off."

"Ignore them," Tabitha ordered Junie. "Think of your happy place."

But Junie didn't have a happy place any more. Her happy place had as good as dumped her the night before. Had he gone out to Chilliwack without her? And if he had, had he told Royce and Jeremy that she was a liar? Would they hate her too now? She thought she heard Wade's van turning off the street, but when she turned to look, all she saw were the curious stares of fellow students as they made their way into the building, and the black maw of the camera pointed at her. It would be a long day. A long and horrible day.

SEVENTEEN

. . . .

It was exactly as awful as she'd thought it would be. And worse, actually. Because she'd barely stepped into the school when she spotted Wade at the far end of the hallway. He looked up at the commotion, as the curious murmurs reached him. He caught Junie's glance and held it, his mouth set in a firm, critical line. Her heart thumped gracelessly in her chest as she tried to figure out if she should go talk to him or give him space.

He decided for her by turning into his Math class without so much as a nod in her direction.

"Ouch," Junie said out loud. "That actually, factually hurt."

"He'll talk to you. Eventually." Tabitha, having seen the whole exchange, patted Junie's arm. "Maybe not this morning. Maybe not even today, but he will. Promise."

And all the while, the cameras rolled, the students

stared and Junie wanted to vomit. She couldn't believe any of this was happening, and furthermore, that all of it was being recorded by a professional TV crew.

Ollie and Lulu were waiting for her by her locker.

"We heard," Lulu said with a sympathetic smile.

"Can we do anything?" Ollie added another sympathetic smile.

Junie wasn't sure what to say. She'd never told them about her mother, and now she felt stupid that they'd found out this way when they were her good friends.

"I'm sorry," she said.

Bob stepped back to get everyone in the shot.

Junie rolled her eyes at him. "Bob, please? Please go away? Just for a minute."

He peered out from around the camera. "No can do, kiddo. You can save anything you want private for later."

But the explanation couldn't wait. Ollie and Lulu were waiting for her to say more.

"I didn't know how to tell you guys about it. About my mom. I was embarrassed—"

"It's okay." Lulu gave Bob a surprisingly fierce look. "We can talk about it later. When he's not around. We've got Art. Let's go." She grabbed Junie's hand and pulled her down the hall. Junie was so thankful for her at that moment that she wanted to give her a big hug, but instead, she just let herself be led.

Once the class got underway, with Bob circling the room, his boom guy following him, Junie and Lulu passed notes to each other while they worked silently on their projects.

Lulu: *You don't have to apologize,*

Junie: *I do so. I should've told you guys. I just didn't know how.*

Lulu: *We've all got our secrets. They're part of who we are.*

Junie: *That's pretty generous. Thank you. At least now you know why I've never invited you over.*

She slipped the paper to Lulu, who read it and wrote back almost immediately. She slid the paper back with a smile.

Lulu: *And all this time I thought you didn't like me very much.*

"No, no, no. I do. I just . . ." And there was the camera in her face again. Junie ripped another piece of paper out of her notebook and wrote fast. *I was just so embarrassed. It's been really bad for a long time.*

Lulu: *Maybe Ollie and I can help?*

"That's really sweet, Lulu," Junie said. "But I think it's probably best left to the professionals. It's that bad." Truth was, she didn't want Lulu or Ollie seeing it, even now that her secret was out.

Lulu saw right through her. "We'll all see it eventually," she gestured to Bob and the boom guy with a small flick of her wrist. "Come on, Junie. Let us help at least."

"It's way worse in real life, Lulu. Worse than you can imagine." Junie shook her head. "Sorry, Lulu. I can't."

"Okay," Lulu said with a shrug. "But if you change your mind, you know where we are.

"I just can't." Junie couldn't . . . what? Couldn't accept help? Couldn't let her friends see how bad it was? Well, what was the point? As far as accepting help, want it or not, it had been foisted upon her. And as for them seeing how bad it was, her reality would soon be televised for the entire world to see.

But time was the only tool she had. If she could keep the world at bay for a little longer, she would.

Bob and the boom guy—his name was Nikolai and he didn't speak much English—followed Junie through the halls to Math class, where Ollie tried his best to console her by aiming a drippingly sympathetic glance in her direction at every opportunity. Thankfully, Mr. Benson wouldn't tolerate any chatter, otherwise Junie was sure that Ollie would have laid it on much as Lulu had. They'd probably strategized last night when it was all over the news.

Halfway through class, Bob and Nikolai left, rejoining her in the hall when the bell rang, dashing her hopes that they'd gotten enough footage and had left for the day.

"Too much to hope that you'd dropped off the face of the Earth?" she said when they fell into step behind her and Ollie.

"Oh, my heart!" Bob stumbled back, hand to his chest. "Thou hast wounded me fiercely with thou barbed words."

"Is that a quote?" Ollie asked. "Because if it is, I think you've got it wrong."

"Who's this guy?" Bob aimed the camera at Ollie.

Ollie held out his hand. Bob manoeuvred his equipment so he could shake it. "Bob McGillicuddy. And that's Nikolai."

"Hello and please I am to meet you," Nikolai said.

"Ollie. Junie's friend and math tutor."

Bob laughed. "You need a math tutor?" He raised his voice as Mr. Benson walked by. "If a smart girl like you needs a math tutor, what does that say about the competency of the math teacher?"

Mr. Benson scowled at the group of them, clutching his coffee mug in both hands as if restraining himself from hurling it at Junie. Or Bob.

"I like you, Bob." Junie grinned, feeling light for the first time since chaos had descended on her the day before. "You're good people. Sort of."

But the lightness didn't last. She caught sight of Wade again, at his locker, pulling his Chemistry text out of his backpack.

"Wade!"

He turned at the sound of her voice, but then slammed his locker shut and stalked away.

"Want me to talk to him?" Ollie offered.

"I don't know." Junie felt her throat swell. Tears would be next. She fixed her eyes on the girls' washroom and headed directly for it, leaving the guys stranded in the hallway.

Junie shut herself in a stall and took a deep breath. That didn't help. The tears came anyway. She wadded a bunch of toilet paper and blew her nose. She heard the door open, and through the crack in the stall she saw Mallory Weiss and her best friend, Tara Peters. Junie was about to get out of the stall, but when she heard Mallory mention her name, she froze.

"I heard on the news that her house is so bad that

they're going to bulldoze it." Mallory's voice was casual, which seemed so wrong, considering her words.

"They said that there is shit everywhere," Tara said. "Like, it's flooded with actual shit. Isn't that disgusting?"

"Totally."

Junie peered through the crack. Mallory was putting on lipstick, leaning in to the mirror, blinking. Tara stood beside her, running her fingers through her hair. She didn't hate either of the girls—or hadn't until now, anyway—but she wouldn't have called either one of them a friend, either.

The door to the bathroom creaked open and Junie heard Ollie's voice. "Junie? You okay in there?"

"Oh my God." Mallory spun, lipstick in hand. "She's in here?"

Junie contemplated the toilet, wondering if she should just climb into it and forever disappear into the sewer system.

"I'm fine," Junie bleated. She pushed open the door to the cubicle and stood there. The two girls were blocking her way to the door. They stared at her, jaws slack.

"Sorry, Junie," Mallory muttered. "We didn't know you were in here."

"Yeah," Tara echoed. "Sorry."

They backed against the counter, giving Junie far more room than she needed. Junie could see Ollie standing there, and the door behind him. But she couldn't make her feet move. She felt as if she'd been hollowed out and filled with cement. Heavy, cold, immovable.

Ollie hung back at the door, clearly debating with himself whether or not he should go and physically pull

Junie out. Then Tabitha showed up behind him, quickly pushed him aside and strode into the bathroom. With one glance at the hangdog expressions on Mallory and Tara, Tabitha knew what had happened, if not specifically.

"What did they do?" Tabitha glared at the two girls.

"Nothing," Junie said.

"We didn't know she was in here."

"And that makes it okay?" Tabitha pointed a finger at one girl, then the other.

"Say you're sorry."

"We did!" Mallory slunk toward the door, pulling Tara with her. "God."

"What did they say?" Tabitha grabbed Junie's arm and tugged her out of her paralysis.

"Nothing that isn't true," Junie said. They were back in the hall now, with Bob and Nikolai and Ollie. Students flooded past, slowing to stare and whisper and point. This would be the rest of her life, enduring endless unwanted attention for her mother's dysfunction. It would never end. And furthermore, it would be forever looping in the rerun world of *The Kendra Show*. She'd never get away from it. Her own daughter would come home from school in tears, herself having been teased for it. And then her grandchildren. It was a legacy. A horrible, shit-stink legacy.

Junie groaned, overwhelmed by it all, and slid down the wall until she was sitting on the linoleum floor, watching a sea of legs pass in front of her. Tabitha crouched beside her first, then Ollie. And there was Bob and his damned camera, angling down on her.

"Junie?" Tabitha put a hand on her knee. "You okay?"

"Here." Ollie thrust a paper bag at her, the same softly worn one he used before exams, to calm himself down, even though he always aced them. "It helps. Honest."

Junie bunched the top of the bag in her hands and breathed into it. Out. In. Out. In.

"It's scientifically proven to work," Ollie was saying. "You're rebreathing your own CO_2 instead of wasting it. Studies have been done showing that breathing into a paper bag actually raises CO_2 levels in the blood—"

"Thanks, Ollie." Tabitha's tone was clear.

"Okay." Ollie backed away. "I'll leave you guys. You can keep the bag, Junie. I've got more in my locker. I'm going to go find Lulu."

The bell rang, ending break. Junie had one more period before lunch. World Studies. With Wade. Junie sucked the air out of the paper bag, her head feeling light.

"Want to skip?" Tabitha suggested.

Junie took another breath, and then returned it slowly into the bag before speaking. "You'd *skip*?"

"This one time. I would." Tabitha helped Junie get back onto her feet. "For you. I could convincingly argue that the end justifies the means."

"Wow, Tabitha. That's really sweet." The halls cleared, and the second bell rang. They were late now. Junie was torn. Skip, and also skip the chance to talk to Wade? Or go to class and endure the probable silent treatment? "But I want to see him. And this might be my only chance."

"You're sure?"

Junie nodded, but took another couple of steadying breaths in and out of Ollie's bag for good measure. "I need to see him. Even if he doesn't want to see me. Maybe he won't even be there. Either way, I'll be okay."

Junie pushed open the door to her World Studies class and instantly felt a swarm of curious eyes swing toward her. Not Wade's, though. He kept his eyes forward, on the teacher, who'd stopped speaking mid-sentence when Junie and the TV crew filed into the room.

"Oh no you don't." Mrs. Kepperly wagged a finger at the trio. "Not in my classroom. No way."

Bob lowered his camera for a minute to speak to her. "We've got permission for the whole school, ma'am."

"And has each and every one of these students signed a release form to be on your little show?" She gestured at the rows of desks in front of her. "Have I?"

"That usually comes after, ma'am." Bob sounded as if he was back in high school, trying to talk back to the teacher and failing. He glanced at Nikolai for some help, but he only shrugged his shoulders and set the boom down. "When we got the footage we need."

"When *we've* got the footage . . ." Mrs. Kepperly also taught English, and was a stickler for grammar.

"Yes, ma'am." Bob ducked his head, his camera at his side.

"Off you go. There will be no filming in my classroom. Am I clear?"

"Yes, ma'am." Bob and Nikolai backed out of the room, taking their clunky equipment with them, leaving Junie standing there all alone, which was, in fact, worse.

"Take your seat, Junie." Mrs. Kepperly turned back to the board. "It's just another ordinary day in my classroom. Let's get on with it."

Junie's seat, of course, was beside Wade's. They sat two to a table in this class, and she shared hers with Wade. Until now, anyway. She did a quick scan of the room in hopes that there would be an empty seat. But no. Hers was the only one without a bum in it.

Wade still hadn't looked at her. And still didn't, even as she made her way down the aisle while Mrs. Kepperly talked about the climate change conference coming up in Mumbai. Junie pulled her chair out as far as she could without banging into the table behind her. It felt as if there was an impenetrable force field around Wade. Junie perched on the edge of her chair, clutching her binder and textbook to her chest, her heart pounding so loudly she couldn't hear a word that Mrs. Kepperly was saying.

"Wade?" Junie finally whispered.

He ignored her.

Junie set her books on the table and reached out and touched his shirt. Just with one finger. Just lightly on his shoulder. He whipped his head around and glared at her. Junie yanked her finger away, her fingertip so hot she was surprised it wasn't singed.

She was going to cry. Right there in class. For everyone to see. Another reason to make fun of her. Point and stare. Junie who lived in the house full of useless stuff, fetid and ruined. The house that smelled of shit. Junie the crybaby. Junie who got dumped. Junie who was on *The Kendra Show* for all the wrong reasons, her humiliation filmed, edited and broadcast in high definition for everyone's *schaden-freude* enjoyment.

Junie pulled a piece of paper out of her binder and scrawled *I'm sorry!!!* across the top. She pushed it at him. Without even glancing at it, he slid it back.

She added, *Please, please, please let me explain!* and pushed it back.

He glanced at it this time, and then bent over it to write a reply. Junie waited, her heart in her throat, choking her. He slid the paper back. His writing was messy, but she'd gotten used to it and could read it easily.

I trusted you. You lied to me. I was falling in love with a lie. I don't know who you are. I just know that you're not who I thought you were. What I do know is that you are a liar.

His words were a hard kick to the gut. *Love. In love with a lie.* Her breath was punched out of her. She slid her hand into her pocket and felt Ollie's paper bag in there. She couldn't bring herself to use it in front of everyone. She left the note, grabbed her things, lurched out of her seat and stumbled to the door.

Mrs. Kepperly pointed a marker at her. "Where are you going, Junie?"

But Junie couldn't answer her. She fumbled with the door handle and burst out into the mercifully empty hall. She doubled over, breathing hard into Ollie's bag. Mrs. Kepperly followed her out and put a hand on her back.

"That's it, deep breaths."

Would Wade come out too? To see if she was okay? Junie straightened, eyes on the door, which Mrs. Kepperly had shut behind her.

"Why don't you go down to the nurse's office for the rest of class? How does that sound, dear? I think this business with the media is affecting you more than you think."

On the contrary, Junie was keenly aware of exactly how she was being affected.

She nodded, nonetheless. "Thank you," she said into the bag.

"Shall I get Wade to walk you down?"

"No!" Junie shook her head and waved her off with her free hand. "No. I can make it on my own. Thank you."

Mrs. Kepperly slipped into the room to fetch Junie a hall pass and then sent her on her way.

Junie stopped a little distance down the hall and turned around, her eyes locked on the door to the classroom. She leaned against a bank of lockers, waiting. She hoped Wade would change his mind and come after her. But at the same time, she would rather never see him again if it meant feeling the pain of his rejection. His disappointment in her. What was worse was that everything he'd written was true. She was a liar. And she couldn't blame him if he didn't care how his words had wounded her. Maybe he even wanted her to feel bad. And she deserved it.

EIGHTEEN

Bob and Nikolai came and found Junie in the nurse's room when the bell rang. The nurse showed them in herself, looking a little bit guilty and a lot impressed by the camera and boom and their *Kendra* crew shirts.

"Junie? Is it okay if they film just a minute or two in here?" The nurse looked as though she was begging Junie for a minute or two of her own fifteen minutes of fame.

"Not really." Junie's face was splotched red after nearly an hour of crying. "Whatever happened to patient confidentiality? Just leave me alone. Please."

"But it's *The Kendra Show*! That's a really big deal, Junie."

Junie took a good look at the woman for the first time. She could hardly have been out of nurses' training. Twenty-two at the oldest?

"Who wouldn't want to be you right now? You get to meet Kendra and be on her show. Probably the most famous woman in the whole world!"

"I, for one, do not want to be me." Junie pulled the blanket down and glared at the nurse. "You do know why my mom is on the show?"

"Sure I do. I saw a little bit of it on the news last night. She's not the only one. Lots of people have hoarding problems. I've seen lots of TV shows on it." The nurse smiled at her. "It's good that she's getting help, right?"

"Right." Junie pulled the blanket back up over her head. "Bob, I can't do this any more. This is totally ridiculous. You've got enough footage, don't you? Please, please, please, please, please just leave me alone."

Nikolai started to back out of the tiny room, but Bob pulled him back. "You think Kendra got so famous by leaving people alone?"

Junie sat up. "And do you think it's kind or fair or right to film me when I'm at my worst?" She blew her nose on one of the tissues that had accumulated by the pillow. "Fine. Drive me to the bridge. You can film me jumping off. Charlie says drama makes good TV . . . is that enough *drama* for you?"

"Suicide?" The nurse blanched. "Now, Junie, you know that we have a protocol for kids who are having thoughts about harming themselves—"

"Oh, please." Junie flung off the blanket and swung her legs over the side of the cot. "It was a joke."

"Trust me, it was a joke," Bob reassured the nurse. "Inside joke between the two of us. She's got a dark sense of humour." To Junie, he added, "We film everything. That's how we get the good stuff."

Tabitha pushed into the room, shoving her way around Bob and Nikolai and the nurse. "Junie, you okay?"

"No," Junie said miserably.

"We were just deciding if they could shoot in here," said the nurse. "I don't mind at all. That Kendra is a saint. If I was American, I'd want her to be president. Heck, I'd vote for her to be prime minister!"

"Because that would solve everything." Tabitha rolled her eyes. "Let's get you out of here."

Junie gratefully followed her into the hall and down to the cafeteria, where Ollie and Lulu were waiting for them at their usual table. No Wade. That wasn't a surprise. Especially not after the debacle in World Studies.

With Bob and Nikolai standing over them, filming, Junie huddled heads with her friends and told them—in a whisper—about Wade's cold shoulder and his even colder words in the note.

"Give him some time," Lulu said.

"He'll come around," Ollie said.

"Can you blame him?" Tabitha said.

"Tabitha!" Junie felt stung. But she knew she was right. "No, I can't blame him. But he could at least talk to me. Get mad at me in person. Anything would be better than the silent treatment."

Lunch dragged on and on as people wandered by, hamming it up for the camera, talking in not-so-hushed whispers about Junie's mom.

Compulsive hoarder, like, mountains and mountains of junk.

Filthy . . . they say she hasn't showered in years.

Dead cats all over the place.

I heard there's a foot-deep swamp of shit in the basement.

She sits in diapers all day so she doesn't have to go to the bathroom.

"Dead cats? Where do they get this stuff?" Tabitha said, exasperated. She spun, and hollered at the nearest gawkers, "Get out of here! You guys don't have a clue what you're talking about, so scram!"

But they didn't. They just laughed some more and stayed put, hoping the camera would swing their way.

Halfway through lunch, the PA system crackled on and Junie was summoned to the principal's office. That was just what she needed. The whole cafeteria erupted with a chorus of, "*Ooohs.*" Junie dropped her head into her hands.

"This day cannot possibly get any worse."

"It's probably nothing," Tabitha said.

This made Junie laugh, kind of a desperate, strangled laugh. "How can you say that? With everything going on, how can you say that? For all I know Kendra herself could be waiting for me."

But it wasn't Kendra. It was Junie's father, his cheeks red and eyes ablaze. "I have to hear about this from the news? The goddamned *news?*"

"It's kind of old news, Dad. Where were you last night? Or this morning?"

He blushed slightly. "Evelyn and I were doing a silent retreat."

"You didn't tell me you were going anywhere."

"We didn't. We were at home." He aimed an angry finger at Bob. "Turn that thing off. You do not have my permission to film me or my daughter."

Bob, to Junie's amazement, lowered the camera. "Parents have veto power," he explained in response to Junie's astonishment. "Didn't know there was a father in the picture. Falconetti's going to be pissed," he said to Nikolai. "Might have to scrap all the stuff we got today."

"Oh no, say it isn't so!" Junie's voice was thick with sarcasm.

"Might just mean we have to come back," Bob warned as he and Nikolai made their way out of the office. The principal excused herself too, so Junie and her father could talk privately.

"What do you mean you didn't go anywhere?" Junie asked once she had her father to herself.

"We do the retreats at home. Once a month or so. Reset. Recharge. Renew."

"That has 'Evelyn' written all over it. Her idea, right?"

"Yes, as a matter of fact." Her dad steered her out of the office and out the front door, where his car was parked at the curb. "It's a very healthy thing. We turn off the cellphones and TV and the radio and don't go on the Internet. We have a nice meal and a bath with essential oils—"

"TMI, Dad." Junie held up her hand. He gave her a confused look. "Too much information. Spare me."

"Sorry."

"You should be." Junie threw her bag into the back seat and climbed into the front. "The only good thing I can think of about your weird silent retreat is the thought of Evelyn not speaking."

"Junie!" Her dad spun in his seat. "Enough!"

Junie was taken aback. "What?"

Her father gripped the steering wheel and glared straight ahead. "You know exactly what I'm talking about. I have absolutely had it with you bad-mouthing Evelyn. No more. I won't have it. Especially not with everything else going on. Understood?"

Junie pushed her inner nasty bitch out of the way. She knew when she was pushing it too far with her dad, and this was one of those times. "Sorry."

He started the car. After a long moment, he spoke. "It pains me to say it, but I don't think you're sorry at all. I'm sad that you're not more empathetic toward others."

For a brief moment, Junie felt a deep, aching shame. But then it flipped, and she was just plain mad again. "Dad?"

"Junie."

"How about you don't ask me to be empathetic about the woman who broke my parents up and I'll just stop talking about her altogether." She managed to make the words come out calmly, which she was grateful for. "Deal?"

There was another long pause, during which—Junie was pretty sure—her dad was choosing his own words just as carefully.

"Fair enough. Deal."

They drove a few blocks without saying anything more, until Junie's curiosity got the better of her. "Where are we going?"

"My place."

But Junie didn't want to go there. Because That Woman would be there. Her father, knowing that was what she was thinking, added, "She's working."

On breaking up another family, likely.

"Oh," was all Junie said, to avoid saying anything worse. Another long silence. "Can we drive past the house?"

"You want to?"

"Yeah."

There were only three media vans out front today, now that Kendra herself had left. The Got Junk trunks were parked in the driveway. There were three of them, and all three were already half full.

"That's good!" Junie leaned forward, her mood suddenly brighter. "Look at how much she's gotten rid of already!"

Her father slowed in front of the house. When he stopped, Junie opened her door.

"Junie, wait!" her father called after her. "I don't want you involved in this!"

But Junie ignored him and ran across the lawn to the front door. She found her mom in the dining room, surrounded by a fortress of file boxes, a tall, slender man beside her, a camera crew behind them, filming.

"Hey, sweetheart," her mother said. "Aren't you supposed to be at school?"

"Not if you want me to survive this. It was terrible. I might never go back."

"Well, we'll talk about it later," her mother said. "Missing one afternoon isn't the end of the world." She gestured at the man beside her. "This is Nigel. Nigel, this is my daughter, Juniper."

She didn't need to introduce him. Anyone who'd watched *The Kendra Show* on a regular basis would know exactly who he was: the polished-for-TV psychiatrist Kendra brought in to deal with the worst cases. He was dressed in a smart-looking suit, with narrow pinstriped pants and a matching vest. No jacket. The sleeves of his pressed shirt were folded up in neat sections. He wore disposable gloves on what looked like quite small hands for a man of his height.

"Nigel Carley, psychiatrist." His posh British accent sounded very out of place, considering the squalor surrounding him.

"Juniper Rawley, daughter. You can call me Junie."

"Pleased to meet you."

"And you, I guess."

Junie scanned the room. Despite the loaded trucks outside, it didn't look as though anything was happening inside. If anything, it looked worse. What had once been disorderly but compact stacks and piles were now all undone and in shambles as her mother sorted through them.

"I'll be working with your mother for the week. We're going to be aggressively addressing her situation. Her Obsessive Compulsive Disorder, and hoarding in particular."

He was speaking for the camera, obviously.

"Obsessive what?"

"OCD. Obsessive Compulsive Disorder. It's a mental disorder characterized by intrusive thoughts that result in severe anxiety, which leads the person to perform ritualized behaviours in order to reduce the anxiety." He sounded as if he were reading from a textbook.

Junie glanced at the cameras, wishing they would spontaneously combust. She placed a protective hand on her mother's arm. "You're saying my mom's mental?"

"It's okay, Junie. He's explained it all to me, too."

"Not 'mental.' Not at all in the way that you're thinking." Nigel smiled at her. It was a genuine smile, too, not fake or condescending, like when Evelyn St. Claire tried to do the same. "But she does—you do, Marla, suffer from OCD, and that is, in fact, a genuine mental disorder."

Before Junie could ask any more questions, her father showed up behind them.

"What the hell is going on, Marla?"

"It's not really any of your business, now, is it?" Her mother turned to Nigel. "This is my ex-husband, Ron."

"Ron." Nigel pulled off his glove and held out his hand. Junie's father didn't shake it, just glared at Nigel instead. "Pleased to meet you, Ron. Do you have any questions for me?"

"Not a question. An order. Get the cameras out of here."

"If that's what needs to happen to make you feel comfortable, we can do that for now." Nigel sent them out of the room with a wave. "There. Now what's on your mind, Ron?"

"I want everyone out of here, that's what!" Junie's dad

took a step forward and tripped on a garden hose. "This is still my house, and I haven't given anyone permission to be here. So out. Go, and clear everyone else out with you."

"Let's take a minute to talk this out, Ron." Nigel's voice was smooth, but not too smooth. "Can I explain how this works?"

"This? What is 'this,' exactly?"

And so Nigel explained about how Junie's mother had contacted them, and how the intervention was going to work. They'd be there a week, all expenses carried by the show. Junie's mother would get help. The house would get in order.

"That can only be a good thing," Nigel finished. "Don't you think?"

"Please don't ruin this for me, Ron." Her mother's voice was shaky. Junie looked at her. She held a plastic grocery bag full of old bills in each trembling hand. "This is going to make things better. Isn't that what you want?"

"Better?" Ron swept his arm wide. "You think a week is going to fix this?" He turned to Nigel. "What you don't know about my wife is that this is the product of years of dysfunction. Decades! You think you can fix her in a week when I couldn't fix her in seventeen years?"

"I do."

"You do? How can you—?"

"The difference is that now she is ready." Junie was rapt. She could listen to Nigel say pretty much anything and it would sound exquisitely right. "The difference is that we have endless resources available to us. The differences are vast, and should not be brushed aside."

Ron paused. Junie could see that he had been swayed, if only just enough. For better or for worse, she wasn't sure.

"I don't have to be on the show, though."

"I think we can arrange for that."

"Because I don't want to be on the show. Not even for a second. Not even in a background shot. Is that clear?"

"As a bell."

Charlie strode into the room, clipboard in one hand, phone in the other. "This is the ex?"

"Charlie, this is Ron Rawley, Marla's estranged husband and Junie's father."

"Sign this." She thrust the clipboard at him. Junie winced. Not a smart move.

Her dad glanced at it before flinging it at her feet. "I'm not going to be on your salacious little talk show, so you can shove that release form right up your ass, lady."

"Ron!" Junie's mother flung the bills down with a flourish. "Don't talk to her that way."

"It's all right, Marla," Charlie said, her eyes on Junie's dad. "Mr. Rawley makes his own decisions. We can do the show without him. From the sounds of it, he's not been in the picture for quite some time now anyway."

"Let's go, Dad." Junie tugged on her father's sleeve.

He glared at Charlie. "Just what are you insinuating?"

"You left your family." Charlie shrugged. "You don't have much say in what goes on here now."

"This is still my house."

"Meh, any reasonable judge would award it to the wife and child you left behind." Charlie sounded even more

New York, if that was possible. "Or should I say ex-wife. Whatever."

Before her dad could erupt again, Nigel stepped between him and Charlie, reaching a manicured hand toward each of them.

"Let's take a minute to collect our thoughts."

"No thank you," Junie's dad barked. He grabbed Junie's hand. "We're getting out of here. Junie can come back when it's over."

"What?" Charlie's eyes widened. "No way, she's part of the show. Nigel," she aimed a finger at him, "make him understand. The kid is a big hook. We need her. We can sacrifice the dad, but Kendra will flip if the daughter is out. She'll totally pull the show. We already talked about it when the daughter was putting up her own fuss. Make this issue go away, Nigel. Do your magic."

Pull the show? Jargon or not, Junie could figure out what that meant easily enough. Cancel it. Stop the intervention. Leave.

Her dad was physically dragging Junie toward the front door. "Come on, Junie. Enough of this crap. Let's get out of here. And you vultures can talk to my lawyer if you have anything more to say to me. Good luck with your fifteen minutes of fame, Marla. The extraordinary squalidness of it particularly suits you."

"Ron! Come back!" Junie's mother yelled after them. Junie could hear Nigel murmuring to her. But her mother kept yelling. "You can't take her! You can't take her, Ron!"

The camera crew was getting all of this, because while they'd left the dining room, they had only gone as far as the living room. They aimed their cameras on the scene now, and Junie's father was too absorbed in his exit to notice.

"Oh yeah?" he hollered over his shoulder. "If I don't take her, then Social Services will. Because you are an unfit mother, Marla! A friggin' mess! I've been nice enough until now, giving you time to get your life together. And you haven't! So now it goes to the courts. And who do you think will win custody? Me! That's who! Sole custody! Because you are a sick, filthy woman living in a sick, filthy house. And I won't stand it any more. Our daughter deserves better!"

"Mom!" Junie yanked free of her father and ran back to her mother. She gave her a hug, and her mom held onto her tight. "Don't listen to him, Mom. You're doing great. I'll be home later. I promise. I'm doing this with you. Okay?"

"He's right. He's right, he's right, he's right." Her mother wiped at her tears. "I am a horrible mother."

"You're not. You're *not*." Junie tossed a glare at her father, but he wasn't having any of it. He held her look, his jaw clenched, face tight with anger. "He's just mad. Everything will be okay."

"Junie," her dad barked. "Now!"

"I'm coming, Dad. Just *wait*." She gave her mother another hug. "I love you, Mom. Do you hear me? I love you."

This started the tears again in earnest. "I love you too," her mother choked out as the cameraman stepped closer.

Turning on her father, Junie shoved him toward the door. He'd already made quite a scene for the camera crew.

She just wanted to get him out of there before he created any more drama.

He stormed toward his car, waited until Junie was buckled up and then stomped on the gas pedal, squealing his tires as he sped away. Junie looked behind them. The camera crew had followed them and was filming him racing off. If drama made good TV, then *The Kendra Show* was going to win awards for featuring Junie's screwed-up family.

NINETEEN

:
:
•

Evelyn St. Claire's loft was sleek and modern, the décor lifted right out of *Home & Style* magazine. Everything was staged, so that no matter where your gaze landed, you saw something that was most definitely meant to be there. Whether it was a throw angled over the edge of the white leather couch, or a carefully aligned stack of art books on the coffee table with a wrought-iron candelabra resting on top, Evelyn St. Claire had put a lot of thought into it all. Even the candles in the candelabra seemed to be artfully, stylishly melted.

Junie kicked off her shoes and slumped on the couch, kicking the throw to the floor and pushing the books askew with her toe. She wondered if they'd had the candles lit for their stupid silent retreat. Who did that? What New Age weirdos did that?

Her father brought her a glass of water with a slice of lemon floating on top. The same New Age weirdos who put lemon in their water. He was turning into a pretentious snob, just like Evelyn St. Claire.

"Where's Princess?" Junie didn't know what else to talk about. The business back at the house, the whole Kendra thing, seemed overwhelming and dangerous.

"With Evelyn." Her father settled on the couch beside her, cupping his own glass of water with both hands. "She's working with this eccentric old millionaire who has an art collection like you wouldn't believe. She's helping him create a gallery in his home, and then she's cataloguing the rest that he hasn't got room to show."

Junie didn't care. She really didn't care. "That's interesting."

She and her father sat side by side, ignoring the hugeness between them until they couldn't any longer.

"I think it's going to help," Junie finally said.

"Well, fine and great if it does. I don't want you on that show."

"But I'm part of her life, Dad. A big part." Junie was surprised at her reaction. She'd spent the whole day wishing the cameras away, but now that she'd gotten her wish, she wasn't so sure she wanted it. "I'm part of the story too." *And so are you*, she wanted to add. But she didn't. He wasn't really a part of her mother's story now. Never mind the seventeen years they'd been married. He'd walked away. He was gone now. "You don't really have a say any more," Junie said gently. "You can't have it both ways. You left. It's me and Mom now. Not you, me and Mom."

Her father looked at her with steely, dark eyes. "I'm still your father."

"But I'm not six." Junie set her glass down on the polished coffee table. Her father scooped it up and slipped a coaster underneath. This irked her more than it should have. She took a deep breath before she spoke again. "So you can't really tell me what to do."

"You're not an adult yet, either, so technically, I can." When Junie didn't reply, he shifted uncomfortably beside her, first placing his hands on his knees, and then crossing them across his chest. Finally, he got up and climbed the stairs to the loft bedroom.

It had been a long time since her father had parented her. Even before he'd left the house he had already checked out emotionally, years before. He'd spent all his time sitting at a small desk in the corner of the master bedroom, surfing the Internet, chatting online, ignoring the mess around him. Junie had never really been parented, she realized. She'd been growing up with a mother and father, but hadn't really experienced either. She'd been ripped off. She figured that she should be angry about the realization, but she wasn't. She was tired, and sad. Nebulously, viciously sad.

Junie folded her legs under her and gazed out the window at the tall orange cranes down on the docks, the stacked shipping containers and the harbour beyond. She wanted to talk to Wade. More than anything. She didn't want to be there with her father. She didn't want to go home. She wanted to go find Wade. She wanted him to put his arm around her and pull her into him. She wanted to be tucked away, somewhere wonderful. And that was with Wade. Or had been, until she blew it.

Junie looked at the time on the massive clock halfway up the exposed brick wall. Evelyn had bought it at an auction of items from a tiny train station way up north that had been decommissioned. Junie liked it, actually, but had never told her so. She wasn't particularly interested in ever giving Evelyn St. Claire any reason to smile. It was after two o'clock now. Wade was probably on his way to Chilliwack. Without her. Junie closed her eyes. She was in the passenger seat in his van, staring out the window at the blue sky, the power lines zipping by. Patsy Cline on the stereo. She glanced over at Wade. He smiled at her. Winked.

Junie opened her eyes. Not the van. No blue sky. No smile.

What would it take for him to forgive her? She would ask him. As hard as it would be to make those words come out of her mouth, she would do it. She missed him. She tried his cell but he didn't answer. She got his voice mail and left a message, her voice low so her father wouldn't hear.

"Wade? Talk to me? Please? Let me explain? I miss you." Junie's voice caught. "I really miss you. I screwed up and I just want to explain. I'm at my dad's. Call me." She hadn't asked what it would take to forgive her. It didn't seem like a question for voice mail. She didn't think he would call. Not anytime soon, anyway. She wouldn't have, if she'd been him. She clutched the phone and stared at it, wishing she could make the call over again. She'd sounded desperate. Nervous. Pathetic. No one she'd want to love.

Her father came down the stairs and disappeared into the kitchen. Junie heard the fridge open, the kitchen tap running, and then he returned to the living room with two shiny apples.

"A peace offering." He set one on the table in front of her, and took a bite from the other. He chewed, every crunch like road construction in Junie's head. She stared at her apple, knowing that she had to pick it up at least, if not eat it. She slid her eye to the side, to catch a glimpse of her father without him knowing. He took another bite, his lips smacking, the apple glistening and wet. Junie's stomach lurched. She picked up the apple, the phone still in her other hand.

"Can I take this with me?" she asked him, meaning both the phone and the fruit.

Her dad waited until he'd swallowed before asking, "Where are you going?"

"To lie down for a bit. I don't feel so good." Junie put her other hand to her stomach. She wasn't faking. Her stomach felt like so much hardening cement.

"We should talk."

Sure, now he wanted to talk. Almost a year after he'd left with hardly two words to say about it, now he wanted to talk. Well, Junie didn't. She wanted to lock herself in a cool, dark room and come out when everything went back to normal. Or ahead, to a better normal where her mom was better and Wade had forgiven her. Ahead to normal.

"I just want to be alone for a bit. Okay?"

"I don't want you on that show, Junie. I'm going to be firm about that. It's not healthy. It's not sane."

Junie was too tired to argue any more. "Later, Dad. Please?"

"All right." His expression softened. "I'll wake you up for dinner."

⋮

But Junie didn't sleep. Her room at Evelyn St. Claire's had actually been a walk-in closet before, just off the hall by the front door. So there was no window, and not much room for anything but the single mattress on a low platform and a small bedside table with a reading lamp on it. Her dad had drilled hooks into the back of the door so she could hang up her things, but other than that, there was nowhere to put anything. When he and Evelyn had first showed her the transformed closet, she'd been outwardly horrified and inwardly pleased. She'd told them it was cruel to keep a child in a closet, when, really, the small room was warm, inviting and ultimately cozy. It felt like a cocoon.

Evelyn had painted it turquoise blue—Junie's favourite colour—and had strung fairy lights along the edge of the ceiling, along with a big silver star lamp that hung down in one corner. She'd sewn throw pillows to match the comforter (also turquoise), and a few more in a light purple, which was the colour she'd painted the bedside table. It was delicious and private and all Junie's, even if she'd never admit to loving it. Like the clock. Truth was, Junie could easily understand why her father loved living here. It was so deliciously unlike home. If only it hadn't included Evelyn St. Claire, who was so not like Junie's mother. That was why her father wanted her instead. Junie knew that. She might want it to be different, but she knew why it was the way it was. Evelyn was put together, beautiful, organized, interested in life and interesting. Her mother was . . . not.

Junie flopped down onto the bed and crawled under the comforter, even though it was already warm in the tiny room. She set the phone beside the pillow and stared at it when her eyes adjusted to the dark. She should call her mother and see how she was doing. But she didn't want to know how she was doing. Instead, she willed it to ring. She wanted Wade to call her back. That was what she wanted. Badly.

It didn't ring. For minutes, and then an hour, it didn't ring.

She checked that it still had a dial tone. It did.

She told it to ring.

It didn't.

She begged it to ring and be Wade. It didn't. It wasn't.

After what seemed like several hours, she turned the phone on just to see the time illuminated in the screen. It was only just past three now; barely an hour had passed.

⋮

She eventually did fall asleep, much to her surprise. When she woke up, she checked the time again. It was almost seven o'clock. She hadn't meant to sleep that long. She reached over and turned on the lamp and sat up, groggy and thick. It took her a few moments to remember everything that had happened over the last twenty-four hours. But then it came at her in a rush.

Kendra, her mom, Wade, school.

With a groan, she fell back onto the pillows. If she turned off the light and closed her eyes, could she just sleep through it all? She didn't think so. She could hear That Woman and her father talking in low voices in the kitchen, which was just at the end of the hall. She crawled closer to the door but still couldn't make out what they were saying. After a couple of minutes, their voices grew more animated. Heated. Junie reached up and turned the door handle as slowly and soundlessly as possible. She pulled the door open a crack and peered down the hall.

She saw Evelyn's shiny red high-heeled shoes first, and then her crisp white dress with big black polka dots. Her dad's bare feet and then jeans. He'd changed out of his work clothes. Then Princess, curled in her bed by the fireplace just past the kitchen, even though there was no fire.

"I think you're being unreasonable," Evelyn said.

"This is my daughter we're talking about. Not one of your clients."

"And what an opportunity for her!" Evelyn opened the fridge and pulled out a head of lettuce. "*The Kendra Show* is not just another trashy afternoon talk show. She deals with serious matters, and has a legion of highly qualified experts on staff. Hell, I'd love to be one of them."

Junie's father murmured something she couldn't decipher, but it wasn't what Evelyn wanted to hear.

"That's not fair! Ron, you can't think that!"

"And why not?" Junie could hear her dad just fine now, as he'd raised his voice again. "This is a perfect opportunity for you to get your foot in there and try to make an impression on Kendra. Well, this is not a job fair, this is my family."

"Your family?" A long pause. "I thought Princess and I were your family now."

"Yes." Another pause, short but packing the required emotional punch. "Of course you are."

"And of course you still have your first family." Evelyn's tone softened. "But Junie is part of our family now too." She moved in and put her arms around Junie's dad, who turned to let her kiss him. "I'm sorry, Ron."

"I am too, Evelyn. I didn't mean to question your intentions. Of course you want what's best for Junie."

"Of course I do. You're her father. That will never change. I just need you to reshape things to include me. You want that, don't you? You want me?"

"Yes, yes, yes and yes. I want you, Evelyn. My life is so much better with you in it. So much better. I love you."

Evelyn murmured something. Junie knew she was saying it back. Again, nausea flooded her stomach. She wanted to stomp out there and inform That Woman that she would never be a part of her family. What her father thought was love was just infatuation. He'd get over it. Over her. Kendra would fix her mom and her dad would come home and Evelyn could keep her stupid clock and lemon water and creepy dog. She would never be family to Junie. Not ever.

But Junie didn't stomp out there and speak her mind. She stayed put, listening. Watching. Evelyn and her father didn't say anything more for another long while. They puttered about in the small kitchen, bumping into each other, touching lots. Hands on bums, elbows knocking, hips bumping. And finally, when her dad was brushing up behind her, Evelyn turned and pulled him against her, her hands—dripping wet from washing the lettuce—on his butt. He leaned over her, his hands braced on the cupboards above her and kissed her long and hard. Evelyn tilted her pelvis to him and let loose a soft moan.

Junie sucked in her breath and sat back, closing the door silently. She did not need to see that. Not in the least. She might actually puke. Up until how, nausea had only ever threatened. But seeing that? Junie swallowed hard, willing the bile back.

What was worse was that she could hear them moving upstairs to the loft bedroom now. They were going to do it. Right now. It was obscene. Truly obscene. She heard Princess follow them up, padding softly on the hardwood stairs, and then Junie made her move. She got her backpack, slipped out of her room and out the front door, opening and then closing it as silently as possible as the bedsprings upstairs creaked grotesquely.

She stood in the hallway for a moment, deciding what to do next. Call Tabitha and have Mrs. D. come get her? Make her own way home on the bus? Wander the streets aimlessly? Try Wade again?

She took the elevator down to street level and pushed through the tall glass doors to the street. It was getting cool, but the sky was clear and cloudless. There was a payphone at the end of the street outside of a convenience store. She headed for it, dropped in some change and dialled Wade's number.

"Hello?"

"You picked up!" Junie's heart pounded. She'd expected to leave another pathetic message.

"I didn't recognize the number."

"Don't hang up!" Junie pleaded. "Please, Wade."

"Where are you calling from?"

"Downtown. I just left my dad's, I mean, Evelyn's place. I'm out front at that store on the corner."

"Not exactly the best place to be hanging out. It's kind of rough down there."

"I'm okay." Her heart warmed a little. He was worried about her. That meant he didn't entirely hate her. "Where are you? Royce and Jeremy's?"

"Look, Junie . . ." He sighed. "I don't really want to talk right now—"

"You're pissed at me, I get it. I totally get it. But can I explain?"

A long pause. Junie took it as permission.

"It's worse than you can imagine. Way worse." Junie held the phone tight, as if clutching it would make him stay on the phone with her longer. "I was embarrassed. I *am* embarrassed. So embarrassed. I didn't want you to know they were my parents after you saw them in the driveway that day. I didn't want you to know that was my house because then what if you wanted to see inside someday and I'd either have to show you or make up some excuse to keep you out. It's bad, Wade. So bad that I had to lie about it. I'm sorry. Maybe it was stupid—"

"Maybe?"

"Okay, totally stupid. I'm so sorry that I lied to you. But you have no idea what it's like, Wade."

"I can imagine."

"No. You can't. However bad you think it is, it's worse. Worthy of lying. I promise." Junie took a deep breath, about to offer him something she'd never thought she would. "Let me show you all of it? Let me show you where I'm coming from. Maybe it can help you understand. Maybe you won't be so angry with me."

Wade sighed. "I'm not angry, Junie. I feel stupid, like I should've figured it out. And I'm hurt that you'd lie to me about your home. Where you come from. Who you are. I thought I knew you, but I don't."

"You know *me*," Junie whispered. "I'm more than where I come from. I have to be." Wade was silent on the other end. "I'm so sorry, Wade."

"I know you are. And I'm sorry that I made fun of your parents. That was totally uncool. Really. And hey," she could hear his voice brighten a little, "the whole world is going to see your house pretty soon, right? So that should make it easier to show me."

"But I don't want the whole world to see it."

"You can practise with me." They let a moment linger, a wordless moment that seemed all that much easier now. "Can I come get you, Juniper Rawley?"

"Yes, please, Wade Jaffre." Junie felt a lightness come over so suddenly that it made her feel faint. "Right now? I thought you were out in the valley today. Working on the movie."

"I finished up there about an hour ago. Royce was getting tired. I'm on the highway. About twenty minutes away."

"Is he okay?"

"I'll tell you when I see you. Go down to that café and wait. It's not safe on the street down there."

"It's not so bad."

"It is. I'll see you at the café."

Junie made her way to the café and ordered a latte and sat in a chair by the window, watching the sun fade into dusk, looking for Wade's van. This part of Vancouver had its share of bums and hookers, or "transient citizens" and "sex-trade workers" as Evelyn called them, and was more than a little rough around the edges. Junie watched the mix of street people and the professionals who'd taken over their neighbourhood. The twenty minutes went fast, and before she could even finish her drink, she saw Wade park across the street and hop out.

Junie set down the mug. Her hands were shaking. *Don't blow it. Don't blow it.* She repeated those three words like a mantra. *Don't blow it.*

Wade came in, the bell above the door chiming happily, even though Junie was far from happy. She was a milkshake of nerves, quickly melting.

"Hey." He had his hands jammed in his pockets and stood well away from her, as if she smelled bad.

"Hey." Junie flung an arm at the chalkboard menu on the far wall. She felt gangly and graceless. Awkward. "You want something?" Loud.

"Nah. Thanks." He shook his head. "Let's just go, okay?"

Cut swiftly and it will hurt less, right? "Sure. Okay."

With that, he turned and went out, not holding the door open for her, for the first time since they'd met. With her heart sinking, Junie climbed into the van and pretended that her seatbelt required her complete attention. Neither of them spoke.

The silence felt so heavy between them that Junie was afraid she was going to suffocate if it continued. She decided on a safe topic.

"How is Royce? You were going to tell me."

"He had a pretty rough day. No energy. You know how he loves to talk. He could barely get three words out in a row."

"Oh, no."

"Yeah." Wade signalled and turned. "He was lying on the couch, and I walked by and I swear he wasn't breathing. I was freaking out. Just about to go get Jeremy, and then all of a sudden he sucks in this great big breath. Scared the crap out of me. I really thought he'd died right there. And you know what?"

"What?"

"I was going to film him like that."

"On the couch?"

"Dead." Junie wasn't sure what to say to that. Wade shook his head. "I had the camera to my eye and every-thing, I was going to go in there and film his dead body. What the hell, you know?"

"It's how you see the world."

"But I don't know if that's okay. It made me think. Really made me think. That's all."

There was her house.

Three Got Junk trucks still lined the driveway. The dressing room trailer and production trailer with *The*

Kendra Show signage on the side still sat at the foot of the lawn. The catering truck was gone, and there was only one media van, parked across the street. No cop cars this time. It was pretty quiet. And for that, Junie was eternally grateful.

Wade pulled up behind the Got Junk truck nearest the street and cut the engine.

"Wade?"

"Yeah."

"It's not all that different. Not really. It's a way of showing the world what is real."

"The talk shows have an agenda."

"Filmmakers have an agenda too." Junie didn't actually want to have a philosophical debate about it in the least, because it was not philosophical at all. It was real and it was happening, and it was a fact. She sighed. "Look, please, please, please just promise me that you won't judge me based on my mom. Or the house."

"I'll try." Junie could hear what he wanted to say: *I'm judging you on the fact that you lied to me.* It was as loud as if he'd hollered it.

Junie took a deep breath. "Let's get this over with." Because she did think it was over. Why would he want to forgive her for her lies, and after seeing the way she lived, he wouldn't want anything to do with her. Might as well get the hardest part behind her. The anticipation of a difficult event was always worse than the actuality of it. That was something Evelyn St. Claire had said when she was working with Junie's mom. She was right. Absolutely right.

She led him to the front door. The house was dark. The door was locked.

"Where's your mom?"

"I don't know." Junie dug for her key and opened the door. "Mom?"

There was no answer. Junie turned on the light and left Wade by the door while she went to look for her mom. She wasn't in the living room. She wasn't in the kitchen. Junie checked the master bedroom, filled to each wall with heaps and heaps of clothes. A musty smell pushed out of the room and caught her throat. She hated to think what they would find in there once they shovelled out all that mouldy fabric.

Her mom wasn't there. Junie went for the phone. Maybe her mom had called her dad, looking for her. Maybe they were out looking for her. She hadn't left a note for her dad. She'd just left.

She called his cell. "Dad? Do you know where Mom is?"

"More importantly, where are you?"

"Home. And Mom's not here."

"It's rude and disrespectful to just leave like that."

Junie wasn't about to remind him that screwing his girlfriend while his daughter was downstairs and could hear everything was also rude and disrespectful. Her silence must have said it for her, because he was quick to apologize.

"Look, I'm sorry. But it wasn't okay to just leave like that. You could've at least left a note."

Junie didn't want to discuss it. Not at all. Not ever. "Do you know where Mom is?"

"I do. Just hang on." She heard him rustling some papers. "She's at the Sheraton. Downtown. Room 408."

"A hotel?"

"Last time I checked the Sheraton was a hotel, yes. A nice one. She left a message saying you can take a taxi there and the show will pay for it. Or you can come back here."

"That's okay with you? If I spend the night at the hotel?"

After a moment, he answered, "I guess so."

Thank you, Evelyn St. Claire. Whatever she'd said (or done, Junie cringed to think) had shifted her dad's thinking, even if just a bit.

"We still have a lot to talk about, Junie. The discussion is not over. Not by a long shot."

"I know."

"But if you want to be part of this so called 'intervention' then that's up to you, I guess. You're old enough to make that kind of decision." He cleared his throat, then again. "I just want you to think hard before you decide to go ahead and be a part of it."

"I will."

"You're a smart girl, Junie. I trust your decision."

Thank you, Evelyn St. Claire, miracle worker.

"Thanks, Dad."

"Night, kid."

"Night."

When she hung up, Wade was standing behind her, his eyes wide. "I think I'm starting to understand." He held out his hand. "Come on. Show me your room."

TWENTY

⦁
⦁
⦁

First, Junie showed him the basement. Not because she wanted to, particularly, but because she was nervous to take him to her room and be alone with him. She might have been a smart girl, and her father might have trusted her decision-making process, but Junie wasn't sure that she trusted herself. They passed the phone on the way to the stairs, and Junie wondered if she could sneak a few minutes alone in the bathroom to call Tabitha. Maybe later. She left the phone where it was and opened the door to the basement.

The smell hit them in the face like an angry apparition. "Whoa." Wade scrunched his nose. "What happened down there?"

Junie told him, trying to laugh it off. But Wade wasn't laughing.

"You think it's okay to go down there without hazmat

suits?" Junie laughed again, nervous. He wasn't joking. though. "Seriously, Junie. I don't want you to get sick. Or me."

"Well, I was down there for the better part of a day, shovelling out crap and trashing shit-soaked junk. I'm not sick." She knew she sounded defensive, but she couldn't help it. This was the most embarrassing part of it all. Her basement, the sewer. That was why she wanted to get this part over with. Start with the worst, and it could only get easier after that, right?

She turned on the light and went down the stairs ahead of him. It was not the basement of a few days ago. This was clearly where most of the cleanup work had been done so far.

"It looks amazing!" Junie surveyed the big open room. Before, it had been packed up to the ceiling with garbage and junk and broken furniture that her mother had collected from alleys with every intention of repairing and selling it to make a little money. All the broken chairs and tables had been taken away, along with what must have been masses and masses of garbage that had been festering down there for years. She could even see the floor in a few places. The junk left was only about chest-high now. It was the worst of it, sure, as it had been rotting under the rest forever, but this was progress. Real, genuine progress. Junie's eyes brimmed with tears. "It looks so great."

"Junie?" Wade held her shoulders and turned her so he could see her face. "You're being serious?"

Junie nodded. "You can't even imagine what it looked like down here before. There's no way I can even begin to describe it. There just aren't enough different words in the English language for 'garbage.' This is a huge improvement. It hasn't looked this good for years." Junie stepped onto the carpet, blackened with dirt and neglect and mould and shit and damp. It squelched underfoot. They'd started to pull up the carpet nearest the bathroom, revealing the concrete below. "I can't even imagine how hard this was for my mom." She shook her head, marvelling. "I'm surprised she isn't hospitalized. Or drugged." Junie laughed. "Then again, maybe Kendra's clinical psychiatrist guy comes with a stocked pharmacy."

"Tranquillizers," Wade said. He hadn't stepped off the stairs. "A beautiful thing." He was trying to be funny. Junie could tell by his tone. But he just sounded weird. Junie knew why.

"You think this is gross."

Wade said nothing. He held her glance, and then slowly nodded. "It's a lot to take in, let's put it that way."

"It's okay, Wade. It is gross."

"Okay. Yeah, kinda gross, to be honest. Sorry."

"You don't have to apologize," Junie continued. "Of course I know that. But it's an improvement. I almost wish that you'd seen it before, so you'd know how much better this is."

Wade leaned against the stair rail and gave her a sad little smile. "But you didn't give me the chance. Remember?"

"Yeah. I remember. And I'm sorry. But if you think this is gross, can you imagine how you would've reacted seeing it before?" Junie wanted out of there all of a sudden.

She shouldn't have brought him down there. Not even Tabitha had been down there for years and years. It was a mistake. "I'm sorry." She spun, and was happy to find that they'd cleared a path to the basement door that led outside, to the steps that climbed up to the back yard. It had been blocked by a heap of broken furniture for as long as Junie could remember. They'd probably been using it to cart out the overwhelming quantities of trash. The door was warped from the damp rot that pervaded the basement, and sticky after not being opened for so long, but it gave after she yanked hard.

Junie stumbled up the concrete steps, gulping in the fresh night air. Wade followed her. She'd thought he would, but still, she wasn't sure she wanted him to. Being this honest . . . showing him how bad her house was . . . it was too raw. Too real. It hurt her heart in a way that felt dangerous. Like she was ruining herself. Forever. Like she was betraying the carefully spun web of lies that had served her so well for so many years. Like she was losing herself to the truth. Like she was losing herself, period.

"I hate this." She collapsed onto the damp grass, feeling the cool wetness seep through her clothes. It felt good, to feel something real and earthy instead of the nebulous muddle inside her head. "I hate all of this mess."

Wade sat on the grass beside her. "I can see why."

"Can you?" Junie didn't turn to him when she said it. She stared up at the sky. It was a clear night, but she couldn't see many stars with the city lights sharing the dark. She kept staring up, hoping the night sky might unzip and invite her in. Dark, cool refuge. She'd stay up there until this was all over, watched over by the constellations. *Delphina, Orion, Perseus.*

"I can." Wade lay back too. He put one arm under his head, and slipped the other under Junie's.

Junie felt almost warm with him near her. He radiated heat. She turned toward him. From the crook in his arm, she could see the angle of his jawbone. She reached up a finger and traced it, stopping at his chin. He lifted his head so he could see her.

"Thanks," she said. "For letting me explain."

Wade nodded, silent for a moment. "You know, when I saw Royce on the couch and thought he was dead . . ." Another long pause. "When my first instinct was to film him. It made me think of your mom."

"Yeah?" Junie barely whispered. "How come?"

"The way that she's just letting them in. To film everything. So raw, you know? Like being naked in front of the whole world. I don't know if that's okay."

"Because it's a talk show?" Junie worked hard to keep the defensiveness out of her voice. "Because, other than that, how is it different from your documentaries?"

"I know, right?" More silence. "I would film this." He sat up and gestured at the house. "I would film all of it, if it were for a documentary. I don't know how it's different." It was dark, but not so much that Junie couldn't see him shrug. "I'm trying to figure that out. I just wanted to tell you that. That I get that it's not all black-and-white."

"I wish it were. I wish I could just wave a magic wand and all of a sudden my mom and I would be living in a different house. A perfect house. That's how I'd like to deal with it."

The two of them lay back down for a while and watched the stars until they both got a chill. "Well, the magic wand didn't work," Junie finally said. "Come back inside the horror with me?"

"Sure."

"I'll show you my room."

He squeezed her hand. "I thought you'd decided it was off limits or something."

She'd already told him that her room was the tidiest space in the house, along with the upstairs bathroom. She'd told him so that he wouldn't think she chose to live like this. She'd told him so that he would know that she was different from her mother. To prove that she was neat. Orderly. Organized. Of course he wanted to see it. But there was something behind that request. An urgency that Junie could relate to. There was a bed. They were alone. There was a natural progression of events ahead, and Junie wasn't sure she knew how to handle herself.

"Not off limits, no. But I have to call Tabitha first. Super-quick. Then I'll show you. Okay?"

"Okay." He grinned at her. "You can tell her that I will be the perfect gentleman. Tell her not to worry."

Junie left him outside and hurried in to find the phone. When Tabitha answered, Junie rushed an explanation of what had happened at her father's, and afterwards.

"So let me get this straight," Tabitha said. "You and

Wade are alone at your house, and your dad thinks you're staying with your mom, and your mom thinks you're staying with your dad, and Wade's brother doesn't care where he stays."

"I never said that," Junie said. "He might have a curfew. I don't know."

"Just . . ." Junie could hear the anxiety in Tabitha's voice. "Just don't do anything stupid."

"Meaning, don't have sex."

"Exactly."

Junie sucked in a loud breath. "Really?"

"Junie!" Tabitha yelled. "Do I have to come over there? I can bring a deck of cards. We could play cribbage. How about that? Sound good?"

"No."

"Then don't be stupid. Or I will come over there. Armed with my Hello Kitty cards and popcorn. It could be fun."

"I'll be good?"

"You'll be good!"

"I'll be good."

"Good." Tabitha sighed. "Because you know I hate playing card games."

Junie said goodbye and hung up the phone. She stared at it for a moment, as if it might ring and the voice on the other end would tell her what was coming next.

⋮

Junie went back outside to find Wade on the back step, still gazing up at the sky.

"You talked to Tabitha?"

Junie nodded.

"Is she coming over to chaperone?" He stood up and took her by the hand. "Not that I want her to, but I'd understand if she was."

"She threatened to." Junie's heart raced. "Do you play cribbage?"

"The card game? No. Why? You're going to teach me?"

"Maybe. Come on. Let's go inside."

She led him upstairs to her room. "See?" she said as she pushed open her door. "My oasis."

"That's not surprising." Wade slung a damp arm across her shoulders. "Even your handwriting is neat." They stood there side by side for a few awkward moments until Wade finally dropped his arm and went ahead into the room, plopping down on the edge of the bed. "I promise I won't bite, Junie. Seriously."

Junie took a tentative step into the room. No guy had ever been in there. Other than her dad, and that didn't count. Really, no one had ever been in there, besides Tabitha and Junie's parents and her grandma. And that one time that Mrs. D. came in. Other than that, no one had ever set foot in there. It was bizarre that she had a boy in there, and no one was home to stop her.

Junie reached to plug in the fairy lights she'd strung after getting the idea from her room at Evelyn's. She switched off the overhead, so that the tiny punches of glow dangling around the room were the only light. Junie sat beside him on the bed, not touching him. If she did touch him, she wasn't sure where she would stop.

He reached for her hand, and they sat there like that for a very long, awkward moment. Eventually, he fell back, still holding her hand. "Coming?"

Junie laid back too, staring at the fairy lights, her heart pounding. She changed her mind and sat back up. He did too.

"Want to play cards?" He laughed, a short laugh that Junie had never heard before. So he was nervous too. That made everything seem a lot easier.

"Seriously, you could teach me to play crib." He brushed her bangs off her face and kissed her. Junie felt as if all the bones in her body had melted, leaving her a floppy, spineless soup of person.

"I hate crib."

He kissed her again. "Me too." And again.

"Wait." She put a hand on either side of his face and held him away as he leaned in one more time. "Wait." But she didn't know what to say after that.

"For?"

For what? Junie searched her brain for the next thing to say and came up empty. She was all feeling, and all of it was in her stomach, and lower. She'd lost her brain somewhere on the back lawn. She put her hands to her own head, willing her thoughts to pull together. "Don't you have to get home? It's a school night."

"I don't have to go anywhere."

So much for that.

"I've got to get out of these wet clothes. And so do you." As soon as she'd said it, Junie realized how it sounded. "I don't mean that we—"

"Of course not—"

"I've got pyjamas. For both of us."

Wade laughed. "I'm not wearing some pink flannel capris with puppy dogs on them."

Humour. Thank God. It was what she needed to get back on track. She slapped him playfully and pushed herself off the bed. She went to her bureau and pulled open the drawer where her pyjamas were neatly folded in sets. She pulled out a black-and-green-checked flannel bottom and a big black T-shirt. She tossed them at Wade.

"That's as unisex as I can find."

"You said 'sex.'" Wade pointed at her.

Junie had to laugh. Then so did Wade. And just like that, it got easier by another notch again.

She rummaged through the drawer, wishing she had something a little cuter than her usual ratty old cotton sets. She settled on a purple pair of short bottoms with lace on the trim, and a white tank top that was a little snug on her.

"I'll change in the bathroom," Wade offered.

When he came back, he asked if she could put their wet clothes in the dryer, and Junie had to admit that their washing machine and dryer hadn't worked in several years.

"I take laundry to Tabitha's house once a week or so. My stuff, anyway. My mom just wears the same thing over and over. And when it gets really bad, I take a load of her stuff to the laundromat." From the look on Wade's face, Junie got the idea that taking your laundry to the neighbour's was just one more thing that didn't fit within the box called "normal behaviour."

Junie hung their wet clothes on the shower rod in the

bathroom instead. When she went back to her room, Wade was already under the covers. He'd pulled a book off the shelf and was thumbing through it.

"I thought I'd read you a bedtime story. Better than crib. Serves the same purpose, right?"

Junie climbed in beside him, her heart thumping so loudly she could barely hear herself speak. "What's the book?"

"*Grimm's Fairy Tales.* 'Rabbit's Bride.'"

He started reading. "'There was a woman and she had a daughter and they lived in a beautiful cabbage garden.'"

"Who knew there was such a thing?" Despite the fact that she was lying in bed with a boy, Junie yawned. It had been a very, very long day.

Wade kept reading. Junie knew it was a very short story, only a couple of pages long, but even still, she was asleep by the end of it. Her night was busy with dreaming, in which Wade was a rabbit with long whiskers and tall, soft ears, and she was the girl he talked into coming into his hut. And she went, happy to leave the cabbage garden behind her.

TWENTY-ONE

. . .

The front door slammed and Junie woke with a start. For a moment, she was confused. This was her room. This was her bed. But there was a boy in it, which did not make any sense whatsoever. And then all that had happened the night before thundered into her thoughts like an earthquake. She sat up with a start, clutching the blankets to her, even though she was wearing pyjamas and had nothing to hide—except for the events of the night before, from her mother. Wade slept soundly beside her, tucked against the wall. He lay on his stomach, his hands shoved under the pillow, as comfortable as if he'd slept there all his life, while Junie had spent the night tossing and turning and dreaming of marrying rabbits.

Loud voices drifted up the stairs.

"Oh my God." Junie suddenly realized the severity

of the situation. There was no way Wade could get out of there without everyone finding out. "Get up!"

Wade sighed and rearranged his limbs and pulled the covers up higher. But he didn't wake up. Junie thought she heard Kendra's assistant's voice.

"Wake up, Wade! They're here! The *Kendra* people!"

He sat up, groggy. "Huh?"

"*The Kendra Show* people." Junie leapt off the bed and pulled a pair of jeans over her pyjama bottoms. She tugged on a sweater, fetched Wade's clothes and chucked them at him. "Get up! We have to get you out of here."

"Wha—?" Wade rubbed his eyes. "Okay. I'm up. I'm on it. Operation Hide the Evidence." He flung the covers off and was on his feet, wrestling himself into his clothes.

They crept to the top of the stairs. "They can't know that I was here, either," Junie said. "I'm supposed to be at my dad's, remember?" The two of them crouched as the boom operator brought his gear in through the front door. Charlie Falconetti came in behind him, BlackBerry to her ear.

"Gotcha, babe. Understood. Hang on, Kendra . . . disaster pending." She pulled the phone away from her ear and hollered at the boom guy, "What the hell you doing with that? Take it downstairs." She returned to her call with Kendra. "So yeah, Marla's a friggin' mess. A total train wreck. I don't know what kind of television you're going to get out of this, babe. It's bad, Kenny baby."

Junie and Wade exchanged a look.

"Yeah, well," Charlie continued, "you're a friggin'

saint, then. Because I'm not so sure I agree. This place is the worst I've ever seen, and that's saying a lot."

Junie wished she could cover Wade's ears. She didn't want him to hear Charlie talking about her mom, her house . . . her life like that. Wade caught the pained expression on her face. He gave her a wink, and then stood up.

"Hey!" Wade called down the stairs. "We can hear you, in case you give a shit."

Charlie looked up the stairs. "Oh, Christ. Disaster pending, part two. Gotta go, babe." Phone still in hand, she started up the stairs. "Hey, Junie. Good morning! And you're Wade, the guy who stormed off in a huff, right?" She reached out her free hand, but Wade didn't shake it. With a calculating glance at the two of them, their tousled hair and the open bedroom door behind them, Charlie grinned. "Well. Looks like you know a little something, and I know a little something."

"You can't tell my mom!" Junie blurted. "Please, Charlie. Don't tell her we were here."

"What is she going to tell?" Wade put a steadying hand on her shoulder. "That we got here before the crew? Big deal. You're an early riser. Me too. We both got up early and met here. What's wrong with that?"

That was good. But Junie had already blown it, and Charlie knew it.

"So I take it that your mom doesn't know about you two being here all night. And I take it that she wouldn't take it so well. Correctamundo, kids?"

"We just got here," Wade insisted.

"Right." Charlie raised her eyebrows. "Look, I'm

taking my leverage where I can get it. We all know that Marla has no idea that you spent the night with Mister Lover Boy here. Come on, fess up. Let's not waste time."

"Of course she doesn't know," Junie said. She sank down onto the top step. "Please don't say anything. She'd kill me."

"She probably would," Charlie said. "So I won't tell Marla if you don't tell her what I said to Kendra. And you don't tell Kendra that you heard me at all. Deal?"

"Deal." Junie sighed with relief. "Thank you."

"I don't know what you're thanking her for. I still say we just got here." Wade shrugged. "But okay. Deal."

Wade shook Charlie's hand, and Junie followed suit. They all went downstairs together, and whether the crew didn't care or didn't notice, no one said anything and there were no fishy looks, even though it wasn't even seven o'clock in the morning.

Wade and Junie made their way to the catering truck, which was already in full swing, with carafes of coffee and baskets of muffins and doughnuts and those little boxes of cereal, bowls of fruit salad, and a menu board with a list of hot food that they could order.

"What do you want?" Junie asked Wade, but he was distracted, watching the crew bring in the cameras and lights and the rest of the gear. "Wade?"

"Do you think I could hang out here today?" The question was for her, but his eyes were locked on the gear truck and the folding table outside, where the crew was checking out their equipment for the day.

Junie wasn't so sure she wanted him there, but there

wasn't any real way of saying that without making it into a big deal. He sensed her reservations, though.

"Not in a watch-the-freak-show kind of way," he added. "To be here for you."

"Yeah, right." Junie laughed. "You want to see the whole behind-the-scenes business, don't you?"

"I won't lie. It's true. But the bigger reason is that I want to be here for you."

Junie grinned at him. "If I recall correctly, you called *The Kendra Show* 'crap.'"

"Sure, I totally think it's crap. But it fills a niche, you know? She's figured out what the people want. I can admire that, even if I don't like how they work, or how they edit, or how they produce the whole package."

"You think they'll make my mom look bad?"

"Yeah." Wade nodded. "Really bad. But you know how it works. The first part of the show is how awful it all is, and then the second part of the show is how Kendra made it all better. Maybe that's what makes it different from documentaries."

"Well, even if you put it that way . . ." Junie thought carefully about what he'd said. She knew he was right. "If Kendra can make her better, then I'm okay with it."

"And I can stay and watch what's going on?"

"Sure," Junie said. "And I'll be here anyway. There's no way I'm going back to school today. Or possibly ever again. I'll introduce you to Bob."

Just then, the black SUV pulled up and the driver opened the door for Junie's mother. She climbed out, her face pale, clutching her purse to her chest like an old lady worried about it getting snatched. Junie could tell just by looking at her that her mother had had a hard night. She didn't like being away from her chair in the living room, for one, let alone the house. Add to that the reason why it was all happening, and Junie was pretty sure that her mother was mere degrees away from a complete and total meltdown. Her house was being gutted, along with all its clutter—which defined her life—so in essence, her life was being gutted. And all on one of the most popular shows in the history of modern culture. Junie felt a genuine pang of sympathy for her mother, something that she hadn't felt for a very, very long time.

"Mom!" Junie ran over and gave her a big hug. "Dad said I could come back. How are you?"

"Morning, sweetheart." Her voice was flat, almost robotic. She let Junie hug her, while she stood and stared at the house and didn't say anything at all about the argument with Junie's dad. She didn't even notice Wade standing right there in front of her, beside Junie. Instead, she pulled away from Junie and dug in her purse. She pulled out a pill bottle, undid the cap and popped one under her tongue. She caught Junie's disapproving look. "Ativan. Just to get me going, okay? You've got to admit this is a pretty big deal. I think I have the right to feel some anxiety over it. Nigel prescribed this for me, but I'm only taking one in the morning." She tucked the bottle away. "He's counting them. He says I have to feel the emotions, difficult or not."

Junie rolled her eyes. "That sure sounds like *The Kendra Show* to me."

"She's coming today. Just for a bit while they take

away my chair." Her mother chuckled to herself. "I suppose that sort of thing makes 'wicked good television,' to quote Charlie."

Junie could already imagine it. Kendra holding one of her mother's hands, Dr. Nigel holding the other, as the Got Junk boys carted away her precious chair, where she'd been stuck for years. Charlie was right. It would make exactly the kind of television Kendra was famous for. That should make the Falcon happy.

When Bob arrived, Junie introduced him to Wade, and he agreed to let Wade follow him around for the day. Junie's mother was so overwhelmed with everything going on that when Junie reintroduced them, she hardly blinked. Just shook his hand, murmured a quiet apology for how it had gone before and then shuffled inside to face the day.

"Is she going to be okay?" Wade asked, watching her disappear.

"I don't know," Junie said. "I don't know."

Clearing out the house was a most unglamorous process, despite Kendra being one of *People* magazine's "Most Beautiful People of the Year," every year. Junie figured that she maintained her Most Beautiful standing by making herself scarce during the dirtiest, foulest parts of her show.

The Got Junk boys were using shovels on the bottom third of the basement. They all wore hazmat suits tucked into rubber boots. They wore the hoods of their suits up and cinched around their faces, and with the bulky gas masks on top of that, they looked like aliens doing hard labour. Charlie asked Junie and her mother not to wear the suits and masks for a few minutes, "because it distances you from the audience," so Junie was breathing through her nose while she and her mother sorted through a stack of mouldering boxes at the far end of the basement, with latex gloves on. The boxes were all filled with stuffed animals, whose tired plush fur was matted and festering from years of being in the damp basement.

Junie's mother let her chuck the contents of the first box into the large black garbage bag, although she was quietly looking away and wringing her hands as she did. Bob stood behind them, his camera levelled at them. Wade stood beside him, operating the boom with a huge grin on his face, which Junie knew was there even if he was wearing a big mask and she could only see the smile in his eyes.

Halfway through the second box, her mother lunged forward, grabbing a flattened panda bear from Junie's grasp.

"Not that one. We're keeping him."

"Why?" Junie snapped. "It's mouldy, Mom."

Her mother patted the bear, smoothing his fur. "Your father won him for you at the fair. Don't you remember?"

Junie shook her head and grabbed the bear back before stuffing it into the garbage along with the others.

Her mother glanced at the cameras, the garbage bag, Junie, and then hollered, "Nigel!"

Bob peeked around his camera and mouthed, "He's getting a coffee."

"Go get Nigel," her mother instructed.

"Go get him yourself!" Junie threw down the bag. "What do you need him for?"

Behind them, Bob was gesturing for one of the Got Junk guys to go fetch Nigel.

"He's going to remind you that I'm in charge here, not you. Things go only if I say they do. He said that I can say yea or nay when I want. That I can have a say about each and every single thing in this house."

"But Mom . . ." Junie sighed. "Why would you want to keep a soggy, rotten old stuffie of mine that I don't even remember?"

"You might want it later." Her mother fished in the bag and retrieved the bear, setting it in a box marked *Keep* beside her. It was already full, as were several more labelled the same way, circling her feet like puppies. Two other boxes were marked *Toss* and *Donate*, but there wasn't much in them. "In fact, you might want the giraffe, too." She fished in the garbage bag and pulled out a small giraffe.

Junie sighed again. She was trying to be patient, but it wasn't going very well. If the cameras hadn't been there, she'd have been strangling her mother right about now. But then again, if the cameras hadn't been there, they wouldn't have been nearly done clearing out the basement in the first place. "And why, Mother, would I want that stinking, filthy, musty, crusty old giraffe?"

"We bought it for you the day of your grandfather's funeral—"

"Which I was too young to remember. So why would I want a stuffie from the occasion? I don't even remember the man!"

Nigel minced his way down the stairs and through the

piles stacked on the floor. "I understand that I might be of assistance, ladies?"

"Yes," they both said at once.

"Tell her that I'm in charge."

"This is true." Nigel smiled at Junie. "Your mother is in charge."

"Over my things?"

Nigel paused, considering. "Hmm. Marla . . . do these stuffed animals belong to Junie?"

Junie's mother reluctantly nodded. "But we got them for her, some of them, anyway. Doesn't that count as mine, then?"

Junie winced. Her mother sounded like a kinder-gartner bargaining her way into an extra turn with a prized toy.

Nigel put a hand on her mother's arm. "Remember what we talked about? How to let go? How to invite not only real space, but *mental* space into your life, too? Imagine what you can do with that space . . . is it worth giving some of it up for the sake of a couple of stuffed animals that, frankly, need to be professionally sterilized? Is it worth the cost of that? The hassle? When your daughter doesn't even want them?"

Junie's mother clutched the panda bear and giraffe to her bosom.

Junie shook her head. "Unbelievable."

"Talk to me, Junie." Nigel nodded, coaxing her to continue.

"Those mouldy, maggot-ridden stuffies are more important to her than her own daughter."

"Good, good. Feeling is good. This is what you're *feeling* right now . . ." Nigel spun his hands in front of him, rolling with it. "Tell me more."

Junie glanced at the camera. At Wade. But she didn't care. They'd already seen so much. There was no taking it all back now. "She's choosing those over me."

"I'm not," her mother protested, still clutching the bear and giraffe to her.

"And we still have six more big boxes to go. And she's going to keep choosing her shit over me. Over and over, like she has done my entire life."

"Not true." Junie's mother dropped her chin to her chest and rolled her shoulders forward, as if trying to fold herself inward and away from the moment, taking the bear and the giraffe with her.

"Then put the damn stuffies into the garbage bag." Junie held the bag open and stared hard at her mother.

Her mother glanced up. She blinked away tears. Shook her head. "Just these two. I promise you. You can throw away the other boxes without even opening them." Even as she said it, Junie didn't believe her. It was one bargain after another for her mother. She would never let them just chuck everything. If she would, the house would have been cleared out by now.

"Put them in the bag, Mom."

"No."

"Marla. Focus." Nigel gripped her shoulder and looked her in the eye. "Take a moment, Marla. Okay? Deep breath in, let it out nice and slow. In through the nose, hold it, out through your mouth. That's it. Close your eyes, deep breath in. Let it out, nice and slow. Think. Think about your choice. You are in charge. No one here is arguing that fact. You need to be on board with each and every decision being made here today. Deep breath in, let it out. Nice and slow. Let the calm come over you like a warm blanket. You're safe. You're loved. You're strong. You can do this."

With that, he dropped his hands and took a step away and stared at her, like a hypnotist waiting for his victim to start clucking like a chicken, as ordered. Moments passed. Junie snuck a glance at Wade. She rolled her eyes. He nodded, his eyes agreeing.

Junie's mother snapped her eyes open. "I'm keeping them."

Junie gasped. After all that? She was going to keep them?

"You have got to be kidding me!"

Junie dropped the bag. She kicked over the nearest *Keep* box and stormed across the basement to the stairs. Bob and his camera followed her, Wade stumbling behind him, clutching the cumbersome boom. Another camera crew that had been filming the Got Junk guys swung their camera toward her mother.

"You're still choosing all this crap over your own kid! Unbelievable!"

Junie took two steps up the stairs and then shook her head and turned. She stomped across to her mother, yanked the stuffed animals out of her hands and ran out the back door and up the steps to the yard, where a large bonfire was taking care of all the scrap wood and broken furniture and piles of old newspapers. Junie hurled the stuffies into the flames, feeling instantly better as she did. She could hear her mother lumbering up the stairs behind her, crying.

"No, Junie! Please don't!"

Junie spun. "Too late."

Her mother heaved herself up the last step and then crumpled down as Bob and Wade manoeuvred around her to reset the shot. Nigel squatted on the step below her and murmured quiet, comforting words to her, glancing up at Junie as he did.

"Junie," he said as he stood up. "Would you like to come over here and apologize to your mother?"

"Not a chance in hell."

Wade gave her a thumbs-up, and right then she wanted to run to him and throw her arms around him and beg him to take her away from all of this. But all of a sudden the crowd gathered on the street in front of the house erupted in cheers. No doubt about what that meant: Kendra herself had returned.

Junie sank to the grass in front of the fire. She stared at the flames, willing herself to throw herself onto them. Charlie appeared from the side yard.

"Marla! Junie! Come with me, guys."

Junie didn't take her eyes from the flames. She watched the giraffe melt onto the bear, and then the two of them twist and burn into a fist of hot, sticky ash.

"Come on, quick like bunnies, people!" Charlie marched straight to Junie's mother and tried to haul her up, but she was stuck, sobbing, face buried in her hands. "For God's sake. Then you, Junie. Come on!"

Junie didn't argue. She let Charlie grip her arm and drag her around to the front of the house so that she could be front and centre and in the shots when Kendra emerged from the SUV.

TWENTY-TWO

:

Kendra had just celebrated her fiftieth birthday the month before. All the A-list celebrities had feted her, and the president of the United States himself had made an appearance in person at her Hollywood birthday bash to wish her Happy Birthday and thank her for her support during his campaign for office. Yet she didn't look a day over thirty as she let one of her security guards help her out of the SUV. Even though she already had her television makeup on, she didn't look overdone. And she'd sworn time and time again that she was against any kind of cosmetic surgery, so her youthful good looks were all her own . . . unless she was lying.

"Stay here." Charlie propped Junie up against the front door and then muttered to herself, "Screw it, I'm going back for your mother. Kendra will shoot me between the eyes if I leave her back there."

While she ran around the side of the house, Tabitha slid up beside Junie.

"Hey. You okay?"

"No."

"Anything I can do?"

"Shoot absolutely everyone here—myself included—between the eyes?" Junie let out a big, defeated sigh. "Not you. Or Wade. You can be spared. Left alive to arrange to have my ashes strewn along the beach. That's the done thing, right?"

"No can do, Junie. But my mom okayed me skipping. She said being your main support would be education enough for today."

Kendra took a few steps, placing herself so that the crowd could catch a glimpse of her. The hundreds of people broke into a loud frenzy, thankfully distracting the camera crew from the ugly sight of Nigel and Charlie dragging Junie's mother back around to the front.

"Kendra!"

"We love you, Kendra!"

"Sign my T-shirt, Kendra! Please!"

By the time Kendra was done with her brief session of royal waves and a few choice autographs for near-hysterical fans, Junie's mother was looking a little less pale and woozy. She stood close to Junie, as she'd been instructed to, but didn't say a word to her. Junie followed suit, the two of them ignoring each other with steely expressions and glares darkening their eyes. Until Kendra started her stylish stroll up the sidewalk and Charlie growled at the two of them to smile, godammit, smile.

"Ladies, Nigel," she purred as she approached Junie, her mother and Tabitha. "How are things progressing?"

"Beautifully," Nigel replied for them all, when it was clear that Junie's mother was in no state to speak and Junie would only bark negatives at her. "Why don't we step inside, away from all of this hubbub, and we can give you an update? Sound good, Kendra?" Nigel smiled warmly, well practised at the art of working the camera to his and Kendra's advantage.

Nigel let Kendra and Junie's mother inside, leaving Junie alone with Tabitha. Tabitha pointed at Wade, who was trailing behind Bob, boom wavering overhead.

"Explain."

Junie got them coffee and brownies from the catering truck, and then led Tabitha to the front step so they could sit down. She told her about the night before.

"Did you—?"

"No."

"Cribbage?"

"No, Tabitha. No cribbage, either." Junie blushed deeply, and for the umpteenth time swung her head in each direction, checking for cameras pointing her way. This was one moment that she really did *not* want televised.

"Because that's a little too much to be getting up to with everything else going on, and . . . AND . . . you've only been dating Wade for a few weeks. You're not that girl."

"Not the kind of girl to play cribbage alone with a boy?"

"Exactly." Tabitha narrowed her eyes, giving Junie a stern look. "And you know exactly what I mean."

Junie and Tabitha sat for a moment, brownies perched untouched on their knees, until the front door swung open and Charlie popped her head out.

"Kendra wants you inside. *Quel pronto.*"

Junie and Tabitha stood.

"Just the daughter." Charlie flashed a quick, condescending smile at Tabitha. "Sorry, hon."

"That's me." Junie rolled her eyes. "The Daughter. Like it should be capitalized."

"See you later?" Tabitha mimicked Charlie's smile but she'd already disappeared back inside. "*Hon?*"

"Don't you dare go anywhere. I need you." Junie grabbed Tabitha's hand. "Come in with me. It'll be fine. I have a little bit of leverage with Charlie Falconetti, if you can believe it."

There was extra lighting, and four camera crews were set up, one in each corner of the living room. Charlie snapped her fingers at Junie. "Over here."

Junie handed Tabitha her brownie and coffee and went where she was told, which was just to the left of her mother's recliner. Her mother was sitting in it, hands clutching the armrests, looking around the room anxiously. Nigel stood at her other side. Kendra stood directly in front of her. When the cameras were rolling, Kendra squatted graciously, tucking her skirt as she did, angling her shiny golden heels just so. She rested a hand on Junie's mother's knee. No gloves, hand to knee. Kendra, keeping it real. Junie had to admire her. She knew how to make this about her mother, and at the same time, the event always starred Kendra.

"Tell me about this chair, Marla," Kendra purred in a soft voice. "Tell me what it means to you."

Junie's mother ran a hand down the length of each oily arm of the chair. "This chair." She glanced up at the camera, then down at her lap. "I live in this chair."

"Hmm." Kendra patted her knee again. "Tell me about living in this chair. What is your life like, the view from this chair?"

Junie raised an eyebrow, confident that none of the cameras were on her, given that they were all angling for a different take on the same moment about her mother, starring Kendra. Junie turned her head, looking for Tabitha, who stood in the front hall, arms crossed, watching. Tabitha gave her head a little shake. She wasn't so sure the cameras weren't watching.

Junie very badly wanted to move this "event" along faster. She wanted to whistle for the Got Junk guys to come in and remove the chair, with her mother in it, if necessary. She'd rather deal with her mother screaming her head off, indignant, than this quiet, painful version of her mother, a woman trying to find words for a deep, devastating dysfunction.

"My life in this chair . . ."—Junie's mother patted the arms again, and then set her hands in her lap—". . . has been very, very hard."

Junie wanted to snort. Hard? How hard was it to sit on your ass all day, ordering crap from the Shopping Channel? How hard was that? Junie would rather have done that on any given day than write a math exam.

"Yes . . ." Kendra's mouth made a comforting little moue. "I can tell, honey. I can tell."

"I sit here all day, wondering how it got like this."

Her mother was choosing her words carefully, Junie could tell. She was censoring herself for television, and Junie wondered why. After everything, what did she have left to hide? The whole world would soon know just how bad it was, so why start mincing words now?

"Marvelling at what a mess I've made of it all. How I've failed my daughter." She looked up, and Junie could hear the near-silent shift of a couple of cameras angling toward her. "How I've failed you so terribly."

"It's okay, Mom." It wasn't okay. Of course it wasn't. But what else was she supposed to say? From behind his boom, Wade gave her a small smile. Junie knew that he meant it kindly, but she wished he weren't there to see her mother's humiliation tumble out like so much dirty laundry.

Her mother quietly tut-tutted. She stood and put a hand on Junie's shoulder. Her touch was hot, and Junie wanted to shove her hand away. "But it's not okay, Junie. Is it?"

"It's okay."

"Junie, be honest, sweetheart. Tell your mama how hard it is for you to see her live her life from this smelly old chair."

"It's fine."

Nigel stepped forward, lips already open, as if his words had come ahead of him and he was only trailing after. "Now is your time to tell your mom how you feel about the way she's been living her life, and how it's been affecting how you live yours."

"She knows." Junie swung her eyes to the floor. Embarrassment had cemented her feet where she stood; otherwise she would have gotten her ass out of there already.

"Do you, Marla?" Kendra's voice was firmer, inquisitive. "Do you really understand how all this affects your little girl?"

Junie's mother nodded, tears rolling down her cheeks, collecting at the point of her chin. "I know she's ashamed of me."

"I'm not—"

"Don't, Junie." She held up a hand. "I know how you look at me. I know you feel you can't bring anyone home. I know you felt you had to hide your boyfriend from me."

That did it. "I *feel* I can't bring anyone home? *Feel* like I have to hide?"

"You could've brought him home. You could have. He's a nice boy. He wouldn't have judged you. He might have judged me, and that's okay, but I don't think he would've judged you."

"Oh, for Christ's sake, Mom! Are you serious? Put yourself in my shoes for one godforsaken moment, would you? Do you honestly think I had any choice?"

"We all have choices," her mother snapped.

"And look at yours," Junie barked back. "Are you proud of them?"

"No."

Kendra nodded sagely. "And that's why we're here today. Let's go to break, and when we come back, we'll see if Marla can make the choice to let go of the cage that has kept her trapped for so many years, this old easy chair."

At the magic words, the camera crews started rearranging themselves, and Charlie swooped in with a coffee and a bottle of water for Kendra.

"Making some great TV today, Kendra. You're smokin' hot."

"You want a coffee, Marla?" Kendra asked, offering hers before she took a sip.

"No." Her mother shook her head. "Thanks."

"It's kind of abrupt, taking breaks like this," Charlie explained in a rush. "But it's best if we work them into the natural pace of things, in case we want to place them in the final edit."

Junie rolled her eyes and laughed. "I would've thought you'd want to 'stay with the moment,'" she said, tossing one of Kendra's common phrases back at her.

"We'll get it back," Kendra said with a smile. "I'm not worried. Excuse me, would you, lovely ladies? I'm going to go to the powder room."

⋮

When Kendra came back, the Got Junk boys were set up, waiting behind Junie's mother with their arms crossed, feet shoulder-wide, like heavies waiting to drag out a psych patient, and not a chair. Nigel squatted beside her, whispering his manifest destiny babble into her ear.

Junie stood beside Wade, waiting to be ushered back into the fray. He'd asked her how she was doing, but she hadn't wanted to talk about it, so she'd got him talking about operating the boom instead. She wasn't really listening, but it was nice to be close to him and hear his voice, even if it sounded like she was underwater. No matter that the cameras were there. No matter that Kendra was there. No matter that Junie's mother wanted to be better, wanted the house back to normal. Removing the chair was not going to be pretty.

Charlie snapped her fingers. "Over here, kid."

Junie made her way to her mother's side.

"And . . . roll!"

And just like that, they were being filmed again.

Kendra made her way through the teetering piles of junk, eyes on the camera as best she could without resulting in a fall.

"Welcome back, friends. We're here in Marla's living room, where she's spent the better part of the last decade, accumulating objects that would appear useless to you or me, but which are, to her, vital. This is the burden of those who suffer from the disease that is compulsive hoarding. Often—"

"Oops, sorry." Junie's mother stumbled over a stack of shoeboxes.

"Well, fudge," Kendra said with a smile. "Let's do that little bit over again." Junie marvelled at how Kendra backed up and redid the spiel, as if she'd simply pressed rewind, and then play. This time, she didn't stumble. Instead, she talked easily to her imaginary audience, about Junie's mother and her pathological dysfunction.

"Today is another hard day for Marla as we and the good folks at Got Junk clean up her house, and her life.

Marla, how are you feeling about saying goodbye to this chair?"

Junie wrapped her arms around herself, preparing for the worst. For another replay of the stuffed animal memorable moment earlier.

"Doing okay, Kendra. Doing okay."

Junie doubted that. But then her mother pushed herself out of her chair and gave it a half-hearted kick. "I'm looking forward to getting rid of this ratty old prison."

All for the television. Junie was sure once the cameras were turned off, her mother would be the first to go outside and try to pull the armchair out of the Got Junk skip.

Junie's mother whistled. Actually whistled. Put two fingers in her mouth and whistled like a baseball fan in the stands. "Take it away, boys!"

"That's my girl!" Kendra clapped her hands. Nigel clasped his together under his chin, his eyes glistening with well-practised, impeccably timed made-for-TV tears.

"Good riddance!" Junie's mother hollered as the Got Junk guys each took a corner and wrestled the heavy, awkward thing out of the room and outside, where they dumped it unceremoniously in the middle of the front lawn.

Someone produced a can of lighter fluid seemingly out of nowhere, but no doubt it had been planned. All of a sudden Junie's mother was holding it in her hand. The crowds on the other side of the hastily erected security fencing started rustling when they began to realize what might be going on. All they were sure of was that Kendra was standing on the lawn, her hands on her hips, grinning satisfactorily as Junie's mom danced an awkward dance around the chair, spraying lighter fluid onto the uphol-stery, her ample bosom bouncing in a most untelevisable manner.

"You're sure about this, Marla?" Kendra asked, raising her voice above the cheers of the crowd.

"I am!"

Junie kept back, not wanting to be a part of the spectacle. Her mother was flushed from the excitement and the dancing, which was the most movement she'd under-taken in years. It was embarrassing watching her make a fool of herself.

Tabitha held her arm, her grip tight. "Look, Junie!"

Junie lifted her eyes; her mother was striking a match. The flame caught and wavered in the wind before dying. The crowd gave a collective *Awww* before erupting into a chant of *Burn it, burn it, burn it!*

With another humiliating whoop, her mother struck another match, and then Junie was watching the chair catch fire, the flames skirting around the bottom and then settling into the seat and stretching into fiery orange plumes that heated the air, turning the crowd beyond into a watery mirage.

"This is all very weird," Junie said simply.

"Very, very weird," Tabitha echoed.

Wade came out from the house and joined them, resting the boom against the wall. "How about we get out of here?" he suggested.

"You guys go," Tabitha said. "My mom wants me home." She narrowed her eyes at Wade. "And Junie's mom would want her home too, if she was in any state to realize it."

"Yes, ma'am." Wade gave Tabitha a salute.

Tabitha wagged a finger at Junie. "And no cribbage, understand?"

"Yes, ma'am!" Junie gave her own salute, before Wade pulled her back through the house and out the rear door, and along the alley to the end of the street, where his van was parked.

⋮

He headed toward the valley, without asking Junie where she wanted to go. That was fine with Junie. The farther away from it all, the better. They didn't say anything until they were well onto the highway, and then it was Wade who asked her if she wanted to get some food. She wasn't hungry though, so they kept driving, pulling into Royce and Jeremy's driveway well after dark.

Wade had phoned to tell them they were coming, and so the porch light was on, and when Jeremy opened the door to them, the smell of curry wafting from the kitchen was enough to bring Junie's appetite to life.

TWENTY-THREE

:
⋮
●

Jeremy and Royce were surprisingly old-fashioned when it came to having a teenage couple in the house. Junie had assumed that she and Wade would be given a bed to share, but no, when it came time to go to sleep, Jeremy led Junie up to a little attic room with a musty double bed tucked in the corner under the eaves, while Royce helped Wade get settled on the couch all the way downstairs in the living room. Their hosts had said their goodnights, and told both Wade and Junie that the dog would be sleeping on the landing and would be sure to let them know if there was any midnight wandering.

Junie was the last one up, finally lured down to the kitchen by the smell of dark, rich coffee.

"Good morning, princess," Jeremy said as he poured her a cup. "Did you notice the pea I placed under the mattress?"

"I must not be a princess, because no," Junie said, "I didn't notice it."

"But you still have your prince," he said with a wink.

"Morning," Wade said as she took a seat beside him. "I actually tried to come up to see you, but Lucy stopped me."

"We said she would, didn't we?" Jeremy gave the dog a pat on the head. "We don't know how you two got permission to stay here overnight, but we can do our part to make sure that it is a perfectly innocent experience. You have plenty of time before you need to submerse yourself in the murk of such things."

Junie had spun the same lie as the night before, telling her father over the phone that she was staying at the hotel, and leaving a message for her mother at the hotel that she'd be staying the night again at her father's. Junie held Wade's hand under the table as they ate big bowls of hot oatmeal with maple syrup and cream poured overtop.

"Not many kids like oatmeal," Royce commented from across the table, where he was drinking muddy-looking green tea, a piece of dry toast abandoned on his plate.

"We're just thankful that you let us stay over," Wade said.

"Can I move in?" Junie added. "I'd be happy if I never went home again."

Jeremy leaned against the counter behind Royce, frowning. "Better not have brought that woman's people out here."

Wade shook his head. "No one followed us."

"Better be sure about that."

Royce winked, his pale face coming to life with a grin. "You never know, you just might be worthy of a little paparazzi, what with all the hype."

"Why do you say that like it's a good thing?" Jeremy growled.

"Oh, come on, Jer. A little excitement does a body good." Royce took a sip of his tea. "I remember when Marlon Brando took us all out to the Brolly pub. Remember that? And the paparazzi showed up out of nowhere—"

"Vultures to the carcass," Jeremy muttered.

Wade glanced at Junie.

"Didn't mean you," Jeremy added, when Royce shot him a look.

"Didn't think you did." Royce waved him away. "I'm not dead yet. Go get me the photo album with the paisley cover. That's got the pictures of Brando."

"Wait." Wade got up. "Let me go out to the van and grab my camera. I'd like to shoot this, if you don't mind."

"Of course not." Royce grinned. "What's a frail man have to do with his long last days but star in the story of his life? That is what this will be, isn't it? The story of my life? You won't go selling the footage to Kendra?"

"Never," Wade said. "I'm way more interested in seeing your pictures of Marlon Brando. Never mind Kendra."

The mention of the queen of daytime talk TV set Junie's heart thumping. She would have to go back home, to another day consumed by *The Kendra Show*.

"Can't you guys adopt me?" Junie asked as Wade left.

"Can't I just live here in the purple house and pretend that I don't have any other family? At least for a little while?"

"Absolutely not," Jeremy barked, startling Junie with his tone.

"He means that you're meant to live your own life," Royce offered. "All of it. Not just the easy-peasy-lemon-squeezy bits."

"I mean, you don't abandon your family when it gets hard." Jeremy looked away from Royce as he said this. But then he looked back, and smiled sadly at his partner. "I mean, you feel all the hard feelings. And you do the best that you can. And you do not, under any circumstances, run away."

Wade came back with his camera, and the moment passed. But it wasn't lost on Junie. She knew Jeremy was a man of few words, so to hear him talk so frankly about something so difficult felt exceptionally precious, as if she'd found a beautiful, sparkling geode inside of a hard, grey stone.

While Wade set up his camera, and Jeremy went to get the photo album, Junie sat with her worries piled in her lap like a tangled ball of yarn. She could get through this. If Jeremy and Royce could cope, then she would too, and with something that wouldn't kill her. Not really. And when she finally got through it, she would be stronger. At least she hoped so.

⋮

They headed back to Vancouver shortly after breakfast, and by the time they pulled onto Junie's street, it was already filled with media trucks and curious onlookers hoping for a glimpse of Kendra herself. It was the last day that the crew would be at the house, and Junie was eager to see what progress they'd made since she'd left.

Wade reluctantly went off to school, and Junie went in through the back, in search of her mother. She found her, surrounded by cameras, in a heap on the living room floor where her easy chair used to be. Nigel was standing by, his pressed pants not yet creased by the day, his face set in an even expression, revealing nothing. How he could deal with this kind of thing day in and day out and not be disgusted was beyond Junie. She was disgusted, and this was her own mother. She stood in the doorway, and was pushed aside in a flurry as Charlie ushered Kendra into the room.

"Morning, kid," Charlie muttered. "Excuse us. Coming through."

"Morning, darling." Kendra smiled at her. She was good at that. Actually seeing people, if only briefly.

"Good morning, Kendra." It was the first time she'd addressed her by name, and it felt weird. Kind of like calling a teacher by their first name, when she didn't actually even know the first names of most of her teachers.

"Marla, dear!" Kendra bent over Junie's mother, placing her hands firmly and sympathetically on her shoulders and giving them a squeeze. "Tell us what's going on."

"I didn't want to get rid of it!" she wailed. "I wanted to keep it. As a reminder of where I came from!"

"But you don't need any reminders like that," Kendra said. "You have your memories. Your story will always be yours."

Junie's mother looked up. "But I burnt it. I didn't mean to burn it. It meant so much to me."

"Here we go," Junie whispered under her breath to no one in particular. She couldn't watch. Not one more minute of it. Not one more second. She backed out of the room, called her father and asked him to pick her up at the end of the block.

⋮

Junie didn't have to wait long, and she was relieved to see that her father was alone in the car.

"How's the three ring circus?"

"As to be expected."

"I've been seeing what the news crews can catch." He turned the corner, going in the opposite direction from the fray. "Mostly just about *The Kendra Show* being in town. But some shots of the house."

"Yeah?"

"Saw her dancing on the front lawn, watching that old chair burn. It looked like it was shot from a helicopter."

Junie could not escape it. Wherever she went, her mother and her mountains of clutter followed her. Even here in her father's car, where she had been hoping to find peace.

"Dad?"

"Junie?"

"Can we not talk about it?"

A pause. Then he looked at her and grinned. "Sure, sweetheart. Want me to take you to school?"

Junie shook her head. "Absolutely not."

"You can't keep missing days."

"Dad. Please, please, please don't make me go there. It's Friday. Just let me have one more day off and then I promise I'll go back on Monday. Okay?"

Another pause. "You go back on Monday. No questions asked."

"Fine."

But Junie wasn't sure that she really would go back. She wondered if this whole Kendra experience had actually and seriously ruined her life to the point where she'd need to drop out, or transfer, or finish online. She wondered if the glorious gift of an intervention had, in fact, demolished her, while at the same time healing her mother. If that was what was happening at all.

"Do you have to go to work?"

"I can skip too, if you want to hang out."

Junie winced at the way he said it, so eagerly and so casually that it was clearly forced. He wanted so badly to be her friend, her "bud." And Junie just wanted somewhere else to be for the day, and it didn't matter if it was with her father or holed up in the reading room at the public library.

"That'd be nice, Dad." Junie heard the fakeness in her voice, but she couldn't do anything about it. "Thanks."

⋮

They went for coffee at the Buckled Star, where if anyone recognized her as the victim of Kendra's attentions they didn't say anything about it to her. Her dad sat across from her in one of two comfy chairs, eyes bright, waiting for the conversation to begin. Junie didn't want to disappoint, but she was just not in the mood to struggle through an awkward conversation in which her father pretended to know a thing or two about her, and she pretended to care about his job and his life with That Woman, and both of them ignored the elephant down the street that dominated their thoughts. Instead of putting them both through the pain, Junie picked up a newspaper from a coffee table and offered him the business section.

"Want this?"

"Sure," he said with a little audible relief. "I'll check on my meagre stock portfolio."

Junie picked up the front section. A seventeen-year-old boy had fallen or jumped to his death from the suspension bridge, a famous tourist attraction. He'd sailed from a dizzying height through the air to a sudden death on the jagged rocks below. Police were interviewing witnesses to see if they could figure out what had happened. Junie had been to the suspension bridge a handful of times. She'd stood at the same lookout, her hands on the railing, never feeling the urge to fling herself over. But she could understand it now. Once he was dead, nothing else would have mattered. It would be a blissful, silent void.

Not that she wanted to kill herself.

But she could understand craving the quiet. She could understand needing a final, lasting peace. She wondered if Royce was looking forward to that at all, or if he was worried about leaving Jeremy behind.

Junie glanced up at her father. He'd put his reading glasses on and was scrutinizing the stock pages, column after column of numbers about which Junie had no clue.

Did he feel about That Woman what Jeremy and Royce felt for each other? Would he be sad if she died? Would he be lonely for her?

Her father looked up and met her gaze. "Want a muffin or something?"

"No thanks."

"You ate at the hotel?"

Junie dropped her eyes to the paper and didn't exactly answer. "I'm not really hungry."

"Well, I'm going to get me a Danish. Live on the wild side."

"Whoa, Dad. Better not let the yogurt-and-fruit police find out."

And all of a sudden, the day wasn't so bad. Junie could admit to herself that she actually liked sitting in a fairly companionable silence with her father, while her mother's mess raged on without her, halfway across town.

⋮

Inevitably, though, Junie was drawn back in. They decided to catch a movie, for the complete playing-hooky experience. Halfway through a matinee showing of *A Fistful of Dollars*, Junie got a text from Charlie Falconetti. It read: *Do I need to pull out the big guns in order to get your ass back here?*

Junie glanced over at her father, who was intently watching the old spaghetti western unfold. Junie had been staring at the screen but hadn't really been watching. She'd let her mind wander, and had no idea what was happening in the plot, other than that some dusty guy was about to shoot another dusty guy in the middle of a dusty street in a tiny, dusty town. It was funny that Charlie had mentioned guns. Almost as if she were omniscient. Junie eyed the mostly empty rows surrounding them, half expecting to see Charlie herself waving at her in the half-dark.

"They want me back at the house," she whispered.

"They aren't the bosses of you, Junie." He offered her the bag of popcorn. "It's totally your call."

Junie texted Charlie back. *Less than an hour. I'll be there.* She had no doubt that Charlie would blackmail her, if that's what it took.

When the movie was over, Junie's dad took her home but dropped her off in the alleyway, not wanting to be on camera for even a minute.

Junie found her mom and Kendra in the much-improved basement, going through yet another box of stuffed animals. Of course Charlie wanted her back for this, what with the tantrum it had caused the other day. As Charlie liked to say, it made for great television.

"Come join us, sweetheart," Kendra called when she came down the stairs. A camera swung in Junie's direction. Even though the crew had been there for three days now, it still was weird that this was happening in her house, to her and her mother. Junie wasn't sure that it ever should feel normal to have a celebrity talk show host hanging out with one's mother in a filthy basement that still smelled like shit.

Junie reluctantly made her way over to where a large folding table had been set up, to help with the sorting. The same three boxes again: *Keep, Toss, Donate.* This time, though, the *Toss* and *Donate* boxes were more full, and the *Keep* box was almost empty. This stirred a small pool of hope in Junie. Perhaps her mother was getting better. Perhaps all of this was actually going to end up making things better.

Junie picked up an old doll from the box. It was one her grandmother had made, and Junie had forgotten about it until now. The doll wore a gingham dress with a white apron overtop, and had thick yarn hair in two braids and black felt shoes on her feet. The facial features had all been embroidered by her grandmother, and the eyes were an eerie turquoise blue because her grandma had let her chose the colour.

"You want to keep that one, hon?"

Junie wished that Kendra would just vanish. Just for a few moments while Junie had a private moment all to herself. Holding the doll now, she remembered wondering where it had gone. The morning she'd thought she'd lost her came flooding back, and all of a sudden Junie was eight years old and rifling through her toy box, looking for the doll, which she'd called Laura, after Laura Ingalls Wilder.

"You told me I'd lost this," Junie said to her mother, an accusatory edge to her voice. "But you'd packed it away."

"I guess I had." Her mother shrugged her shoulders, not realizing the seriousness of the moment.

"You were always doing that. Sorting and moving and packing. Even *my* stuff! Without asking!"

Nigel stepped in out of nowhere, as if manifesting out of the ether. "Sometimes, hoarders need to control their belongings, categorize them in a certain way that only they understand."

"You were always getting rid of your toys," her mother said, petulant. "I wanted to make sure that I set aside a few things so that you'd have them when you had children of your own."

"You could've asked me."

"Well, I didn't. Clearly." She reached out to pat the doll, and Junie pulled away, clutching the doll protectively. "But here it is, in good shape, years later, for you to enjoy."

"Ah, yes," Nigel intoned, "but don't present this kind of preservation as a good thing, Marla. It isn't healthy to steal from other people for their own good."

"Steal?" She pulled her chin in, offended. "I did no such thing."

"What else did you take that was mine?" Junie set the doll in the *Keep* box and opened a box that was sitting to one side, waiting to be sorted through. She reached in and pulled out the first thing she grabbed. It was a soft, knitted blanket, blue. Not anything she recognized. She pulled out the next thing. A blue teddy bear, with the name "Thomas" embroidered on its little white T-shirt.

Junie's mother let out a strangled cry. "No! Put it away!" She shoved Junie aside, grabbing the blanket and the bear and shoving them back into the box. She lifted the box into her arms and ran up the stairs, crying. Junie heard a distant slam. Her mother had locked herself in the bathroom.

Behind them, from where she'd been watching the scene unfold, Charlie Falconetti whistled. "That right there, folks, is good television turning into *great* television!"

Kendra stood, her hands on her hips. "Zip it, Charlie." She turned to the camera and spoke to it as if speaking to a real person. "Obviously, we've stumbled onto a very painful part of Marla's past just now. Stay with us as we uncover the story behind it." She waited a few seconds, all the while gazing at the camera with her trademark sympathetic smile on her face. "And cut. Thank you, folks. Let's give this a moment to settle before we go back to it." She turned to Junie. "Honey? You know what this is about?"

Junie shook her head. She was as confused as the rest of them, and that did not feel good at all. She ran up the stairs and pounded on the bathroom door, demanding that her mother open up. But all she could hear was her mother, weeping, the taps turned on full to mask the sound, but failing to.

TWENTY-FOUR

:
•

Two hours later and Junie's mother was still locked in the bathroom. She'd stopped crying but would not come out. She wasn't even refusing to, she was simply not responding at all. Tabitha and Wade had joined Junie outside the bathroom door, from where Junie had not budged since coming up the stairs. Wade pulled her so she sat against him, his arms wrapped around her. Tabitha sat in front of her, one hand on the door, as if that would coax Junie's mother out.

"Have you called your dad?" Tabitha asked. "He'd know what this is about."

Junie had called her dad, and he was on his way over, very reluctantly. He'd been short with her on the phone, telling her to leave her mother alone and let it go. But Junie had insisted that he come, or else she was going to call the police to come and break the door down and haul her mother away to the loony bin, where she clearly belonged. Junie had practically yelled all of this into the phone, so she could be sure that her mother heard every single word. But even the threat of being carried off to a mental institution hadn't persuaded her mother to open the door and explain what was going on, and who Thomas was. When Junie had mentioned the name to her father, he'd fallen silent. After a long moment, and then an even longer, sad, sigh, he'd told her that he'd be over in ten minutes.

When he arrived, he headed straight for the bathroom door and knocked on it gently. "Open the door, Marla. It's Ron." When there was no response, he knocked again. "I know this is hard, but you're right in the middle of it and you've dragged Junie into it now, and you're going to have to come out eventually and tell, right?"

There was no response from Junie's mother, just the sound of quiet whimpering. Her dad banged hard this time. "Open this goddamn door, Marla. I'm not going to explain this to Junie all by myself. That's not fair, Marla. And you know it"

"Explain what?" Junie stayed on the floor, safe in Wade's arms, not wanting to stand up but wishing instead for all of this to sort itself out without her for once.

The whole situation got worse, though, because Evelyn St. Claire came in next, a wide, pained grin on her face, proving that she knew what was going on while Junie did not. This got Junie up on her feet.

"What's she doing here?"

"She came with me."

"But why, Daddy?" Junie was surprised to hear herself call her father that. She hadn't called him "Daddy" since she was a toddler, she was sure. This whole day was warped, and Junie was too. "What do you need her for?"

"Not your concern, young lady."

"Kendra!" Evelyn chirped as Kendra and Nigel swept into the room, Charlie Falconetti at their heels, clipboard in hand. Kendra had gone to do a conference call in her trailer and was coming back, ready to make another try at getting Junie's mother to open the door and talk. "And Nigel!" Junie hated that she was greeting the two of them like old friends. And they didn't take too kindly to it either.

Nigel looked down his nose at her. "And you are?"

Evelyn offered her hand. "Evelyn St. Claire, certified personal life coach."

"The one we hired to help my mom last year," Junie added. "Who then had an affair with my father. He lives with her now."

"Is that true?" Kendra fixed wide, horrified eyes on Evelyn.

"Well, their marriage had been in disrepair for some time, and so when I—"

"So it is true. I can smell your kind a mile away. No need to try to explain yourself. An affair. My, my, my." Kendra shook her head. "Is that included on your list of services? Home wrecking?"

It was common knowledge that Kendra strongly disapproved of adultery. Her first husband had cheated on her, and she flayed him repeatedly, offering up his failings on any show that touched even remotely on the subject. Had Evelyn been thinking, she might have thought twice about showing her face, Junie thought. But then, the lure of fame was a pretty compelling thing.

Evelyn's face flushed red. "There are two sides to every—"

"I'm sure there are." Kendra cut her off. "And right now, I do not care to hear yours."

"But I—"

"Come here a minute, honey." Kendra ushered Evelyn back to the front door. She pointed to the crew trucks lining the driveway. "See what's written on the side of those trucks? *The Kendra Show* . . . in big sparkly letters. Right? See that there?"

Evelyn nodded. "And I'm a big fan, I really am—"

"It's my show. I decide whose story we're telling, and when. This is not your moment, honey. Understand?"

Evelyn nodded again, but it was much tighter, and her lips were pinched into a bleached, flat line. She was about to erupt, Junie was sure.

"So why don't you head on over to the catering truck and get yourself a nice Venti skinny latte. Okay?" And with a little shove, Evelyn was on the front porch, looking at them with blank anger as Kendra shut the door in her face.

"She goes," Junie's father growled, "I go. That was totally uncalled for, lady."

"Do you honestly think that your ex-wife will come out at all with that woman here?" Kendra stared at him, unapologetic.

Junie wanted to cheer. Kendra had called Evelyn

"That Woman" in the exact same tone that she herself used on a daily basis. She wanted to jump up and down and say, *See, Dad? I'm not the only one who hates her!* But at the same time she did feel a tug of sympathy for Evelyn, having just been told off by one of the world's most famous women, and an idol of hers.

Junie's father's angry expression did not change, but he knew better than to demand that Evelyn be invited back.

"I want the cameras off."

Charlie Falconetti wagged a finger at him. "Not happening."

"Turn them off."

"No." Charlie tapped something into her BlackBerry. "Not at the expense of great television."

Junie's father paused. "Then how about at the expense of Marla's broken heart? How about the expense of grief? Shut the cameras off. Now."

Charlie looked up, slipping her BlackBerry into her pocket so she could give Junie's father her full attention. "The cameras stay on."

Kendra lifted a hand, silencing Charlie. "Five minutes. We'll leave you alone for five minutes. And then we come back, and one of you," she pointed at the door, then Junie, then Ron, "one of you will tell us the story here. I can tell it's a sad one. And so we'll leave you alone with it."

With a wave of her arm, the camera crews left, and so did Nigel, and Charlie. Then it was just Tabitha, Wade, Junie and her father.

"You want us to stay or go?" Wade gave her hand a squeeze. "Whatever you want, Junie."

"Go," her father barked. "Now. Please."

"I don't know what's happening." Junie sounded so unsure of herself, and she was. This was strange territory, and she didn't know where to place her feet. "Mom!" She banged one more time on the door. "Open up!"

"Let's go, Wade," Tabitha said, letting Junie off the hook of having to make the decision herself.

Tabitha and Wade joined the others outside, and Junie stared hard at the closed door while her father hugged his elbows and stared at the floor. After a long moment during which absolutely nothing happened, Junie finally said, "Dad, she means it when she says five minutes. Do something. Before they come back."

Ron knocked half-heartedly on the door. "It's time to tell Junie, Marla."

"Tell me what?" Junie whispered.

But she knew. Somewhere very deep down inside her sat the knowledge of exactly what this was about. She couldn't put words to it, but she knew all the same. On a visceral level. And she wasn't sure how that was possible.

There was a rustling from inside the bathroom, and then the knob turned with a creak and Junie's mother opened the door. Her face was blotchy and red from crying. She pulled Junie's dad to her and planted her head on his chest and wept anew. Junie stared in disbelief at her parents. She would never have thought to live to see something like this happen. Junie's dad held onto her mother, too, and after a moment of stoicism, fell to pieces himself, leaning his chin on her head and crying in great big sobs.

"Mom?" Junie put her hands to her own cheeks, feeling the prickly heat of confusion and fear. "Dad?"

Her mother said something but her words were muffled against her father's chest. She pulled away, still clutching her ex-husband, and sniffed back another set of tears.

"Thomas was your little brother," she said. "He was perfect and new and smelled so delicious and fit in my arms as if he'd been there forever and . . . and—" She lost herself to the tears and sank her face back into Junie's father's shirt.

"He died," her father finished simply. "One night. In his crib. He was blue when your mother went to him in the morning."

Junie didn't know what to say. She held her face, still hot, and now damp with silent tears. "Why don't I know this?"

"We thought it best to put it behind us." Her father shook his head sadly. "For better or for worse, that's what we did."

"When?"

"You were two. Just two. We didn't think you'd remember." Her father reached out to put a hand on her shoulder, to touch the child who'd lived. "And you didn't."

Anger was pushing the sadness and confusion aside, and Junie wasn't sure that was such a good thing. She wanted to have nothing but sympathy for her parents, for surviving such a terrible loss, but she was angry with them too.

"I can't believe you lied to me! About my own life!"

"No, no. No." Her mother shook her head, protesting. "I wasn't lying to you. I was lying to *myself*! I had to pretend that he'd never been here. I had to push the memories away.

It was too painful to live them every single day! To see the nursery, and his tiny clothes. His receiving blankets, the pictures, the mementos, the diapers! The tiny newborn diapers. It was too hard. Too hard. Too hard. Too hard. *Too hard. Too hard*—"

"It's okay, Mom." Junie was frightened to see her mother like this, unhinged. "Maybe it will be better now? Right? Now that the truth is out?"

"No, no, no, no, no. No!" She shook her head. "It will never be better. You never recover from the death of a child. Never, never. Never."

What Junie wanted to say was that she still had one child left. And that she deserved a full mother, and not the fraction of one that she had. Even if the fracture made some sense now, she still resented it.

"His name was Thomas?" Junie pushed past her parents and into the bathroom, where her mother had pulled out every item from the box and set it neatly along the counter and the floor, in tidy lines. Everything was blue, just as all of her infant things had been pink. Blankets, onesies, rattles, a tiny pair of cloth sneakers. Junie picked up the crib shoes and felt a wave of what might have been a memory. She'd been too young to truly remember, but somewhere inside of her was that two-year-old girl, trying to figure out why the baby had been there and then was suddenly not. Why her mother was crying all the time. Why the house had become such a sad, bleak place.

The shoes sat in the palm of her hand, tiny and empty. She imagined that morning. Her mother finding Thomas in the crib, lifeless and blue. She could see it easily, and could only wonder if she'd been standing in the door, clutching her doll, watching, her thumb stuck in her mouth.

"Where was I?"

Her parents shared a look, and then it was her dad who explained, because her mother couldn't speak through her tears.

"It was a Saturday. You'd gotten up out of your bed and gone to see if Thomas was awake. I don't know how long you were in there, but you came in and woke us. You took your mother's hand and dragged her into the nursery, telling her Thomas was too sleepy. 'Too sleepy, Mama,' you said. 'Baby Thomas too sleepy.'" Ron's voice caught. "And then I heard your mother scream. She came running into the room with Thomas in her arms. He was blue, and cold. He'd died during the night."

"All alone. I wasn't there!" Her mother wailed. She grabbed fistfuls of Ron's shirt. "We weren't there! He was all alone!"

"The paramedics came. The police. The coroner." Her father stared into a middle distance, as if watching it all over again. "They took him away in a tiny body bag. It looked like they'd come to collect the laundry."

"Where was I?"

"Your grandmother came to take care of you," her dad said.

Junie expanded her anger now to include her beloved grandma. Why hadn't *she* told her? As a way to explain her mother's dysfunction? The look on her face must have announced her thoughts, because her mother was suddenly defending Junie's grandma.

"She would've told you. But I made her promise. On Thomas's grave. Never to speak of him. He was only seven weeks old. I thought it would be easier if we just pretended that he'd never been here at all."

Their five minutes were up. Junie could hear the front door open, and Charlie barking into her phone. Kendra hushed her, and then the trio of them were back again, Charlie, Nigel and Kendra.

"Ready to share your story with the world?" Charlie asked, sounding more as though she was ordering them to do so.

"No," Ron said. He gave Junie's mother a long hug, and then pulled Junie to him before continuing. "Marla can decide for herself, but I won't have anything to do with it. Junie can make her own decision." Her dad stroked her cheek, a gesture both tender and possessive. "She can come with me, or stay here with her mother."

"I'll stay." Junie didn't even need a moment to make up her mind. She would stay with her mother and help her through this, because, while it might have happened many years ago, it felt like a sudden breakthrough at last. Junie felt as if the entire house and the family it had held within its walls had shifted into a new shape, giving her mother the space to reshape herself after so many years of being defined by such a tragic, heavy secret. Junie wanted to be there to see what would happen. As sad as it was to hear about her tiny baby brother who had died, she was hopeful, too, that by unearthing his story, her mother could finally move past her grief and take control of her life now.

TWENTY-FIVE

. . .

Two months later, *The Kendra Show* flew Junie and her mother down to Los Angeles so they could be onstage with Kendra during the broadcast of the intervention.

Since talking to Nigel and Kendra about Thomas's death, Junie's mother had begun to deal with her long-buried grief. Nigel had stayed two extra days to help her get on her feet after the revelation. Of course he'd pointed out the obvious on camera, that she'd been filling the void of the lost baby with things upon things upon things, but that no thing would ever replace a lost child. And Junie's mother could only tearfully agree. They'd set her up with what they called "after-care." That meant that twice a week she got on a bus and went downtown to see her new psychologist, an internationally recognized expert in compulsive hoarding and post-traumatic stress. She'd be doing that for a good long while to come.

By the time all the crews had left, the house had been restored to a certain tidiness but still suffered from the years of neglect. Junie's mother had booked a paint crew to come in and repair the walls and paint them a creamy yellow, to bring in a bit of sunlight. She'd hired a carpet-layer to rip out the ruined flooring and replace it. She'd ordered a new living room furniture set, with a matching couch, ottoman and loveseat. All of these seemingly normal things pointed to a much larger, more important change: Junie's mother had started to take care of herself. She rose each day from her new bed in her remade room and pulled open the tailored drapes to let in the day. Then she showered and did her hair, and came downstairs to put on a pot of coffee.

Telling all this to Tabitha and Wade, it sounded so normal, but it was beyond thrilling to Junie. That her mother was functioning was a gift, and she had to admit that it was Kendra who had made it happen, and her mother, too, for contacting the show in the first place. It had seemed so far-fetched and impossible at first, but now Junie was just deeply grateful.

As for Junie, she was going to flunk Math. There was no doubt. But Ollie had a plan. He was going to help her catch up over the summer, and he was hopeful that she'd be able to nail grade ten Math the second time round, do summer school for grade eleven the next year and go into grade twelve Math on track. Normally, this would have devastated Junie, but considering how well everything else was going, she was more than willing to accept this failing as her one big awful deal.

Wade's Virginia Woolf project was nearing comple-
tion, and was due just a week after Junie was going to
Los Angeles for the *Kendra* taping. It was going to be on
hold while she was gone, but she'd join the rest of them at
Royce and Jeremy's to finish it when she got back. They
were all helping now, Tabitha, Ollie, Lulu, curmudgeonly
Jeremy and Royce, too, energy permitting. Either Royce
was feeling a bit better, or the movie was letting him forget
about his heart problems, because he seemed to have a lot
more energy lately.

When it was time for their flight to L.A., Junie and
her mother had multiple offers of a ride to the airport.
Mrs. D. had been the first to offer. Then Junie's dad, even
though he still didn't want anything to do with the show.
Junie didn't want to jinx things by being too hopeful, but
it seemed to her that her father and mother were getting
along a lot better since everything had come out in the
open. But it was Wade who drove them in the end, because
Junie wanted to have her very own Leaving Your Boyfriend
at the Airport moment, even if her mother was there and
Tabitha had come along for the ride, too.

Wade kissed her rather chastely, one eye on Junie's
mother, and then gave Junie a bag of goodies for the plane:
expensive chocolate, a deck of cards, earphones for the
in-flight movie and a tiny four-leaf clover sealed in resin
for her to put in her pocket as a talisman. Tabitha cried
when she handed Junie a stack of trashy magazines for the
plane and waved them off. Junie knew why. She would
have cried too, if she hadn't been trying so hard to be the
strong one. It was amazing to Tabitha and Junie to see her

mother looking so put together. She had makeup on, and looked quite a bit lighter already, which might have been due to the fact that she was going for a walk once a day before making supper. She was wearing purple capri pants and a matching sweater, and slingbacks with large purple plastic flowers on top. Junie couldn't expect her mother to get any kind of fashion sense overnight, and she didn't care. She was very proud of her mother, just the way she was.

After they landed they were taken straight to the TV studio, which was enormous and industrial, like an airplane hangar. They were met at the edge of the lot by Charlie Falconetti and a driver in a golf cart and taken into the building and down wide concrete corridors, until the cart stopped in front of a room that had a star on the door, with their names on it in smart cursive lettering.

"Whatever you need should be in there. Give me a shout if you think of anything else." Charlie handed Junie a walkie-talkie. "Best way to get a hold of me. We go on the air in three hours. Hair and makeup and wardrobe will be by to collect you in about fifteen minutes."

By the time they were ushered onto the stage, Junie didn't recognize herself, or her mother. After being dressed in clothes that they'd never wear, but which looked fantastic on them, they'd sat in the stylists' chairs for the better part of an hour, their hair being worked on and their faces being carefully made up by women talking about their boyfriends and texting in between putting on dabs of this and spritzes of that.

The whole experience was very surreal. Junie wasn't sure that she liked it at all.

The audience was abuzz, talking excitedly while they waited for Kendra to appear. Junie and her mother sat awkwardly in two orange leather chairs, centre stage, the lights up in the rafters so bright that it almost felt as if they were alone in the studio.

"Quiet on the set!" a voice called from the darkness. The crowd fell silent. Kendra's theme music, upbeat and youthful, exploded out of the speakers lining the edge of the room, and the audience leapt to their feet as Kendra swept into the room, walking confidently in her high heels, holding out her hands so that the crowd of mostly women could reach out and touch her as she made her way to the stage.

Junie and her mother stood, as they'd been directed to earlier. Kendra parked herself between the two of them and took their hands.

"Welcome, everybody! You're all looking so smart today!" She turned and gave Junie's mother's hand a squeeze. "Especially you, Marla." Back to the audience and the teleprompter, where her script was scrolling down in slow, big letters. "Marla here has come a long way to be with us today, both in real life and in her heart and mind and soul. Marla is a compulsive hoarder, and today on *The Kendra Show* we bring you her story, and her miraculous recovery. We'll be back in a moment."

Crews rearranged the enormous cameras on tracks laid along the floor while the audience murmured and Kendra invited Junie and her mother to take a seat. They hadn't seen Kendra since that last day when she'd sat alone with Junie's mother in what had once been Thomas's nursery.

A room that had been used for storage for as long as Junie could remember.

Seated, Kendra reached for Junie's mother's hand again and gave it another squeeze. "Won't be any surprises, hon. Promise you that. Nice and easy, a few tears and some laughs and you can go back home and start living that life of yours to its fullest. Okay?"

"Okay," Junie's mother said, struggling for enthusiasm.

Now the director said, "Going live in five, four, three . . ." Then she held up two fingers, and one, and finally pointed to Kendra to indicate that they were live on air.

Kendra turned on as if a switch had been flipped. Her teeth gleamed white in the hot lights. Her eyelashes looked larger than life, like her smile.

"When I first walked into Marla's home, I couldn't believe anyone could live in such squalor. The stench. The filth. The detritus of life. The decay of a life abandoned . . . to junk."

Junie nervously crossed and uncrossed her legs. Nice and easy? She doubted it. Her mother had taken something for her nerves before the show and was seeming to hold up okay in its lazy, warm glow. Junie glanced at her and wished she'd helped herself to a pill too. Behind them, shots of the house before, filled with the familiar mountains of crap, the rotting takeout boxes, the stacks of mildewed laundry, room after room filled to the ceiling with useless, unnecessary stuff. Junie's skin broke out in goosebumps, and she had to grip the arms of the chair to resist leaping up and running out of there, screaming.

Everyone she knew, and eleven million or more people she didn't know, were watching right now. Wade and Tabitha, along with Ollie and Lulu, had driven out to Royce and Jeremy's to watch it there in their home theatre, which had real theatre seats and a popcorn machine and a screen that took up one whole wall. Junie imagined Evelyn watching it alone, cursing Kendra for snubbing her but too curious to refuse to watch. The only person Junie was sure was not watching was her father. He'd be at work, adding and shifting columns of numbers, reaching for a perfect order that he could not attain in his personal life. He quickly clammed up whenever Junie brought up Thomas, and he hadn't mentioned Kendra since her trucks had pulled out of the driveway. He was as solidly parked in denial as he'd ever been. He might not have been the one with the hoarding problem, but he was just as screwed up as her mother for trying to ignore the son he'd lost so suddenly and tragically.

They cut to footage of Kendra mincing her way around the heaps of garbage to meet Junie's mother in her long since torched easy chair.

It went fast. It was true that living through the intervention itself had been far harder than actually being on *The Kendra Show* stage. This was all old news to Junie now. Her life had already moved on in the two months since Kendra had come to town. The cameras had left, along with the media and spectators. At school, the kids had moved on from her drama to the new drama of a girl who'd been arrested for smuggling drugs across the border for her boyfriend. Not that Junie was happy that the girl had been caught with five baggies of pot on her, but she was glad that the focus had shifted abruptly off of her. Of course there would be talk after the show, but honestly, Junie didn't care. It was done. It was over. She'd lived through it, and, more importantly, so had her mother. And for the better.

Was her mother healed, as Kendra was claiming? Junie didn't think so. She knew that it would take more than a couple of months and a celebrity at your back to change the dysfunction that had accumulated over so many years. But Nigel had given her hope, assuring her that if her mother kept working with the psychologist she might very well go on to live a normal life.

Normal life.

What was that?

Kendra put a hand on Junie's knee. "A penny for your thoughts?"

Junie glanced beyond the lights to the rows and rows of shadowed heads. It wasn't normal to be sitting on the set of one of the world's most famous talk shows. It wasn't normal to have a mother who'd been locked in her grief for so long, finding comfort in packages from the Shopping Channel and other people's garbage left in the alley for her to take home. It wasn't normal to have a dead brother you didn't know about. Had forgotten about. A little boy who had been born and loved and then buried in the ground, and buried a second time under all of the trash Junie's mother had stuffed into the great big hole of sadness.

"Tell us about what it's been like for you," Kendra prompted her. "How has it been to grow up in a house like this?" She gestured behind them, to a photo on an

326 · · · ●   CARRIE MAC

enormous screen. It showed the basement, with its teetering archives of garbage.

"Hard." Junie couldn't find the words. She felt suddenly very private about it all. She wanted to take her mother by the hand and lead her away from the stage, out through the fire exit and into the blazing California afternoon. She wanted to get a taxi to the airport and get on a plane back home. She wanted to go home. For the first time. To her house. Because it was finally a home. She should be there. With her mother. Not here.

"Tell us more." Kendra was giving her a sympathetic smile, leaning forward, her elbow cocked on the chair's arm, chin resting on her fist. Earnestly being her famous self. "Tell us what it was like for you."

Junie looked for the camera that was trained on her. She realized that she didn't actually have to open her soul to the world. There was no way that Kendra could take back her mother's transformation now. She wasn't obliged to describe the years of sadness and shame about the state of her home and the state of her mother. Junie blinked a couple of times and then said, "I always wanted my mother to be happy. And she is now. And that's all I have to say."

Her mother reached for Junie's hand with one of hers and for the box of tissue with the other.

The rest of the taping seemed to go quickly. Kendra asked her a couple more questions, to which Junie answered again, "I just wanted my mom to be happy." Kendra gave up on Junie then and focused solely on her mother, bringing Nigel into the conversation halfway through. The show took its shape, without Junie, and that was fine by her.

Afterwards, Kendra was cold to her, not saying goodbye. Not offering one of her trademark hugs or even one last smile. She gave Junie's mother one last hug and shook her hand, too, snubbing Junie altogether.

"Thank you, Marla, and all the best."

"No, no," Junie's mother said. "Thank you. I can't even begin to tell you how much—"

"Okay, you take care now." Kendra was looking past Junie's mother at one of her producers, who was waving her over. "Safe trip home."

"I am so very grateful," her mother still gushed, oblivious. "So many people don't get this second chance."

"Okay, kids." Charlie swept in between them, letting Kendra escape. "Let's get the two of you on your way back to your charmed life!"

The Kendra Show and Kendra herself were done with them. Moving on, or having already moved on, to the next bleeding-heart story, the next headline. The next people to exploit. Anger turned Junie's insides molten, but she kept her mouth shut. Exploited or not, she and her mother were better off because of it.

"They're busy, Mom." Junie kept her voice low, restrained. "Let's go." She was afraid if she started to talk she'd turn on Kendra, hollering across the soundstage that she was an opportunistic leech, feeding off people's misery in order to stuff her bank account. And while she believed that, she also believed that Kendra left a lot of good behind her, so she kept her trap shut and steered her mother toward the dressing room.

⋮

Wade met them at the airport that evening. He had two bouquets of flowers, a small one for Junie and an enormous one for her mother. On the way home, her mom sat in the front and talked about the show and the trip, about all the shiny, glossy people in L.A., the smog, the city that never fell quiet, not ever. Every once in a while, Wade would glance back and give Junie a little smile. Each one warmed her, like small sparks to her heart. She was glad to be home.

When they got back to the house, Wade came in too, following Junie into the kitchen, where her mother was rummaging around in the tea cupboard, newly organized with everything needed for making a pot of tea all in one place. The house still had a certain ruined smell, but Junie hoped that, in time, that would fade.

"Peppermint?"

Junie grinned. This moment was so ordinary. So normal. This was life, lived normally. As it should be.

"Actually, Marla," Wade clasped his hands under his chin, "I was hoping that I could take Junie out for a little bit."

"It's a little late to be going out, don't you think?"

"Well, actually, I was hoping to take her to Chilliwack for the night—"

"Absolutely not!"

"Mom—"

"Scout's honour, nothing fishy about it." Wade held up three fingers and placed his other hand over his heart. "Tabitha is coming too. And Ollie and Lulu. I'm running out of time on my term project for English and I really need to finish the filming so I can get to the edits. The weather tomorrow is going to be perfect. We'll have mist, or at least Jeremy says so. That's what we've been waiting for to finish."

Her mother knew about the Virginia Woolf project. Tabitha as Vanessa, Junie as Virginia, they'd all been out there for several entire Saturdays but had never spent the night.

"You're wondering why overnight, Mrs. Rawley, and it's a good question. The sunrise with the mist. It's perfect for the scene in the river. I scoped it out. Spectacular. I thought it'd be easier to spend the night. We'll be with adults. And Tabitha will chaperone. You know she's up to the job."

"That much is true." Her mother poured the boiling water into one mug, instead of the teapot, which meant that she was going to let Junie go.

"I can go?"

"It's so late." Her mother lifted her eyes to the clock hanging over the dining table. It had hung for years in Junie's grandma's kitchen, and then had been lost in the basement chaos, only to be found and restored while *The Kendra Show* was there. Again, Junie felt her heart leap. So much normal, all of a sudden . . . she could hardly contain herself. "I suppose. But separate rooms—"

"Mom! Please."

"*Please* nothing. I'll call and make sure they know my wishes. Got it?" She glanced sternly at Junie, then at Wade.

"Yes, ma'am," Wade said for the both of them. Junie was too embarrassed to say anything. This new, more attentive, more involved mother would take some serious getting used to.

"And call me when you get there. And don't let yourself get too chilled if you're going in the river. And be careful."

"Thank you, Mom! Thank you!"

Junie ran upstairs to get a few things. She passed the room where Thomas had died. It was a guest room now. *The Kendra Show* designer had furnished it with a new bed, and a comforter that played on the burgundy walls and the custom drapes. Three square picture frames hung above the bed. In them were black-and-white shots of Thomas. Nigel had helped her mother pick them, and then had sent them away to be restored and blown up. He'd had a set made for Junie's father, too. When the photos had shown up at his place, he'd called and spoken with Junie's mother for over an hour. Now they were in counselling together, talking through what they had not even been able to mention just weeks before. Junie wasn't naive. She didn't think her family would ever go back to the way it was. And she didn't want it to, anyway. But it was nice that they were being human to each other. Gentle, even. Even if it was years overdue.

This was an adult room now, maturely decorated, but Junie could see Thomas there if she closed her eyes and took herself back. She wasn't sure if it was a memory or a creation of her mind, but she could see the blue curtains dotted with clouds, the crib with the bird mobile above, the little baby kicking his chubby legs, turning his head to look at her as she stood on her tippy-toes, fingers gripping the wooden slats.

There was a moment while *The Kendra Show* was

there that Junie had known things were going to be okay. The camera crew had been wedged into the corner of the room, right about where there was now a small leather chair sitting at a smart angle, a reading lamp leaning over from behind. Nigel had been at her mother's side while she went through boxes of old books. She'd slowed down, wanting to keep most of them.

"You can't keep this much," Nigel reminded her. "You need to get rid of at least 90 percent of everything in this room, 90 percent of everything in this house. I'm going to give you five minutes, and I want you to get what you want from this room."

Junie's mother just stood there, looking around, a book in each hand. "I can't."

"Four minutes."

"That's not enough time!" Panic filled her voice. Junie stood in the doorway, wanting to go help her, but knowing better. Her mother had to go through this on her own. "I can't!"

"Three minutes, Marla. Think. What in here is truly important to you?"

"Thomas," she whispered at once. "But he's gone."

"He is gone. You're right. He's not here any more." Nigel softened his tone, but persisted. "Your house is burning down, Marla. You have a minute to get out of here, what do you take?"

She looked at Junie just then, her eyes clear, her gaze solid, expression warm. "Junie. She's all that I would take. Everything else doesn't matter."

⋮

Junie and Wade drove along the highway, not saying much. Lulu and Ollie and Tabitha sat in the back. Lulu and Ollie shared a pair of earbuds, heads together. Tabitha had fallen asleep five minutes into the trip.

It grew even darker as they left the city behind them, crossing the bridge, the traffic thinning on the other side, stars dotting the sky over the farmlands. Wade fiddled with the stereo, and on came Patsy Cline, singing "Crazy," the same song that had played when he'd first driven her home. He glanced over at her and smiled. Junie took his hand, and held it while they passed under the slices of light from a highway exit ramp.

This was what it was like, she thought, when things were normal. Room to breathe. Room to screw up. Room to be right. Room to wonder. Patches of darkness, and patches of light, and the moon overhead.

ACKNOWLEDGMENTS

:::

Thank you to my agent, Suzanne Brandreth! Here's to our first project together. And thank you to my editor, Lynne Missen, for all the work you've done to make this book shine. Many thanks to Mary Ann Blair, for her care and attention to the manuscript, too. Thank you to my mom for providing free child care so I could write, and thank you to Esmé for going along with it. Thanks also to Jack, for being the best partner and personal chef and co-parent. Without her, I could not write at all. And thank you, Hawksley, for being an easygoing baby who happily nursed while propped on my lap while I wrote.